Hat

A. Zavarelli

CHAPTER ONE
STELLA

"Sorry I'm late." My father flops on to the back seat of our Town Car with his briefcase in tow. He's still dressed in his office garb, but the wrinkles in his shirt make it look like he just woke from a nap. The shadows beneath his eyes are more prominent than the last time I saw him, and I can't even recall how long ago that was. He's been holed up in his apartment in the city while my mother reigns supreme over the manor house in Greenwich. I've barely seen either of them over the summer, and it feels like it's taken a small miracle just to bring the three of us together now.

"Really, Brady?" My mother huffs from the front passenger seat. "Would it kill you to be on time for once in your life?"

"Would it kill you to wait until noon for a drink?" he fires back.

Ignoring the hubbub, our driver, Luis, merges into traffic as my parents continue to bicker all the way up the I-95. I pop my headphones in and thumb through the latest tracks on my Spotify playlist to drown them out. Once I've settled into a good vibe, I reach for the camera hanging around my neck and sort through the photos I took over the summer. Lucky for me, the drive to New Canaan is short, and we seem to survive without any major bloodshed.

By the time we pull up to Loyola Academy, a wall of silence has been erected between my parents, which is preferable to the constant bickering. They tactfully go about the business of ignoring each other while Luis retrieves my suitcases from the car. My mother stands on the curb, twisting the gold bracelet draped over her delicate wrist as she studies the crowd that has gathered just inside the gates of my new home. Or prison, depending on how I choose to look at it.

"I should go speak with some of the other parents," Mom says.

"Of course." My father shoos her away. "Wouldn't want to miss an opportunity to let the world know Lila has arrived." She ignores his parting jab, and my father helps me roll my suitcases over the cobbled entrance to the campus of one of the nation's finest boarding schools. At least that's what the brochure said. In this case, I'm convinced finest is interchangeable with expensive. At first glance, it looks more like a university than a boarding school. The campus is massive, and while they boast about having one of the largest libraries in the nation, it looks like the acreage itself is more impressive. I could easily get lost here, and I don't doubt that I will. From my research, I know that many of the brick buildings that dot the plush green landscape are historical. And beyond all that well-manicured grass lies the best preparatory education money can buy.

As we venture onto the grounds, a knot forms in my throat as multiple pairs of eyes roam my direction. Amongst the scattered parents and faculty are the modern-day Jackie Os and John Kennedys of the world. And then there's me, Stella LeClaire. Unlike my peers, I'm not American royalty. I'm not even American aristocracy. The best thing I have going for me is that I'm the daughter of Lila Monroe, the once sort-of famous jet-setting model who refused to change her last name when she married my father. She's beautiful and elegant and spins a wonderful tale about my father being a Wall Street fat cat and her daughter's aspirations to work in fashion public relations. That isn't even slightly true on my part, but she read something about it in a magazine once and decided soon after that would be the path for me. The next thing I knew, she was plying the admissions committee with expensive gifts and calling in all sorts of favors to get that golden ticket and the bragging rights that come with it. Now here I am with said ticket, signed up to take courses she thinks will eventually get me in the door at Cornell.

As I watch her make the rounds, I wonder if any of the other parents are falling for her respectable family act. Lila always wants to be the woman others look up to and not just because of her sky-high legs. In her mind, she's the woman who gets invited to dinner and charity galas. The head of the table at the country club, and the fashionista who rules on and off the tennis court. What she fails to realize is that those same women who invite her into their circle are talking shit about her just as soon as she leaves.

In my brief interactions with the upper crust, I've learned they can sniff out a fraud better than anyone else. I don't doubt for a second these alums and their offspring haven't figured out we aren't from old money. The majority have probably already deemed me unworthy of walking this hallowed ground with their trust fund babies. Honestly, I can't say that I disagree with them. Loyola was never my dream. But with the current climate at home, and my parents' eagerness for their own freedom, I'm forced to make the best of the situation.

"You're in Lawrence Hall." My father squints at his iPhone, scrolling through the information the school sent him. "Looks like we can check in at the student center."

I traipse after him as he marches across the quad in the direction of the central brick building. There's already a flock of eager parents and students hovering around the check-in, and I'd rather be anywhere but here right now. My dad still hasn't looked directly at me, and I catch myself staring at the side of his face, wishing he'd just acknowledge me. He used to be my rock. My stability. For so long, he was my sole caretaker while my mother remained a passive participant in family life. Everything has shifted, and I barely recognize him now. I don't know when our relationship fell apart, but it did.

Things haven't been easy for any of us, but they especially haven't been easy for him. Lately, it seems like all he does is work, and the long hours in the city have monopolized his time. Gone are the days of vacations and birthday dinners. I can't even remember the last meal we had together. As my parents' marriage crumbles and their attention drifts in separate directions, we've all become our own islands. I haven't made things any easier on them. Abandonment issues are a bitch, and the only way I manage to get their attention now is by getting into trouble, which I've been doing often lately. And this is how Loyola Academy came into the picture. As my father says, this is my chance to turn over a new leaf. But to me, it just feels like he's sending me away.

"Welcome." A bright-eyed faculty member greets us as we move forward in line. "Are we checking in?"

"Yes," my father answers. "Stella LeClaire."

"Ah, Stella." She drags a manicured finger down the sheet of names in front of her. "There you are." After checking me off like an item on her to-do list, she retrieves an envelope with my information printed across the front. "Here is your room number, map, class schedule, and orientation information. Welcome to Loyola Academy."

"Thanks." I stuff the envelope beneath my arm, pinning it to my side. Dad doesn't waste any time herding me toward my dorm. As it turns out, the map isn't necessary because he already studied the materials they sent him, and he knows exactly where it's at.

The iconic brick building that once housed several now famous alums squats on top of the hill surrounded by trees and well-coifed shrubs. The main entrance is smack in the middle; a solid set of double doors flanked by white columns. Three rows of paned windows stack neatly along the length and depth of the building, indicating three separate floors. Or in the case of teenage girls, a whole lot of hormones. Dad blows through the entrance and past the flurry of activity in the common room, an enormous space filled with books, a central fireplace, and plenty of comfy sofas. He's hell-bent on finding my dorm as soon as possible, and I'm certain he's already counting down the seconds until he can get back to the city. Meanwhile, I'm just trying to catch my breath. Lawrence Hall is aged but well cared for. Solid oak floors squeak beneath my red Dr. Martens, and a pervasive scent of lemon cleaner lingers in the space. Along the corridor, I catch glimpses of mothers and daughters fussing over bed linens and furniture in the rooms. As usual, my mother is notably absent, and I can't count on Dad to fuss over anything.

"Here we are." He opens the door numbered 203 and examines the space. The room is small and basic, with a twin-sized bed, a desk, a dresser, and a few shelves for my things. My mother arranged for a private room because she said roommates are for commoners, and in her eyes, everything comes down to appearances. As my dad sets my suitcases aside, I doubt he'd care one way or the other.

"Well, what do you think?" I sit down on the bed and test out the mattress, which is surprisingly comfortable.

"Stella—" My father's eyebrows pinch together as a knock on the door interrupts whatever he was about to say. Another faculty member wearing a Loyola emblem on her blazer steps inside with a stiff smile.

"Mr. LeClaire, I hope you don't mind the interruption. I'm Marcy from the financial office. We spoke on the phone a few weeks back regarding the remainder of the tuition payments."

"Of course." My father kneads the back of his neck with his fingers, undoubtedly trying to relieve some of the tension gathered there. "I thought we already cleared that up."

"You had a business meeting to get to, and unfortunately, our call was cut short." Marcy's eyes wander over me as she speaks, and she doesn't attempt to hide her obvious disapproval of my tight red dress and black leather jacket. "We understand you're a busy man, so we extended the deadline as a courtesy, but I just need your reassurance that you will have the remainder of the payment to us within two weeks."

"You will," he assures her. "I'll have it sent over before that." He sounds confident, but she doesn't look like she believes him, and I'm not sure I do either. Though he hasn't made it overtly obvious, I've seen the worry in my father's eyes over the past six months. Something has changed with our finances, and I don't know exactly what it is, but I've noticed him in his study, poring over bills whenever he's home. As always, my mother remains clueless, content to maintain the status quo with frequent shopping trips and designer luxuries.

"All right then." Marcy offers up a tight, disingenuous smile. "I'll leave you to it. Welcome to Loyola, Stella."

As soon as she shuts the door behind her, my father turns back to me, and suddenly, he looks like he's aged twenty years.

"Is everything okay, Dad?" I fidget with the spinner ring on my finger as I wait for his assurances.

"It's fine." He flippantly waves away any other possibility. "Just an accounting snafu. I'll get it taken care of, Stella. You don't need to worry about it. The only thing you need to worry about is your education."

"Okay." I offer him a weak smile.

He sits down on the bed beside me, and in a rare moment of vulnerability, I recognize the concern on his face. He seems nervous, but I don't know why. "I need you to make the most of this opportunity, honey. This is important. I'm sure I don't have to tell you that Loyola is going to be a challenge. I should have sent you to better schools from the beginning."

"My school was great." I shrug. "They offered advanced classes too. You know I never cared about the money, Dad. I was happy even when you were a photographer."

He cringes at the reminder of his past, but those are the years I like to remember most. At least then, we weren't just three strangers living together in a house. My mother wasn't completely consumed by her social status, and their love hadn't yet turned to hate. We didn't have a house in the suburbs or the best of everything money could buy, but I still had a father.

"I need you to do well here," Dad reiterates. "This is your last year of high school. From here, you can go straight to college. I think the plan your mother has laid out for you is a solid one. It's important you follow it and don't get into any trouble." Disappointment lingers in his eyes, but I don't know if it's for me or himself. "I'm putting everything on the line to send you here, Stella. This is all I can do for you now."

My breath catches as his eyes become glassy, and he turns away from me. My father isn't an emotional man. At least, he hasn't been since he became a corporate robot five years ago. If he's admitting that things aren't as good as they seem, then I know they must be pretty bad.

"You don't have to send me here," I tell him. "It's so expensive, and if we can't afford it—"

"No." He shakes his head, adamant. "This is the last good thing I can do for you before you're out on your own. I want you to go to Cornell. That degree means something in this world we live in. It will open doors for you that our name won't. But they aren't going to give it away. You have to put your head in the books and work hard. Can you do that for me?"

The knot in my throat makes it too difficult to speak, so I nod instead. And I really do mean it. I know I've disappointed my father lately with my stupid antics, and I want him to be proud of me. I want to be one less thing for him to worry about. If that means getting a degree in communications, then so be it. Even if it feels like a prison sentence, I make myself promise what he needs to hear.

"I'll do it." I offer him a watery smile. "I'll make you proud, Dad."

CHAPTER TWO
SEBASTIAN

Entering the grounds of Loyola Academy, freshly sharpened pencils aren't the only scent lingering in the air. The stench of wealth and pretension invades every porous surface around me. A new wave of faces blurs together among the old familiar. Trust fund brats and their parents eye the competition in the courtyard while I narrowly avoid them all. The ever-present noose around my neck strangles the air from my lungs as I walk the sacred grounds of the asylum doubling as an educational institution. I hate this place. And yet, I find myself coming back here for the fourth year in a row.

I did not choose to be a teacher because I love the job. Prior to taking the position here, I'd spent the entirety of my life being groomed to work in a corporate skyscraper. The title and matching desk plate were mere formalities at the end of my tunnel to success. But when the time came for me to take the rightful place I'd earned through literal blood, sweat, and tears, I turned my back on all of it and came back to the establishment that represents everything I despise.

The New England boarding school tucked away just a short distance from Yale has a campus that rivals its Ivy League neighbor in size and prestige. And why shouldn't it? With tuition fees totaling over sixty thousand a year, this isn't a boarding school at all. It's a machine designed to churn out America's best and brightest. The future one percent. I know because, once upon a time, I was one of them.

Ten years ago, I walked these hallowed halls as a seventeen-year-old with his entire future laid out before him. My goals were lined up in militant fashion with little chance of deviation. AP classes, respectable extracurriculars, advanced standing at Harvard. I was on the fast track and set to graduate with a master's in four years. Like a puppet, I soldiered on through the plan. I did and accomplished everything I'd been told to. But I'd learned the hard way that life was a fickle bitch, and the end goal crashed and burned the night I graduated. I traded a corporate office on the sixtieth floor for a teacher's desk. And after three long years, I'm eager to finish what I started.

"Sebastian." Misty Hargrave's eyes light up as I enter the mail room. "It's so good to see you back. How was your summer?"

"Not much to report." I scan her from head to toe, noting that she's come back with a tan. Misty is the resident English teacher at Loyola, and the reason hordes of teenage boys suddenly develop an interest in the subject. She's classically beautiful, graceful, and eloquent. All the signature traits of fine breeding. Yet when she bats her eyelashes in my direction, my dick remains as limp as a noodle in her presence.

"Come now." She laughs softly. "You must have done something interesting."

I know how this game works. She wants to ask me about my summer, so that I'll ask about hers out of politeness. It's evident she wants to tell me about her days on some cliché of a tropical island. Misty still hasn't quite figured out that I'm just an asshole who doesn't care what she has to say.

"I stayed at my cottage in Nantucket," I inform her as I reach into the wooden box designated with my name.

"That sounds lovely." She sighs dreamily. "Were you there with family?"

"No." I tuck the mail into my briefcase and duck through the door before she can ask any more probing questions. I imagine her standing there, mouth agape as I make my way across campus to my living quarters.

Teachers at Loyola Academy live in a separate village on the north side of the campus. Far enough from the dorms to have a reprieve from the endless chatter of students, but close enough that they could still knock on your door if they really want to. Since our job is to act as surrogate parents throughout the school year, we are encouraged to develop bonds with our students. It isn't uncommon to see them traipsing across the quad in the middle of the night to knock on the math teacher's door when they have a fight with their boyfriend or a pressing need to discuss some other teenage drama. However, in the three years I've resided here, only one visitor has bothered to darken my doorstep. After I'd numbly accepted Misty's welcome basket of baked goods, she hasn't bothered to come back, and neither has anyone else.

The house I chose when I moved in happens to be the one that affords the most privacy on campus. Tucked away behind a thicket of New England trees, there is little chance of others accidentally stumbling upon it. And given that most of my students refer to me as some form of Satan, it's unlikely they would ever bother to seek it out.

I dust off the doorknob and turn the key, hesitating in the entryway as I step inside. There's a faint note of my cologne along with the musty smell of a house that's been locked up all summer. Other than that, everything else remains the same.

I drop my mail onto the table and set my briefcase aside as I hit play on the answering machine. The endless reel of voicemails from my father echoes through the space as I discard the letters he'd sent over the summer months. Numb to the pleas to return his calls, I delete his messages and spend the evening unpacking in the tomb of silence that's become my life.

In my restless state, I consider going out for a run. But when I scoop the necklace from the bottom of my suitcase, I find myself collapsing into the nearest chair instead. In my haphazard packing, I knew it had been stuffed somewhere in the void of my clothes and toiletries, but I'd managed most of the summer without looking at it once. Now, it can't be avoided.

I roll the chain between my fingers, studying the symbol rooted in Dharmic religion. I'm not a man to believe in the afterlife. Once things are gone from this earth, they just cease to exist. But if there were such a thing as signs, this would be hers. The ever-present reminder of why I'm here in the first place. What I came here for, and what I've yet to accomplish. Katie told me once that if she could just change one person's life, then she could say she'd really lived. I never got the chance to tell her that she already had. It was her dream to come back here and show these students that there's more to life than Ivy Leagues and test scores and corporate jobs. She believed she could save someone else from the acute misery she felt growing up under the dictatorship of my father and the pressures bestowed on us. But Katie never got the chance to prove herself. She lost her life because of me, and now the only way to make it up to her is to follow through with what she started. That has always been the goal. But in the three years I've been here, every one of my projects have failed. I am not a teacher. I am not a mentor. I am simply a man without passion trying to honor the memory of the most passionate person I knew. And as I clench the necklace within my fist, I know this year I have to leave my mark. Leave my mark or be done with this existential crisis.

But for tonight, the necklace will remain in the cabinet.

CHAPTER THREE
STELLA

"Is it just me, or is the tension at this table so thick you could cut it with a chainsaw?" Sybil whispers under her breath.

"It's not just you," I assure her.

"I have a headache," my mother mutters before she drains the last of her wine from lunch.

"Unfathomable." My father eyes the empty bottle in front of her.

She shoots him a withering glare. Sybil and I stare at our plates, shoveling in food as fast as we can so this train wreck can be over already.

Unlike me, Sybil is a boarding school veteran. She's an actual descendent of American royalty, and it just so happens that her father works with mine at the Arthur Group. That connection is how she came to be tasked with hosting me for the summer at her family's house in the Hamptons. Neither of us were exactly thrilled at the prospect, but we quickly learned that despite our lack of common ground, we have a keen ability to be real with each other, which goes a long way in our world.

In just a few short months, we became fast friends. Friends with a double lack of parental supervision and a lot of time on our hands. Trouble seemed to find us. We spent countless nights raiding her father's liquor cabinet and sneaking out past curfew to parties on the beach while Sybil single-handedly charmed every wealthy heir to their father's fortunes on the East Coast. A few times, to my utter dismay, we even ended up in New York gossip columns because of Sybil's socialite status.

Beside her, I found myself identified as the "unknown friend" in photographs, which suited me just fine. But while Sybil's parents write off her shenanigans as harmless teenage fun, my parents seem to think I'm in a field of lava, narrowly avoiding a PR disaster for our family at every turn. Though they don't exactly care for Sybil, they like the fact that her family has connections, and therefore, our friendship is beneficial to them. Naturally, when my mother heard that Sybil attends Loyola Academy, she decided that was the place to send your daughter when you'd rather not deal with her yourself. The only silver lining in this whole equation is Sybil. At least I won't be facing my senior year entirely alone.

"I'm going to rest in the car," my mother announces dramatically as she gets up and leaves without waiting for a reply. What she really means is she's going to sneak off with our driver, Luis, who I'm pretty sure she's having an affair with. I caught them kissing in the car once, and she tried to play it off like he was helping with her necklace. She never could explain the lipstick smeared all over her face.

"Your mom is super-hot." Sybil wiggles her eyebrows and laughs as she watches Lila Monroe sashay out of the restaurant with the authority of a first lady.

"She was a model." I offer the stock explanation I use whenever someone remarks on my mother's appearance.

"And she'll never let anyone forget it," Dad chimes in, tossing his napkin down onto his plate. "Excuse me."

"Ouch." Sybil glances at me as he leaves the table. "And I thought my parents were bad. At least they make an effort to hide their resentment. How are you still sane?"

I laugh because sarcasm is the only defense I have left. "My mom feels like we ruined her life. She had a glamorous career and then she got knocked up by a photographer. My dad promised her they could make it work. He believed he could make her happy. I still don't know if he did it to keep her or me."

"Yikes." Sybil cringes, obviously at a loss for words.

"Yeah."

"You know what?" She reaches into her purse and pops a piece of gum into her mouth. "Forget them. You're about to start a new chapter in your life. And the best part is, you'll have me by your side. Pretty soon, we'll be eighteen, and we can rule the world."

I swallow the acid in my throat and nod even though I know that isn't true. Sybil has dreams of being a dancer, and her parents are happy to foot the bill while she follows her heart. But my parents have made it more than clear what they expect from me. It's Cornell or nothing. My mother won't be satisfied until she can brag about her daughter with the inside scoop on all things fashion. I guess it's not as easy to brag about the smartass daughter who really wants to be a photographer.

"Ready to go?" My father reappears with the lunch receipt in his hand. "I think it's about time to drop you girls off."

Loyola Academy isn't fooling around when they boast about superior educational resources on their website. In today's tour, with Sybil as my guide, I've learned that there is a dedicated building for almost every subject. College level classes are the norm, and there are a billion languages to choose from. In addition to the plethora of athletics on offer, there's also an Olympic-sized swimming pool at our disposal. Oh, and a student who actually went to the Olympics at fourteen.

If I wasn't intimidated before, Sybil's offhand comments aren't helping as she throws out statistics about how thirty to forty percent of students matriculate at top colleges. I knew coming here that the academics would be rigorous, but Sybil's word of choice is cutthroat. While I've always done well in school, this isn't just about keeping up good grades. It's about being the best at everything, full stop.

"This is kind of insane," I murmur as we stroll across the quad.

Sybil laughs. "Tell me about it. You're in another world now, Cherrybomb. There's a hierarchy here. The girls will see you as a threat, and they will test you. And the boys will all want a piece of the fresh meat. You have to remember these are kids who have been top performers since the age of five. They expect to be the future one percent, and they will accept nothing less. That means trampling over anyone they see as competition."

"Great."

"It's not all bad, though." She shrugs. "The pressure really gets to people. We have some rager parties. The headmaster's deadbeat son will supply weed and alcohol for a price."

"Really?" I question. "Don't people get caught?"

"Nah." She smooths back her long brown hair and knots it at the base of her neck with a hair tie. "I mean sometimes. But usually the teachers here don't pay attention. There are a couple you have to avoid, but for the most part, a lot of shit flies under the radar. Last year, when I was sneaking into my boyfriend's dorm, I crossed paths with my math teacher, who was sneaking into the married science teacher's house. We both just stopped and stared at each other, then went on our merry way. Neither of us ever said a word."

"Holy crap." I glance around the mammoth-sized campus, noting the distance between buildings. In the dark, I guess it wouldn't be too hard to fly under the radar, particularly with teachers who are too busy looking the other way to care.

"Yeah, and that's not even the worst of it," she says. "There are quite a few hookup spots around campus. Let me just say that more than a couple of teachers have been caught making out in the dark too. I guess they get just as sick of these confines as we do."

"I've heard stories about boarding school," I admit. "I just never put much stock into it."

"What do you expect when you put a bunch of kids with affluenza and little parental supervision into one giant melting pot?" Sybil shrugs.

"True." I nod. "Is there anything else I need to know?"

She considers the question for a second before she starts pointing out the dorms and rattling off their reputations. "That's the coke dorm. Don't ever go there. If you needed Adderall to cram for a test, which you don't, you could get it from Lyon's Hall. And if you do ever decide to sneak into the boy's dorms, always work out a system with someone on the lower level. It's so much easier to climb through an open window and work your way to the top inside."

"Right." I smirk. "I'll remember that."

Except boys aren't even a fleeting thought in my mind right now. I have more important things to worry about. Like keeping up with my academics this year and focusing on the extracurriculars I'm expected to cram into my schedule. Long after my father left this afternoon, his words have continued to haunt me. I *put everything on the line to send you here.*

"Well, I think that about concludes the tour." Sybil cranes her neck from one side to the other, stretching it out with the elegance of a dancer. "You ready to venture into the dorm? We can go over our class schedules."

"Sure."

Lawrence Hall is already at full capacity when we arrive, and most of the students have gathered in the common room. Chatter about their summer activities floats through the space, but an undeniable cloud darkens the room when I step foot inside. They look at Sybil, and then their eyes fall on me, deadly and sharp as they appraise me from head to toe.

"Ladies, this is Stella LeClaire," Sybil announces. "Or Cherrybomb, as I like to call her. She's a transplant from Greenwich."

Silence. That's what I'm greeted with. Until the girl who I can only assume fancies herself as queen bee decides to pipe up.

"Who let the scholarship student in?" She snickers.

Red creeps into my cheeks as my fists curl at my sides. Before I can say anything, Sybil answers on my behalf.

"Careful, Louisa. You're letting your green-eyed monster show. Stella's not a scholarship student. Her father works for the Arthur Group, and her mother is Lila Monroe. You know, the model?"

"Right," another girl with a yellow blazer chimes in. "I think I've heard of her. Wasn't she famous in like… the eighties? I heard she's more into day drinking than runways these days."

"It must be hard to swallow what your own future will look like," I bite back. "After all, that's what this machine is all about right? Churning out suburban housewives whose husbands cheat on them while they raise the next generation of trust fund brats to be just like you."

Sybil snorts beside me, but I know I've hit the nail on the head when the trio of girls at the front pierce right through me with looks that could kill. "You better watch your back, Cherrybitch. You've just lost any chance of making friends at Loyola. You're blacklisted."

"Let her reputation forever rest in peace," another girl adds, dabbing at her eyes theatrically.

"I'm shaking in my Doc Martens." I roll my eyes.

"Looks like you won't have another spineless clone to follow you around this year, Louisa." Sybil smirks. "You'll have to let one of your other bots do the grunt work."

We leave them standing there, slack-jawed and fuming while we venture toward my room. Vaguely, I hear Sybil congratulating me on surviving my first standoff with the self-proclaimed Loyola sisterhood. But internally, I can't help feeling like it wasn't an accomplishment at all. Deep down, I know there will be a lot more where that came from to contend with this year.

CHAPTER FOUR
STELLA

"Damn girl." Sybil whistles as she pulls up a seat at my table in the cafeteria. "Your outfit is on point today, and I think everyone in here has noticed."

I glance down at my clothes, wondering what the big deal is. According to my Pinterest board, my white blouse, navy blue cardigan, and polka dot tights are all standard issue boarding school fashion. The only difference is that my dress code compliant pleated skirt is crimson, not black. A signature splash of color to match my Mahogany red hair and iconic lipstick. If there was one thing my mother imparted on me, it was my own sense of fashion. While she always insisted I should wear green, I rebelled by buying everything red I could get my hands on.

"People won't stop staring." I glare at some of the faces who still haven't turned away. "I feel like I'm on display."

"That's because most of the girls have to pay for what God gave you naturally," Sybil teases. "And the boys want to be the first to get under your skirt. It's a huge challenge with the new girls. Don't be surprised if you have a different male suitor trying to escort you to class every day."

"Ha." I fling a noodle across the table onto her plate. "Says the graceful swan of a dancer. Don't think for one second I haven't noticed how many admirers you have here."

"They're just stupid high school boys." She sighs. "This year, I want to dip my toe into the college water, if you know what I mean."

Sybil is unashamedly boy crazy, and I foresee a lot of lonely nights without her this year while she's off chasing trousers. In some ways, I envy that she's able to be so carefree and happy. She knows who she is and what she wants, and she doesn't apologize for it. But those traits are luxuries I don't have.

"Well, you have fun with that," I remark. "I'll just be back at the dorms, painting my nails every weekend."

"Not likely." She snorts. "You'll make friends in no time."

"I have plenty of friends." I count them off on my fingers. "Chaos. Neurosis. Psychosis. Anxiety. The list is never-ending."

"Don't we all." She laughs. "How were your first three classes?"

"They were interesting," I admit. "There was a lot more talking than I thought there would be. Like the teachers actually want to hear what you have to say."

"Most of the classes here are discussion based." She takes a sip of her water and tosses a gummy bear into her mouth. Something I've noticed about Sybil is that between every healthy bite, she rewards herself with a gummy bear.

"I like it." I shrug. "But when I do speak up, there is inevitably someone waiting to challenge me."

"Just try to ignore them," she says. "It will get better. They're testing you out, trying to break you. Eventually, they'll get bored and move on to someone else."

I nod. Everything is a game here, and like a Shakespeare play, I'm merely one of the many players. "We have AP Research together next."

A funny look passes over Sybil's face. "Right. I forgot about that."

"What's wrong?" I ask.

"Nothing." She shakes her head. "Just be careful about speaking up in those classes. Mr. Carter is a grade A asshole. We call him Lucifer. Or the hot teacher of doom. Depends on who you ask."

"That bad, huh?" I swallow a mouthful of macaroni and cheese and wish I'd chosen a salad instead.

"He's harsh," Sybil answers. "His classes are challenging, but that's why everyone takes them. They look good on applications, but if you want to do communications at Cornell, they are a must. Just make sure you're always prepared and never late. In his class, I'd say it's better to blend in than stand out."

"Duly noted." I glance at the papers I stuffed into my binder to see what I need for the class and then check the time on my watch. "Crap. I still have to grab my book. We only have ten minutes left."

"Meet you there?" Sybil asks, shoveling as much salad as she can into her mouth.

"Yep, save a seat for me."

She nods, and I fly out of the cafeteria and onto the quad. It's going to take me some time to get used to planning for the whole day. Without one central location, that means I'll need to carry my books with me or manage my time better. Which, admittedly, I'm not great at. I'm disorganized on my best day, and I tend to lose track of the hour. I take notes on whatever's handy at the moment and then often have to dig around for ages before I find them again. I've always had my own way of doing things. My mother says I'm flighty, and she doesn't mean it in a good way. But I know if I'm going to survive this year, I have to do better.

Entering Lawrence Hall, a few girls are touching up their makeup in the common room, and it doesn't escape my attention that Louisa and her drones are here. Ignoring their jabs as I walk by, I dart into my room and start searching around the scattered mess of my things for my research textbook. I've only got five minutes to grab it and get all the way to the other side of campus, and right now, things aren't looking good. But they start to look even worse when I hear the unmistakable snickering outside my door, followed by the sound of a loud thunk.

"What the hell?" I grumble as I jiggle the handle and discover that they've managed to lock me in somehow. "You've got to be kidding me! This isn't funny. Let me out now."

There is no answer from the other side. It's clear they've already left, reveling in my misery as panic rises in my chest. Sybil said I can't be late to this class, and I still haven't found my textbook. There isn't time now, and no matter how hard I try at the doorknob, it won't budge.

Crap. Crap. Crap.

I glance at the window, realizing it's my only option, and then stupidly berate myself for not thinking of that right away. I'm on the ground level, so the only thing I have to lose is my pride as I fling myself out the wooden frame onto solid ground. With no time to adjust my rumpled clothing, I dart toward the Franklin building, only to realize I mixed up my directions and have to backtrack, adding another two minutes to my journey. Today is not my day.

I bluster inside the building and into the classroom without giving it any real thought, silently crashing right into the teacher as he's heading to shut the door. *Mr. Lucifer Hot Teacher of Doom Carter.*

"Oh my God." The words fall helplessly from my mouth as I look up at him and try to right myself. "I'm so sorry, Mr. Carter."

Deep green eyes fringed with dark lashes gaze down at me, brows pinched together, lips in a flat line. Sybil wasn't joking. He really is the hot teacher of doom. My heart beats faster as I study him, unable to stop this slow-motion train wreck from happening. He isn't like any teacher I've ever seen before. The man is at least six feet tall with the body of an athlete. A body wrapped up like a *GQ* model in black trousers, a crisp white shirt, and a black waistcoat. His cologne has notes of what I think are cardamom and sandalwood, but I drag in a deep breath just to be sure.

My God, this man is beautiful, and I can't seem to stop staring at him. He's older than me, but young enough that I know he isn't quite in his thirties. Silky chocolate locks of hair soften his caustic expression and sharp, angular cheekbones. My eyes blaze over his coppery skin down to the beating pulse of his throat.

This must be what it feels like. That chemistry thing Sybil is always rambling on about. My hormones are firing on all cylinders, and I don't know how to stop this roller coaster of emotions as his eyes cut over my face. That is until he speaks, reminding me we have an audience, and I've just humiliated myself for the third time today.

"You're late, Miss LeClaire."

CHAPTER FIVE
SEBASTIAN

The first day of school is as monotonous as the blur that has been the past three years. One by one, the students parade into the classroom, showing off the latest designer handbags while they humblebrag about their summers on the French Riviera. The endless cacophony of giggling schoolgirls born with Tiffany spoons in their mouth is a long-suffering death. Briefly, my thoughts drift to Katie, grateful that she never succumbed to the peer pressure to be just like them.

I scan the sea of faces, taking note of moods, new haircuts, casual attempts at cool conversation. There aren't any who stand out. Not a single one. Already, I'm convinced that it's hopeless. Finding someone who can think for themselves in this monochrome environment will suck the last of my soul from me.

The steady unfailing tick of my Tag Heuer timepiece alerts me to the hour, and I move on autopilot to seal my fate inside the classroom. It's just another Monday. Just another school year. Another group of students I will forget as soon as they leave. Until it isn't. Until a flash of red crashes into me, making this day one for the books.

Stella LeClaire. I know it must be her when she looks up and stuns me with those kohl-lined eyes the color of honey. I would have remembered those eyes if I'd ever seen them before. Vaguely, I recall glancing at her name amongst the others on my list, acknowledging that I had a new student this year. But after that, I never thought of it again. And now here she is. A banging drum solo in a world full of symphonies. Right away, I know she is the outlier in this group with her red wine-stained hair and ivory skin and her hundred thousand-megawatt face.

"Oh my God." The words stumble from her crimson red lips. "I'm so sorry, Mr. Carter."

Christ, those lips. I can't tear my eyes away from them, and the limp dick in my trousers has taken notice too. My dick hasn't seen any action for far too long, and now is an inopportune moment to remember that. This is new, and it's a fucking problem, but that doesn't stop me from taking stock of this mysterious new creature in front of me. Leggy with a body of a pinup fantasy, she has the figure of a model with none of the grace and only half of the confidence. There is something unapologetically genuine about her, and I am drawn to it like a goddamn moth. Soft lines and retro sex kitten lashes are all I can see. Unspoiled territory demanding to be explored.

Fuck. I'm staring at her, and the entire class is watching. How long have we been here like this? What fucking day is it? It's time to rectify this situation. My eyes cut over her, and my voice turns menacing as I establish dominance. "You're late, Miss LeClaire."

"I'm so sorry." Her eyes dart to Louisa and her gaggling pack of hyenas in the back of the classroom. "I had some trouble finding my way here."

She's lying, and it's evident that she's become the latest target of the self-proclaimed mean girls at Loyola. But regardless of her excuses, I have an example to set.

"Congratulations," I reply flatly. "You've earned the award of fastest detention ever given on the first day of school. Now find a seat, Miss LeClaire, and get here on time from now on or don't bother showing up at all."

Her lips slam shut, and she stares at me in disbelief for a second before she swallows down her humiliation. Slinking to her seat, she leaves me standing at the front of the class alone with an unfamiliar shadow of frustration. I shut the door and take a moment to gather myself before I point out the rules I scrawled on the whiteboard earlier this morning.

"Welcome to AP Research. Those of you who have made it this far are second year students of the Capstone program, so I assume you will understand this is not an easy college credit for your application. If you are ready to put your mind to use, then I will be your guide this year. My name is Mr. Carter, and I expect you to address me as such. Now, let's go over the rules, shall we?"

The class falls dead silent as I begin to ramble off the structure that is better suited for toddlers than teenagers.

No texting. No snapchatting. No selfies. No phones, period.

No eye rolling. No whining.

If I'm talking, you're not.

If you plan to show up late, don't bother coming at all.

My eyes inadvertently move to Stella as I read this line. To my satisfaction, she sucks in a breath, and I continue down the list.

If you're passing notes, be prepared to share them with the entire class.

No gossiping. No food or drinks.

No shirt, no shoes, no classroom. This is not a hippie commune, nor is it your sofa. Come to class in compliance with the dress code and remain that way. Nobody wants to smell your feet when you kick off your shoes.

Do your homework and don't make excuses.

If you are coughing, sneezing, shivering, or otherwise showing signs of an impending plague, you will be sent directly to the school nurse.

There are no participation medals in this class. Grades are earned through sweat and tears.

"Now that we have that out of the way, are there any questions?"

A horde of blank faces stare back at me, but the one I find myself drifting to is hers. The girl who will undoubtedly be a problem this year. She's chosen a seat next to Sybil, which displeases me more than I expect. While Sybil is a decent student, she is also a party girl. They aren't the most likely of friends, but I can see Stella getting caught up in things she shouldn't be with Sybil's influence. Regardless, I remind myself it isn't my concern.

"If there are no questions, then let's proceed. You will note on your desk there is a course syllabus in front of you. Today, we will cover the schedule, course materials, and expectations for this semester. In the likely event that you decide this class isn't what you anticipated, you can elect to opt out this week. Now open your *AP Research Workbooks* and turn to page twenty-seven. You have ten minutes to read the *Getting Started* section on your own."

The class shuffles around, removing books and pencils from their Prada bags. Everyone except for Stella, who has slunk even lower into her seat, failing to go unnoticed as she refuses to follow through on this very basic command.

"Miss LeClaire, do we have a problem?" My voice echoes off the walls, and every student turns to look at her.

"I don't have my textbook," she says, her voice unwavering even though her face betrays the nerves she doesn't want anyone to see. "I'm sorry. I had trouble finding it, and then I was late —"

"You seem to be under the impression that I care about your excuses." I lean against my desk and pin her with my gaze. "Next time, come prepared or don't bother. A sloth catches on quicker than you, Miss LeClaire."

The classroom erupts into soft snickers while red blooms across her cheeks, just as I predicted. Her fists curl at her sides, and it appears that Stella does have some fire in her after all.

"Hey, Mr. Carter," Ethan pipes up, waggling his eyebrows in Stella's direction. "She can share with me. I won't bite."

The muscles in my throat tighten as I swivel my attention in his direction. "Did I ask for your assistance, Mr. Dupree?"

"No." He scratches at his eyebrow with the end of his pencil. "I just figured—"

"You just figured your raging hormones would be a benefit to Miss LeClaire in some way, but they won't. Not today. Not ever. So, think twice before you open your mouth in my class again."

Ethan shuts his trap, and I take a seat at my desk, confounded by my annoyance over something so juvenile. My body is rigid with tension, and I can't dispel this odd sensation in my gut. Every jock in class is staring at her, and my reaction is beyond visceral. What the fuck is this? I haven't been this wound up... *ever*. Stella has captured the attention of everyone in class, the girls included. They know she's competition, and they want to squash her like a bug beneath their Jimmy Choos.

We all need to get a fucking grip. Scrapping my initial plan of discussing the material together, I rattle off instructions for the class to read an additional two chapters on their own. In that time, I take the opportunity to study Stella as she and Sybil share a textbook, quietly flipping through the pages without distraction. She can do that much, but is she capable of more? The fact that she's friends with Sybil makes me question her background. What brought her here? What secrets is she hiding behind those expressive eyes? And why does she keep glancing up at me like she's seeking out my approval?

She is a curious dichotomy of fire and fragility if ever I saw one. But when I glance at her file, I'm not surprised to find that at least in one regard, there is nothing different about her. She's on track to be a communications major, courtesy of the courses picked out by her mother. Her class schedule is nearly a carbon copy of every other Loyola student before her. This is the recipe for the Ivy Leagues. But is it Stella's desire, or is she merely a good little soldier? The answer to that question becomes painfully obvious when I read the administration's note about photography classes being strictly forbidden, per Stella's parents.

She likes to take photos. Yet here she is, doubling down on college level courses like a daughter who wants nothing more than to please her parents. There's something about Stella that makes me believe she will always go the extra mile to seek approval from those with authority. I can see it every time she looks at me. And before the end of the hour, I've made up my mind. In the past, I picked easy, obvious targets for my projects. Without fail, they failed me. They couldn't withstand the expectations of their peers and their family and the machine that is Loyola Academy.

But Stella won't fail. I feel it deep in my gut. A spark of hope that I haven't had with any of the others. A want I haven't experienced since my own college days. I will push her harder than I've pushed anyone else before her, and she will cling to hold onto herself in the face of any storm I might bring her way. I will open her eyes to the realities of this world. And in the end, she will despise me for my ruthlessness, but she will be grateful.

Stella LeClaire, welcome to my final project.

CHAPTER SIX
STELLA

Fourth period Creative Writing passes in a blur as I am yet
again saddled near the Loyola mean girls and their scornful
gazes. After my first run-in with them, I have since learned
their names are Louisa, Libby, and Leah. Just a guess, but it
seems like there's a pretty basic requirement for their club,
and it has everything to do with their names. It probably
doesn't hurt that they all come from wealthy families and
have matching wardrobes too. Through the entirety of the
class, I can feel their gazes boring into the back of my head
while they whisper amongst each other.

The one silver lining is that Ms. Hargrave seems like a decent
teacher, and so far, I haven't earned myself a reprimand from
her. She commends me several times for my correct answers
as she asks questions to gauge our knowledge, and it dissolves
some of my first day jitters. Loyola Academy isn't going to be
a walk in the park, but if I stay focused, I think I can do well
here. I can uphold my grade point average and maintain the
course laid out for me.

I'm putting everything on the line to send you here, Stella.

As Ms. Hargrave dismisses us, I release a celebratory breath
for surviving the first day. Well, almost. There's still the
matter of detention. Something I hope my parents won't be
hearing about. I only have ten minutes to get there, and I'm
determined not to screw this up. But before I can even make it
onto the quad, I'm stopped by Louisa and her crew of
cardigan clones.

"We have a message for you," Louisa says.

"Another one?" I roll my eyes. "Well, in that case, why don't
you write a letter and send it to someone who cares?"

I attempt to step around the trio, but Libby stops me with a pink clawed hand on my chest. "The message is stay away from Ethan. He's off-limits."

I pry her fingers off me and examine the scowl on Louisa's face, and suddenly, it all becomes so clear. I can't even help the laughter that bursts from my lips. Could she be any more transparent?

"I don't want your dumb jock boyfriend," I assure her. "He's all yours. Now if you'll excuse me, I have to go."

I successfully manage to maneuver around them this time, but it doesn't stop Louisa from calling out after me anyway. "You better watch your back, Cherrybitch. That's the only warning you'll get."

I throw a hand up and wave as I pick up the pace, heading down the hill toward the student center. Sybil was kind enough to let me know where detention was since Mr. Carter failed to inform me. He did arch an eyebrow at me before I left, and I almost asked, but it felt like he was challenging me. I think he has me pegged for another run of the mill rich kid with entitlement issues, but I'm here to prove him wrong. While I was undeniably flustered in his presence at first, his abrasive personality was enough to douse me in cold water. The man might be hot as sin, but he's also completely detached from human emotion. Briefly, I wonder how he came to be that way, but I try to forget it as I stride through the student center and find room 206.

Stupidly, I had anticipated I wouldn't be the only one in detention today, but one glance at the empty classroom has dashed that hope. Worse yet, when I see the dark figure lurking at the desk inside, my heart jumps into my throat. Mr. Prince of Darkness, aka Satan, isn't just my research teacher. He's also my warden.

"Are you going to stand there all day, Miss LeClaire, or do I need to give you permission to take a seat?"

Crap.

I'm staring at him again. Why do I keep doing that, and how do I make it stop? Moving my leaden feet, I traipse across the room and sit down at one of the tables in the second row. At least now there's some distance between us, and I can pretend I'm working on something while I doodle in my journal. Even though I have homework, there's no way I can concentrate in his presence.

He doesn't say another word, but our eyes clash as I retrieve a few things from my bag and lay them out on the desk. Binder, notepad, pens, a few books to look legit, and my journal.

When Mr. Carter settles into his seat and begins going over his own paperwork, I settle in too.

Flipping through the pages of my journal, I smooth my fingers over the edges of some of the photos I took this summer. They are mostly sunsets and candids of people on the beach, but also the occasional bird and plenty of shots of me and Sybil goofing around. While nature is great for practice, people are my favorite subject to photograph, and I have some shots of Sybil I'm especially proud of. She even asked me to print them out so she can use them in her dance portfolio.

More than a few times, I considered showing them to my father. Once upon a time, he had a passion for photography. He loved his job, and he was good at it, but he never made it big, so he gave up his dream when he traded his soul as a corporate slave. The dissatisfaction is written all over his face, and now I can't help but wonder if that will be me in ten years. He's told me on more than a few occasions that photography can only ever be a hobby for me. Neither of my parents see it as a viable career choice even though my mother hasn't had her own career in decades. She hates the very idea of me wasting my time behind the camera so much that she even broke one of my lenses last year in a drunken fit.

Darkness infiltrates my vision as I flip through my journal until I find a blank page. A new chapter. This is the part of my life where I focus on the things I'm supposed to be doing. Acing all my tests, getting good grades, and going to the college my mother wants. *But what about my happiness?*

I find myself scribbling that last sentence onto the page with a pink gel pen before a tear inadvertently slips from my eye and splashes onto the ink, splattering it like a sign of things to come. And when I quickly wipe my eyes and sneak a glance at Mr. Carter, I'm mortified to find that he witnessed the entire event. Our eyes lock, but he doesn't say a word, and neither do I. For a moment, I find myself studying the lines of his face again, considering how easy he would be to photograph. There isn't a bad angle on him. But the permanent scowl on his face hints at something darker under the surface. Something broken and jagged and full of pain or rage. Those of us who know can recognize these qualities in each other. He's the first to look away, and it leaves me feeling empty, though I'm not sure why. The loss of that connection is oddly disappointing. I don't even like him. He's an asshole with a heart of barbed wire, and that's what I find myself drawing on the blank page next to my tear-soaked art. A beating heart wrapped in barbed wire. I drew it for him, but when I stop to examine it, I can see myself in there too.

When my forty-five minutes are finally up, Mr. Carter rises from his desk with the authority of someone who should be ruling a boardroom rather than a classroom. His black oxfords clip across the floor with military precision, and he ensnares me with a dark look as he opens the door. I don't dare move. Not until he tells me to. Another standoff ensues, our eyes battling our respective roles in silence. I could almost swear the edge of his lip twitches in victory. He's a man who likes to exert his power, and right now, he's exerting it over me.

"You're free to go, Miss LeClaire."

I stuff all my belongings back into my bag and sling it over my shoulder. When I glance back up, I expect him to be gone, but he isn't. He's still standing there, caging me in with his eyes. I can't figure out what he's thinking, and I don't know if I want to either. There's something mysterious about him. Something sinister, certainly. But something alluring too. Does he know that I feel that way? Can he recognize my desperation for his approval? Even as I'm calculating all the ways I should hate him, I'm wondering how I can win him over too.

I join him at the door, and he gestures me out first. To my displeasure, I find we aren't alone. Along the corridor, Ethan and his Lacrosse buddies are waiting for someone, and when their heads swivel in my direction, it becomes apparent that someone is me.

"Hey, Cherrybomb." Ethan grins as he uses the name he must have heard from Sybil. "You're finally sprung, huh?"

"Yep." I rock back on my heels and glance at Mr. Carter, whose gaze is practically glacial as he examines Ethan.

"Don't you have somewhere to be, Mr. Dupree?" he clips out. Ethan's jaw flexes, and he raises his chin in challenge as he meets Mr. Carter's gaze. The temperature in the building plummets as they stare at each other. If I didn't know any better, I would say the scowling beast of a teacher doesn't want me hanging out with Ethan and his buddies, but the question is why?

"What's the big deal?" Ethan claps back. "She's out of detention, right? We're allowed to socialize in public quarters, and last I checked, this is the student center."

"Miss LeClaire has a maintenance issue to deal with back at her dorm," Mr. Carter answers flatly. "So why don't you boys run along and find something else to do?"

Ethan turns to me, but I'm too busy staring up at Mr. Carter in confusion. Is he referring to my locked room? And if he is, how the hell does he even know about that?

"The door," I murmur though it comes out sounding more like a question.

"Damn. Someone already pennied your doorjamb?" Ethan asks.

"Yeah, your girlfriend." I glare at him.

"Louisa?" He scrunches his nose and his buddies laugh. "She isn't my girlfriend. She wishes she was, but she isn't."

"That's nice." I wave him away. "But I don't need any more trouble, and Mr. Carter's right. I have to go deal with that now."

"All right." Ethan hops down off the table he's perched on and allows his eyes to do one full sweep over my body in slow motion. *Pig.* "We'll see you around then."

They disappear down the hall, and I turn back to Mr. Carter. "How did you know about my door?"

"I know everything that goes on in this school." He pivots on his heel and locks the door behind us. "And you'd be wise to remember that."

CHAPTER SEVEN
STELLA

I spend the next afternoon shooting photos around campus while Sybil finishes up her dance practice, and I'm surprised to see just how many extracurricular activities Loyola Academy has. Everything from fencing to cheer to swim is on offer, and even though my mother requested I choose at least two, I haven't signed up for any yet.

"There's still time," Sybil tells me as she crash-lands into my camera view. "You could do swimming. That's easy."

"Not really a fan of the chlorine," I admit.

"Hmm." She does a triple cartwheel across the lawn and plops down gracefully in a cross-legged position. "What about cheer squad? You could come to practice with me next Wednesday."

"Really?" I laugh. "You want me on the cheer team? I don't exactly have the right look. Or the pep. Or the coordination."

"Why not?" She scrunches up her nose and claps her hands theatrically. "Be aggressive. Be, be aggressive."

"I wish I could bottle up some of your energy." I roll my eyes.

"Come on," she pleads. "What could it hurt to at least try out? We can work on some of the moves over the weekend. Just promise me you'll think about it."

My gaze drifts across the field to where the boys are playing lacrosse on the left and soccer on the right. Everybody is busy doing something. And I know from my mother's incessant nagging that I need something else on my college application, even if it does seem somewhat ridiculous to me. But at least with Sybil at my side, it could be fun.

"I guess it wouldn't hurt to try," I concede.

"Yay!" She jumps up and does a few cartwheels while I continue to snap pictures. And then something in the distance catches my attention.

"What the…?" My voice drifts off as I inadvertently zoom in and snap a few photos.

"What?" Sybil asks.

"Is that Mr. Carter coaching the soccer team?"

"Yep." She squints into the distance, using her hand as a shield against the sun. "He played soccer for the Ivy's. Won a bunch of awards, or so I've heard. I think he was supposed to be drafted into the Major Leagues too."

"Why wasn't he?"

"Don't know." She shrugs. "But the soccer players here practically bow at his feet like he's some kind of legend. I know because I dated one of them freshman year."

"Who haven't you dated here?" I tease.

She sticks out her tongue and throws a handful of grass at me. "Just wait and see. You'll have five or six boyfriends soon too. I've heard you're making waves around the school."

"Yeah, Louisa and her girl gang already threatened me to stay away from Ethan." I make a slitting action across my throat. "Or else."

Sybil rolls her eyes. "Louisa is never going to get Ethan. She's delusional."

"Like he's some prize." I shake my head. "I don't get what she sees in him anyway. He was waiting for me outside of detention."

"Who knows." Sybil agrees. "And that doesn't surprise me. He's had eyes on you since you stepped foot on the grounds. Every time you turn him down, he'll just try harder."

"Oh, yay." I groan. "Just what I need."

"Apart from Ethan's prowess, how was detention anyway?" she asks.

"It was all right. I didn't know it was with Mr. Carter."

"Oops." She slaps a hand against her forehead. "I should have probably warned you, huh? He always does detention. I think he actually enjoys it, miserable bastard that he is. I still can't believe how harsh he was with you. I mean, he's always been a prick, but still, he could have cut you some slack on your first day."

"Doesn't seem like that's his style," I observe, opting not to tell her about our weird stare down in detention.

"No, it isn't. Probably best to stay off his radar if you can. It already seems like he has it out for you."

"That's my plan."

"You want to head back to my room and study for a bit?"

For reasons I don't really know, I snap a few more photos of Mr. Carter, and then Sybil pokes me in the arm.

"Hello, earth to Stella. Are you there?"

"Sorry, got distracted."

"By all those hunky soccer players?" Her eyes light up.

"Uh-huh." I lie because I don't want to admit that I have a weird hate crush on my teacher. "Let's go study."

While Sybil does her math homework, I pretend to read on my phone, but really, I'm checking out Mr. Carter's bio on the school website. I have no idea why, but I can't seem to keep my mind from drifting back to him. What Sybil told me about his almost career as a soccer player has only managed to spark my curiosity about him.

Unfortunately, other than a small blip about him being the soccer coach, there isn't much about his past. There's a mention of his time at Harvard, that he played in the Ivy Leagues, and that with his advanced standing, he graduated with a masters in just four years. It seems insane, but then again, he is insane. I can just imagine him not eating, sleeping, or blinking while he aced every one of his college courses. All to end up here. It's rather odd. Not that Loyola isn't prestigious, but teaching doesn't seem like it would be his career of choice. In fact, I would think it would be the last thing on his list.

"Finally." Sybil slams her book shut with a yawn. "Got that done. Now I can spend extra time in the studio tomorrow morning."

As much as Sybil loves to goof off, she never lets anything get in the way of her dedication for dancing, and I admire her for that. I wish I could be as passionate and free spirited as she is. I wish I could go after what I really want without disappointing my father.

"I think you're going to do great things someday," I tell her with a weak smile.

"So are you," she insists. "Just wait and see."

I nod and gather up my things, taking my cue to leave. We both need to get some sleep, and I need to be on my game tomorrow with time management and organization. That means extra planning tonight for what I'll need.

"Okay, I'll see you tomorrow afternoon."

"K." She flops back onto her bed and nods. "Night."

I shut the door behind me and pad down the hall to my room, trying to stay quiet. Most of the other girls are already in bed, and I don't want to wake them. Sneaking into my room, I change into my pajamas and toss my hair up into a messy bun before flopping down onto my bed, only to be horrified when I do.

The mattress is soaking wet, and now my bedding and pajamas are too. I pull the cold wet material away from my body and groan as I hop up and stare at the mess. Looks like Louisa is up to her tricks again, and I am officially fucking over her shit. Tempted to respond in kind by walking down the hall and throwing a bucket of ice water in her face, I take three deep breaths and calm myself. That's exactly what she wants. Girls like Louisa have everything, and she knows that if we get into a catfight, I'm the one who will get the boot. I have to be smarter. I need to be the bigger person. If I let my emotions win, I could end up losing my place at Loyola. And right now, I just need to get some sleep. I won't allow Louisa or anyone else to deter my focus this year. My parents are counting on me, and I can't waste this opportunity.

Dragging the only spare blanket I have from the closet, I spread it on the floor and wad up a sweater for a makeshift pillow. It's not going to be the best sleep I've ever had, but at this point, it will have to do. I lay down and close my eyes, finally starting to drift off when something taps at my window.

"You've got to be kidding me," I groan.

I get up and slide the window up, only to be greeted by Ethan's face. "Hey, Cherrybomb. Watch out."

"What the—" I squeal as he pushes his way inside and wiggles a bottle in my direction.

"I brought the party."

"What are you doing here?" I demand. "You're going to get us both in trouble."

"It's no big deal." He waves off my concern and takes a seat on my bed. *My soaking wet bed.* His face morphs into an expression of surprise, and he jumps up and stares at the blanket on the floor. "Fucking Louisa. She did this, didn't she?"

"I'm assuming." I throw my hands up. "As you can see, it's been a long day. So please just go."

"Come on." He twists the top off the bottle and offers it to me. "Just do one shot. It will help you relax."

"I don't need to relax," I argue. "I need to sleep."

"Fine." He smirks. "One shot and I'll leave."

"I'm not bargaining with you." I put my hands on my hips and glare at him. "I didn't invite you, and I really don't need Louisa coming after me if she finds out you were here."

"Fuck Louisa." He takes a pull from the bottle. "She doesn't own me."

"Well, that's between the two of you to work out," I tell him. "Now please just—"

"What's going on in here?" The booming voice at my window scares the ever-loving crap out of me, and when I turn, I'm horrified to see Mr. Carter outside in what looks like running gear. His eyes bounce back and forth between Ethan and me, silent accusations lingering in the air between us.

"This isn't what it looks like," I say quickly. But it's too late. Mr. Carter has already disappeared, and I know he's headed this way.

I look at Ethan, wondering what we should do, but like the worm he is, he disappears out the window, leaving the bottle of whiskey behind as if it belongs to me.

"You're a real piece of work," I yell after him. "Don't ever come to my room again."

The door swings open, and there's Mr. Carter, his shadow falling over me like a black cloud. "Miss LeClaire." His eyes dart toward the open window briefly before landing back on me. The bottle of whiskey is still in front of me, and he doesn't miss it. Things only gets worse from there. His eyes move over the blanket on the floor before they roam over me and pause briefly on my chest. It isn't until I look down that I understand why. The flimsy white knitted tank I wear for pajamas is still damp, and my nipples are poking out from beneath it.

"Oh God." I slap my hands over my chest and shiver as Mr. Carter reaches down and seizes the bottle of whiskey, examining it.

"You are really making quite the first impression here," he snarls.

"This isn't fair," I blurt out, realizing how lame it sounds. "I didn't ask him to come here. He just barged in—"

"A convenient excuse." He stalks toward me, and I step backward, bumping against my bed. He leans in, and for one delusional second, I think he's going to kiss me. But instead, he presses his palm against my soaked mattress. His body is so close to mine I can smell him. The scent of masculine sweat and cardamom. I stupidly inhale a deep breath, and he notices. What the hell is wrong with me?

"Is there something you'd like to report, Miss LeClaire?" he asks, his tone acerbic.

I know he's referring to the mattress, but I don't have any proof, and even if I did, that's not a war I'm ready to start with Louisa. I'm not a snitch, and there are better ways to get back at her than involving the school staff.

"No, sir." I tilt my chin up to meet his eyes.

His nostrils flare, and I take note of it. I take note of everything from his sweat-soaked T-shirt clinging to his broad shoulders and muscular abs to the way his pants hang loose from his hips. I've never felt like a hormonal teenager before, but my hypothalamus is working overtime to pump out those feel-good chemicals in his presence. I'm practically biting my tongue to keep myself from saying something stupid. Because right now, his attention, good or bad, is everything. I want his approval like I've never wanted anything else before. I want to tell him to push my knees apart and show me how mad he is. Punish me the way I can see he wants to. But Mr. Carter has more self-restraint than I do. He coldly chooses to deny me, stepping back into his own space and leaving me alone. Always alone.

"If that's the road you want to take, so be it." He holds the whiskey bottle up. "I'll be confiscating this, and I expect you to report to the groundskeepers at six a.m. tomorrow for your punishment. Work hours and detention after school for the next week."

"But what about Ethan?" I demand childishly. "What will his punishment be?"

"That will be all, Miss LeClaire." He turns on his heel and exits just as quickly as he arrived, sealing me into my room with the faint trace of his scent. A glance at the clock confirms it's already one in the morning, and tomorrow is officially going to suck.

Chapter Eight
Sebastian

Back at my house, I drain the bottle of whiskey into the sink and throw the remnants into the trash, taking satisfaction in the sound of it shattering. Leaning over the counter, I close my eyes and try to gather my thoughts, concentrating on what I need to do this week. But instead, all I can see is her. Standing there in soft cotton shorts and a wet tank top with her pink nipples poking through.

Irrational thoughts flood my mind about what happened in that room. Did she let that entitled prick touch her? Kiss her? Did her lips touch that bottle after he did?

It's not fucking logical or sane, but the uncertainties continue to plague me as I sit down at the kitchen table and stare at the wall. This girl is getting inside my head, and I can't focus on what I'm supposed to be doing because my dick is so goddamn engorged, I can't think straight. She's a temptation straight from the devil's toy factory. I've survived years of celibacy without issue, but after two days of Stella LeClaire in my life, I'm ready to fuck anything in sight.

It would be tempting to walk across the campus right now and hate fuck Misty Hargrave. I know she'd let me do anything I wanted to her. Maybe it would even purge these fucked-up thoughts playing on repeat inside my head. But it wouldn't satisfy me. Not like Stella would.

Christ.

I close my eyes, and all I can think about is spreading her thighs apart and stuffing her full of my cock while she screams my name from those blood red lips. Teachers aren't supposed to have these thoughts. It goes against every moral fiber I've ever tried to hold on to. But morality is a blurred line when I wrap my fist around my cock and allow my imagination to run wild. I want her to be a virgin. I want to be the first to ruin her. I want to debase her and torment her and call her every filthy thing I can think of while I fuck her and fill her with my come.

She will be my ruination if I don't get a fucking grip. I suck in a breath and think about her tight pussy wrapped around me, milking me dry. I bet she tastes like honey between her thighs. I bet she would feel so goddamned good I'd never want to let her go. And for that, I hate her.

The fantasy in my head takes a dark turn as I bend her over my desk and beat her ass with the palm of my hand until it's so red, she will think of me every time she has to sit down. She'd let me too. I know she'd let me do anything I wanted, and she'd follow my every command, so desperate for my attention and approval. She'd kneel before me and pant at my feet, begging me with those gold eyes as she looked up at me in worship. She'd call me sir and let me grab her by the throat and shove my cock into her mouth. She'd kiss my body and touch me with her soft, delicate hands.

Fuck, I want her. I want her so much it makes me violent with need. And no matter how many times I stroke myself or what I imagine her doing, it won't be the same. I know this when I finally come, shooting my release across my knuckles, and my dick refuses to fall limp.

Stella. Stella. Stella.

Her name is a mantra in my thoughts. She's supposed to be my project for this year. I want to break her but not like this. Not by corrupting her.

Yet I fear that's exactly what I'm going to do.

Unsurprisingly, Stella arrives on time today, making a show of placing her textbook neatly on the desk in front of her. *See, Mr. Carter, I can be good.*

It's almost too fucking easy. When she offers me a secret smile, she may as well be whispering that she's mine. Briefly, I consider how fucked up it is that she's so eager to please me. And then I remember that I don't care. I'm here to make this year hell for her and wear her down until I get to the core of her emotions. Her desires.

What does Stella LeClaire really want? And how far will she go to get it? Despite her resolve to put her head down and do her best at Loyola Academy, we both know she doesn't really belong here. She is too free spirited to be just another cog in the machine. She isn't chasing her dreams; she's chasing a feather in the wind. And I'm not here to teach Stella. I'm here to open her fucking eyes and wake her up. This path she's headed down is a collision course with misery, and until she sees that, I will take pleasure in reminding her every day that she isn't one of these trust fund brats. Starting right now.

She's obviously exhausted and tense as she waits quietly for class to begin. A girl like Stella has been deprived of her parents' attention for so long that she will look for it everywhere else. And as long as I set the bar higher, she will keep jumping to reach it.

"Let's get started." I rap my knuckles against the desk, drawing everyone's attention to the front of the class. "Stella, shut the door for us, will you?"

Her eyes flare as her name rolls from my lips with a cadence that lulls her into a false sense of comfort. She doesn't hesitate to get up from her seat. Today, she's wearing a crushed red velvet skirt, antique white blouse, and a pussy bow tie. I'm not the only one watching her as she crosses the room. Every pair of eyes is on the exotic creature cloaked in red. She shuts the door with a softness befitting of a mouse and returns to her seat, eagerly waiting for the next set of instructions.

"Today's class will be free form discussion as noted in the syllabus," I begin. "Every second period of the week, you will seek out academic papers on a chosen group topic to discuss. Today's umbrella term is ancient philosophies. Now, who would care to throw some ideas into the ring?"

A few hands go up around the classroom, and I scan the crowd as they wait to be called on. But it's Louisa who speaks first. "I have an idea, Mr. Carter."

"What is your suggestion, Louisa?"

She smirks in Stella's direction before returning her gaze to me. "The curse of the red hair gene throughout history."

Her friends snicker behind her, and Ethan decides to chime in too as he sneers in Stella's direction. "Yeah, we could answer that age-old question. Do gingers really have souls?"

Stella frowns at his newfound animosity toward her, but it's apparent I've made my stance clear. He won't be bothering her anymore. At least not while he's doing dishes in the cafeteria for the next two months.

"There's no need to waste precious time in class on that answer," Stella bites back. "I can already tell you... I sold mine to the devil."

My gaze returns to Stella, and despite her bravado, I can tell she doesn't like this. And why would she, being the only redhead in the class? Louisa's suggestion is designed to make her feel small, and admittedly, I want to see how she responds to the pressure. So even if it is utterly bullshit, I decide to roll with it.

"The curse of red hair throughout history. You have twenty minutes to do your research, and then we will discuss as a group."

Stella's mouth falls open, and Sybil foolishly tries to make her feel better about the situation. Perhaps it is cruel, but Stella will learn. *My God will she learn.*

"I can't believe this," Sybil whispers beside me. "This isn't fair."

"It's okay." I maintain my attempt at stoicism even though I feel anything but.

"It's not okay," she hisses. "This is basically a roast. You're the only redhead in here, and Mr. Carter knows it. He seriously has it out for you."

"I know." I choke back the awful feeling in my throat. Stupidly, I came here this afternoon hoping to make a better impression. But instead, he chose to put a target on my back. I don't get it. I really don't understand how he can be so cruel.

"Just don't let anything they say upset you," Sybil advises. "That's what they want. A reaction. And besides, I wrote down all the good things about redheads. I promise it won't be one-sided."

"Don't get yourself in trouble on my behalf," I whisper. "I'll be fine, I swear."

But as Mr. Carter calls time on our research, I don't exactly believe that myself. He stands in front of his desk, expressionless with his hands stuffed into his pockets. "Who would like to go first?"

"I will." Louisa flips her hair over her shoulder.

He nods to her and gives her the floor, and I glare at him like the traitor he is. I can't believe I ever thought he was hot. He's an asshole. The biggest asshole ever.

"Aristotle is rumored to have said that redheads are of baddish character," Louisa reports gleefully. "And they were often thought to be witches or vampires in certain cultures, which resulted in them being sacrificed, burned, or buried alive. A practice some believe should be resurrected."

"I got one, Mr. Carter," Ethan adds. "In Jewish mythology, Lilith was believed to be a redheaded sexualized demon who wreaked havoc on men."

"The Thracians worshipped gods with red hair," Sybil interjects. "And they have a special gene that gives them a higher pain threshold. Just under two percent of the population have red hair, so that makes them pretty unique."

"Don't tell that to the ancient Greeks," Louisa bites back.

Libby adds, "Yeah, I read that they were thought to be conceived through unclean sex in some religions. Usually with the devil."

"Hitler banned redheads from reproducing," someone else chimes in.

"Mark Twain thought they evolved from cats."

"In one of Michelangelo's pieces, Eve is depicted as a redhead after luring Adam to damnation."

"There are many notable redheads throughout history." Sybil raises her voice, counting off on her fingers as she speaks. "Cleopatra, Queen Elizabeth, Venus, Emily Dickinson. They don't ever go gray, and they can make their own vitamin D."

"I found a German study that says redheads really do like to have more fun, if you know what I mean." Ethan chuckles.

And so, the list goes on. For twenty minutes, I doodle in my journal while I listen to my classmates throw out every possible form of ammunition they can against a single hair color. Sybil is the only one who seems to find anything positive, and eventually, even she runs out of things to say. Silence is my only defense, until it isn't.

"Are we boring you, Stella?" A shadow falls over my desk, and I look up, horrified to see Mr. Carter studying the sketch in my journal.

"No."

"You don't have anything to add to the discussion?" he clips out.

"Not really, no. I think it's all been said."

"Then perhaps you'd like to share what you've deemed to be more important during class." He snatches the journal from my hands and holds it up for the class to see. "Great likeness of me, wouldn't you agree?"

Nobody agrees, of course. The devil with Mr. Carter's eyes and facial structure is undeniably him, and I don't have the will to argue otherwise.

"That will buy you one more week of detention, Miss LeClaire. Now put it away."

He tosses it back onto my desk and returns to the front of the class. "Your assignment for this evening is to articulate what approach and method of research you employed for today's topic. Cite your evidence, detail your own conclusions, and acknowledge any implications of your message. Class dismissed."

I take a breath and look at Sybil, who's glaring at Mr. Carter like she's tempted to say something she'll regret.

"Don't bother." I nudge her in the side. "It isn't worth it."

"We need to do something," she whispers.

I wait until we file out of the doorway and onto the quad before I respond. "I think I should just withdraw from his class. It's clear he doesn't like me, and if I stay, he's probably going to fail me."

"Ugh, I hate him." Sybil pouts. "It's so unfair. That's the only class we have together. But I think you're right. Maybe you should go to the office now and talk to an advisor. They can give you a late pass for the next class."

I nod in agreement, and we hug our goodbyes, going in separate directions. The administration building always has at least one student advisor hanging around during the day to chat with, and though it's typically by appointment, I'm hoping they will make an exception in my case. When I arrive, the woman at the front desk greets me and checks the schedule upon my request.

"I think Mrs. Hart can speak with you for a few minutes. Come with me and we'll see."

I follow her around the counter and into the office where Mrs. Hart resides at her desk, tapping away at her keyboard.

"Cacey, do you have a moment to speak with Miss LeClaire regarding her schedule?"

Mrs. Hart checks the time on her watch and nods, gesturing for me to sit down. "Sure."

The other woman leaves, and the door remains open while Mrs. Hart stares at me in question. "What can I help you with, Stella?"

"I wanted to see if it was possible to withdraw from my AP Research class and transfer to something comparable."

"Hmm." She adjusts her glasses. "Let me check."

I wait quietly while she clicks around my file and studies the class schedules.

"I'm afraid all the other AP classes are full. And I would highly advise that you stick with it if you can, since it looks like your career path is noted as a communications major. Is that still your plan for college?"

"Yes," I admit. "I'm trying to get into Cornell."

Or at least, that's what I'm supposed to do.

"Well, you'll need all the help you can get. Every detail makes a difference on an application. Can I ask why you want to withdraw from Research? It looks like you've already completed the first year of Seminar for the Capstone program. It might not work in your favor to quit halfway, as colleges are likely to notice."

I bite my lip and squeeze my hands together in my lap, fighting my reluctance to betray Mr. Carter, even though he's an ass.

"It's nothing," I assure her. "I think I'm just overreacting. It's all a little overwhelming for me."

"Okay." She tilts her head to the side, studying me. "I know Mr. Carter can be tough on his students, but I assure you he's an excellent teacher. He does have office hours too, if you need extra help. You'll be well educated in his class if you can hang in there."

"I'm sure I will." I swallow and stand. "Thank you, Mrs. Hart."

She smiles, and I move for the door, only to have my heart sink into my stomach when I see Mr. Carter standing in the office. And judging by the scowl on his face, he heard everything.

Chapter Ten
Sebastian

As Friday draws to an end, my irritation increases by the second. My father has called me an additional six times this week, which is unusual, even for him. I still haven't responded, but I am questioning his sudden urgency to speak with me. Three of his latest letters rest in the bottom of the garbage can, and I have no desire to open those either.

In addition to that annoyance, Stella LeClaire is challenging my last nerve. I have to give her credit, she's more resilient than I anticipated. Every day, she shows up on time for class, and every day, I find new ways to humiliate her. On Wednesday, I threw her sorry excuse for notes in the trash and told her to try again. On Thursday, I taped her assignment to the whiteboard as an example of what not to do. I gave her extra homework. I asked her impossible questions and challenged her at every turn. And still, she has not cracked. She remains as stoic as the day she walked out of the office after the little traitor tried to escape me.

In detention, she doesn't bother to doodle in her journal anymore. She does her homework in silence and leaves. She only speaks when spoken to and never asks to use the restroom. Her devotion to perfectionism is getting on my last nerve, and it's written all over my face as I glare at her from across the room.

This week, I took the time to dig a little deeper and do some research on her parents. As I suspected, Stella doesn't hail from the typical wealth and privilege. Her father married above his station and crawled his way to the top in an effort to appease his model trophy wife. Now he works himself to death in the city while she spends her days socializing back in Greenwich. Interestingly enough, Stella has always maintained excellent grades, and her transcripts are proof of that. But regardless, Brady LeClaire had to call in a lot of favors to get Stella in the door of Loyola Academy, which explains her drive to do well here. The enormous cloud of pressure hanging over her head would be motivation enough for any young, attention-starved woman.

My investigation served its purpose, but it had not cured my growing appetite for all things Stella LeClaire. So I did something this week that I've never done before. I snuck into her dorm like a hormonal teenage boy and swiped her journal, proceeding to read through every page, front to back. All of her innermost thoughts. Her drawings. Her photos. And now I understand the thing that makes Stella tick. She has a knack for taking pictures of people. The little creep even snapped photos of me on the soccer field. When I found them on her camera, my dick became unreasonably hard as I considered her spying on me. The little deviant had zoomed in on my face, snapping away as I remained unaware. She captured something in me that I didn't expect to see. A rare moment of passion. Passion for something in this uninspiring world. Without thinking of the consequences, I deleted the photos in anger, and then to make matters worse, I ripped out a page of her journal. The page where she said she hated my guts. It's still sitting on my kitchen table. Maybe I'll frame it, or maybe I'll throw it away. I haven't decided yet.

Looking at her now, I want to forget the entire project. It's becoming too complicated, and she's getting under my skin. In the beginning, I told myself I was doing this to prove something to her, but now, I find that I just want to punish her. That urge only gets worse when I dismiss her, and she refuses to acknowledge me. But she does acknowledge Joshua, who's waiting for her in the hall. He's another lacrosse player and obviously someone who hasn't learned from Ethan's mistakes. I flay him alive with my eyes, but he doesn't seem to notice because his are fixated on Stella's chest.

"Hey, Cherrybomb." He flashes a dimple at her. "What's happening?"

"Hey, Josh." She secures her backpack around her shoulders and shrugs. "Not much. Just another day in the life, you know. I practically live here now."

"Right." He laughs. "I was gonna say, you're always in detention."

They both glance back at me as I fiddle with my keys, taking my sweet ass time to lock the door. He doesn't want an audience for whatever he's about to say next, and I have no plans on going anywhere until I see how this plays out.

"So, uh, I was wondering…" Joshua shifts and stuffs his hands into his pockets. "You have anything planned this weekend? I was thinking you could come to the game tomorrow."

Stella hesitates, and I think she might actually be considering it. My blood boils as I imagine Joshua sloppily kissing her and groping her under the bleachers this weekend, and before I can grasp onto logical thought, the words are coming out of my mouth.

"Stella, I need to speak with you for a moment."

She turns around and meets my gaze with a blank expression. We haven't spoken throughout detention for the entirety of the week, and I know she's wondering what the hell I could possibly want now. I'm wondering myself when I re-open the door and gesture her inside.

"Hang on a minute," she tells Josh. "I'll be right back."

He nods and rocks back on his heels, watching me shut the door behind us. Stella waits for me just inside the room, arms crossed and on the defense. She doesn't want to show her vulnerability, but I know what she needs from me. I know it better than she could ever know herself.

Before I can stop myself, I close the distance between us. So much so that my shoe bumps against her red Dr. Marten. Her breath pauses, and she glances up at me with those warm brandy-colored eyes that betray her sensitivity. A certain disadvantage for her, considering there's a predator in her midst, but I wouldn't have it any other way.

"Tell him no," I command.

"What?" Her eyebrows pinch together, but she knows she's asking a stupid question. She just wants me to spell it out for her.

"Go back out there and tell Joshua no. You will not go out with him this weekend."

"Why should I?" she challenges.

My cock twitches, and I have to fold my arms so I don't venture further over the line than I already am right now. All I want to do is grab her and push her to her knees and stuff her lips full of my cock until she can't think twice about asking me why I tell her to do anything.

"Because I said so, Stella. And you like to do what I say."

She's quiet. Our eyes are locked. Neither of us moves, but I can practically feel the beat of her pulse in my own throat. I want to eat her alive, and right now, she can sense that. But I'll never admit it. I'll never admit that she gets to me. I just need her to know that she's mine to toy with for as long as I want, and that's all there is to be said about it.

"Okay." She drags the corner of her plump red lip against her teeth.

Logically, I know I need to stop this insanity. I can't uncross this line. But it pleases me so much to watch her submit to me. I need her to know just how much.

I pivot on my heel and move around behind her, gently dragging her hair to one side as I lean in to whisper my command in her ear. Her breath stutters, and she instinctively leans back into me, the pleats of her skirt brushing over my rock-hard dick. I know she feels it when she shivers, and I know I need to stop, but my brain isn't doing the thinking as I drag my knuckles down her arm and watch her break out in goose bumps.

"Say yes, sir."

"Yes, sir," she breathes.

"Say I'll do anything you want, Mr. Carter. Anything you tell me."

She swallows, still trying to resist me, but ultimately caves in just as I knew she would. "I'll do anything you want, Mr. Carter. Anything you tell me."

"Prove it." I close my eyes and drag my nose so close to the hot flesh of her throat I can almost taste her.

"How?" she pants.

"Get creative, Stella."

The anticipation of what she might do is almost too much. But watching her turn around and sink to her knees in front of me snaps me back to reality. Her eyes are level with my engorged dick, just inches from her face. So close she can smell my arousal. All she'd need to do is unzip my trousers, and I could be right there between her lips. The lips that were made for sucking my cock and screaming out my name.

Motherfucking fuck.

"I can keep a secret, Mr. Carter," she whispers. "Can you?"

"Stella." I reach down and drag my thumb across her lips before taking a step back and glaring down at her. "You need to leave now."

I turn away from her and drag a trembling hand through my hair. She is so quiet I almost don't hear her get up. I can't look at her, but I know she must be shattered. She must be confused, and rightfully so. I wouldn't be surprised if she walks straight to the office and turns me in for my perverted behavior. But instead of telling her to do that, I call out one last instruction.

"Remember what I said."

CHAPTER ELEVEN
STELLA

After dismissing Josh, I spend the rest of Friday night in a restless state of curiosity. Sybil decided to stay late and put in some studio time and neither of my parents have answered my phone calls, which leaves me with little else to do besides ruminate on the events of this afternoon.

Mr. Carter touched me. He breathed me in. He made me promise him things. Dark things. Things I couldn't even admit I wanted, but now I crave them with the intensity of a scorching flame. His touch, his commands, his presence. When I was under his spell, it was like I was drugged. Intoxicated by him. So much so that I can't even be sure it really happened. Except I can still feel him on my skin. My lipstick is still smeared from his thumb. And the image of myself kneeling before him, obedient and willing to do his bidding, is burned into my mind for eternity. He is undoubtedly Satan, but I want him, no matter the cost to my soul.

I close my eyes and shudder as my fingers snake down between my thighs. I've never touched myself there, but now I want to. I want to touch myself and think of him. What would it feel like to be with a man? What would it feel like to have Sebastian Carter's throbbing cock inside me?

My sensitive nipples scrape against the lace of my bra, and I wiggle uncomfortably as I try to figure out what my body likes. But before I can, someone knocks on my door, dousing my fantasy in cold water.

"Psst." Sybil pokes her head in, and I shoot upright, making an attempt at casual. "What are you doing?"

"Nothing," I answer, my voice way too high. My face feels like it's on fire, but she doesn't seem to notice.

"A few of us are going down to Bryer's pond for a gathering. Want to come?"

"A gathering?" I discreetly adjust my skirt and stand.

"Yeah, it will be fun. A good way to blow off some steam after the stress of the first week." She wiggles her eyebrows.

Sebastian's earlier request comes to mind, and I wonder what he would say about this. Then I realize how foolish I am to consider it. It's not like he's watching me or really cares what I do in my spare time. Something happened between us today, and I can't deny it, but I've already convinced myself numerous times over that he probably regrets it, and it will never happen again.

There are rules about this sort of thing, and we broke a lot of them today. He could lose his job. I could lose my place at Loyola. There are too many consequences to consider, and none of them are good. But even as I try to talk myself out of it, I know that if he came to me again, I wouldn't deny him.

"A gathering sounds fun." I force the words from my lips, and Sybil smiles and rubs her palms together gleefully.

"Thank God, I didn't want to go alone."

Without giving it too much thought, I follow her down the hall and out her bedroom window, which happens to be closest to the shrubbery.

"It's only about a mile through the trees," she whispers. "But we have to be quiet until we get there. Mr. Carter usually takes late night runs around the perimeter, and we don't want to get caught."

"He does?" I ask, getting caught up on his name and forgetting everything else she just said.

Sybil nods and doesn't give me any more details, obviously unaware of how desperately I want them. We trek through a well-worn path between the trees, and when the pond finally comes into view, I'm almost disappointed we didn't get caught. Sybil said it was a small gathering, but it looks like half the lacrosse team is here, including Ethan and his buddies. And if that wasn't bad enough, Louisa is here too.

"Do you really think this is a good idea?" I ask.

Sybil glances at the source of my concern and waves them off. "Just ignore them. We'll make our own party."

I try to do as she suggests and follow her lead as she heads for a guy in the back who's manning the keg. She bats her eyelashes at him and holds up two fingers. "One for me and my friend please?"

The beer smells gross, and I already know from this summer that I don't have a taste for it. But I'm hoping Sybil is right, and I can relax if I just have one or two. We barely even have our drinks in hand before someone calls us over to the larger circle gathered near the pond.

"We're playing truth or dare," Josh informs us. "You should join in."

I'm about to say no when Sybil answers for both of us. "We are so in!"

Crap. I'm pretty sure this would go against Sebastian's do whatever he says policy. I did not know Josh was going to be here. Or Ethan. Or the whole damn lacrosse team.

"All right." Micah, Sybil's crush of the week, slings his arm over both of our shoulders. "Who wants to go first, ladies?"

"Stella will go first." Sybil nudges me with her elbow in good fun.

"Rules are, you can pass on whatever you're challenged or asked, but you have to drain your cup if you do," Josh explains.

"Fine." I roll my eyes. "Let's do this."

"Truth or dare?" Louisa challenges, and of course, she's the one who gets to taunt me.

"Truth." I take a sip of my beer, trying to play it cool.

"How many guys have you been with?" she asks coyly and then giggles. "I bet it's a lot."

Some of the crowd joins in on her laughter, and I try not to let it get to me. There isn't a way I could answer this question that she wouldn't use as ammunition against me, so I decide to skip.

"Pass."

"Lame." Louisa rolls her eyes as the crowd chants at me to chug my beer.

I drain the glass, and before I'm even finished, someone's handing me another one. Sybil goes next, taking on her dare to do the splits with a smile on her face while all the guys ooh and ahh over her flexibility. The circle continues, and I continue to drink from my cup, dreading my next turn. I feel woozy, and I don't know why I even came here when I'm already counting down the minutes until I can leave.

Eventually the circle comes back to me, and this time, it's Sybil who gets to challenge me, which fills me with a little relief.

"Truth or dare?" she asks.

"Dare."

She eyeballs Micah and licks her lips, and already she looks a little drunk. "I dare you to swim with me."

The guys hoot and holler while I bite my lip and consider it. It's not like we didn't do this dozens of times over the summer. Sybil is already running down to the pond, stripping off her shirt and shorts along the way. "You can leave your bra and panties on," she calls over her shoulder.

I chug the rest of my beer for liquid courage and trail after her, stripping off my sweater and then my skirt, leaving them next to hers. I imagine everyone is watching us as I push my way into the water, but my head is fuzzy, and I can't really seem to care what they think right now.

Sybil squeals when she sees that I've joined her, and soon, some of the guys start diving in too. Before long, her lips are locked with Micah's, and I don't really know what to do with myself. The pond is too cold to be enjoyable, and I'm already shivering and feeling sick to my stomach from the beer, I think. When someone grabs me from behind and spins me around, I can't seem to react as fast as I should.

"Hey, slut." Ethan grins down at me.

"Fuck you." I try to push him away, but he's too heavy, and I feel like I'm moving in slow motion. I don't understand what's happening, but something isn't right. My body is too sluggish. I've been drunk before, but this is something different and terrifying.

"Quit teasing me," Ethan growls. "I know you want this." Before I can protest, he smears his wet, sloppy lips all over my face, attempting to kiss me as I try to fight him off. Nobody seems to notice, and I don't know what to do. Screaming for help feels too dramatic, but I don't want this disgusting oaf touching me.

"Get off me." I hiss, shoving him with all my might.

He barely budges, and that's when I know I'm on my own. I try to jam my knee into his groin but even that requires too much effort. So instead, I lean in and bite down on his shoulder until he screams like the little bitch he is.

"What the fuck?" He shoves me away from him, and once my balance is gone, I can't even seem to tread water.

"What happened?" Josh asks.

"Little bitch bit me. She's into some freaky shit."

"Stella?" Sybil calls out from behind me as I attempt to drag my useless body to shore. I don't even realize that I'm not moving until Micah puts an arm around me and hauls me up, allowing me to take in a long breath.

"What the hell just happened?" Sybil appears in front of me with wide, panicked eyes.

"I don't know," I admit. "I feel weird."

"I think she's drunk." Micah observes.

"She's only had two beers," Sybil protests.

Regardless, they help me back onto dry land, only to discover that my clothes are missing. Sybil mumbles something about Louisa, but I'm only picking up every few words. I can barely keep my eyes open, and now I can't even stand on my own.

"We need to get her back," Sybil says. "Micah, can you give her your shirt?"

I try to protest until I realize that I'm only in my bra and panties. And as if that wasn't bad enough, my delusions take on a whole other level of scary when I hear the furious voice from behind me.

"What the hell is going on here?"

"Holy shit! Run!"

Numerous footsteps scatter into the distance as Mr. Carter's voice explodes through the trees. "Party's over. Everyone back to campus, now!"

"Crap." Sybil and Micah utter in unison as they support my lifeless body between them. I realize I'm holding them back and they are going to get into trouble because of me.

I try to tell them to go, but it comes out as gibberish.

"Sybil, Stella." Sebastian appears in front of us, his eyes narrowed in on me.

"I'm so sorry, Mr. C," Sybil apologizes. "I'm trying, but I think Stella's too drunk to move."

There are expectations for how situations like this should be handled at Loyola Academy. If I was doing my job, I would take Stella straight to the school medical office, where they could observe her until morning. Upon which, she would be questioned and most likely suspended. Loyola has an uneasy track record of making examples of students like Stella. Students who haphazardly expose the ugly side of this school. Feeding her to the wolves and leaving her to fend for herself might be the smarter option in this case, but I refuse to do that.

Stella is barely coherent as Jennifer examines her on my living room sofa. I'm breaking more rules than I can even count right now, but all I can think about is beating the ever-loving shit out of whoever did this to her.

"I can test her for benzodiazepines if we can get her to urinate," Jennifer says. "But that could take some time."

"The headmaster's son supplies the kids with prescriptions. It's likely Valium or Xanax."

"Has this happened here before?" Jennifer frowns.

It's evident she's torn about this entire situation, and I don't blame her. Jennifer is a doctor, and an old friend of the family, but those ties only go so far.

"This is the first time I've seen it," I admit. "It's widely known that the students use uppers and downers for studying and partying, but I've never seen them used as a weapon before. She should have known better."

My blood boils every time I look at Stella lying there in her barely conscious state. She put herself into a dangerous situation. She completely disregarded every rule she should have followed.

"She's young." Compassion laces Jennifer's voice. "Teenage girls don't always know better."

"She's almost eighteen," I argue, and I know how it probably sounds. "She should know better. If I hadn't shown up, it could have been an entirely different outcome."

My chest heaves as I pace the length of my floor, unable to hide my frustration. Jennifer studies me and her eyes soften. "We've never really talked about it, Sebastian... but you do know what happened to Katie wasn't your fault, right?"

Her observation stops me in my tracks. "This has nothing to do with Katie."

"Really?" she challenges. "Because it looks like it has a lot to do with Katie. Why are you even here? Why are you teaching at some boarding school in the middle of nowhere?"

I release a breath and shake my head. "It's only temporary."

"You think you can make up for what happened to her by following her dream, but it's obvious to everyone you aren't happy."

"Everyone who?" My voice darkens.

Jennifer looks at the floor to avoid my arctic gaze. "Your father is worried about you."

A dry laugh erupts from my throat. "He's worried about someone other than himself? That would be a first. I think the more appropriate line is he's worried about the company."

Jennifer sighs. "At some point, you'll have to deal with this, Sebastian. You can't put it off forever."

"At some point, I will." I turn my attention back to Stella. "Right now, I need your help, not your therapy. What can we do for her?"

"At this stage, I'm just keeping track of her vitals. When she starts to wake and consents to a drug test, I can give her one. But being that it's most likely benzos, we'll need to wait for them to eliminate from her system. She'll have one hell of a raging hangover tomorrow, but she should be just fine."

That answer isn't good enough for me. Stella isn't fine. She shouldn't be lying here in my living room. She shouldn't have put herself in this position, and when she wakes up, she's going to hear about it. But for right now, I have somewhere else I need to be.

"Can you stay with her for an hour?" I ask. "I have something I need to do."

"Sure." She shrugs. "I'm not going anywhere. But whatever you're about to do, be careful, okay?"

Her warning barely registers as I wind my way across campus to the small cottage where the janitor resides. The janitor, who also happens to be the headmaster's son, Charles. After banging on his door for the third time, he opens it, and a cloud of smoke filters out into the evening air.

"Yo, Mr. C." He grins at me in a haze. "What's going on?"

"Why don't you tell me?" I wrap my fingers around his throat and shove him inside.

"What the fuck, man?" He makes a half-assed attempt to pry me off before I land a solid punch to his gut. He doubles over in a coughing fit, and I grab him by the collar and lean down into his face, ready to destroy him.

"Which of my students bought the benzos from you?"

"I don't know what you're talking about," he spits.

I pummel his rib cage with three more blows before he curls up into the fetal position and starts to whine like the little bitch he is.

"All right, man. Chill. I'll tell you whatever you want to know."

"I told you what I want to know," I growl. "Who the fuck bought the benzos from you?"

"Ethan Dupree. He bought some Xannies. That's it, I swear."

"And then he used them to drug another student."

Charles looks up at me with a panicked expression. "I didn't know, man. I swear. I'd never sell them to him if I knew he was gonna do that."

"You'll never sell them again, period. You're done here. No more drugs, no more alcohol. Do we have an understanding?"

"Man, I'm done with Xanax, okay? I won't sell it no more."

"You're done with all of it," I say. "Or I'll go straight above mommy dearest's head and have your ass carted to prison. Not one more fucking pill, Charles."

He glances at my phone, and his body sinks into the floor as it occurs to him that I'm recording this on audio. While Charles is generally harmless, he will also do anything to make a buck. I let it slide before because it didn't affect me, but those days are over, and now he knows it.

"All right." He holds up his hands. "I'm done. I swear it. I'll only do my business elsewhere. No students."

I release him and stuff my phone back into my pocket. Now that I'm satisfied Charles has been dealt with, I have one more stop to make.

Chapter Thirteen
Stella

After waking up feeling like I've been hit by a truck, the woman who introduced herself as Dr. Jen takes it upon herself to explain what happened. Though my memory is spotty, I'm able to remember bits and pieces of the night before. The party at the pond. Truth or dare. Taking off my clothes. Feeling like I was weighed down. Ethan.

Oh God.

The thought of him makes me want to vomit, but Dr. Jen just made me a nice breakfast, and I'm trying to keep it down.

"You're probably going to feel like hell for the day," she says. "That's pretty typical. But I'm here if you need to talk. Anything you say to me is confidential, of course."

"I'm okay," I insist, and really, I am. What happened was scary, but if Sybil and Micah hadn't pulled me from that pond, it could have been a lot worse. It was just plain stupidity on my part, and I realize that now. "I think I've learned my lesson."

"You haven't even come close." Sebastian's voice comes from behind me, and when I turn to meet his eyes, a shiver moves down my spine.

"Sebastian," Dr. Jen chides.

Ignoring her, he pins me with his gaze. His entire body is rigid, and he looks pissed as hell. I know I fucked up, and I expected him to be mad, but this is something else entirely.

"You put yourself at risk last night," he bites out. "You didn't even consider the consequences."

"I know." I bow my head. "I'm sorry I disappointed you."

"To be disappointed in you, I'd have to be invested in you," he answers coldly. My heart drops into my stomach, and now I really feel like I'm going to be sick.

"Sebastian, a word in the other room please?" Dr. Jen taps him on the arm.

His gaze doesn't move from mine. Not until he's got his point across. I fucked up, and now he hates me for it. Tears spring to my eyes as he walks into the other room with Dr. Jen, and they argue in hushed voices.

I take the opportunity to gather the clothes that Dr. Jen brought me and slip into the bathroom. Sebastian Carter's bathroom. I realize it when I shut the door, even though I knew I was in his house when I woke up. Now the scent that lingers in this space is undeniable. Cardamom and sandalwood.

My curiosity gets the best of me, and I start rifling through all his things. In the hamper, I find a damp tee shirt that smells like him, and if I had to guess, he was probably wearing it on his late-night run. Without giving it too much thought, I roll it up to take with me. Then I open his cabinet, seeking out the source of the delicious smell. When I find the dark bottle of cologne, I spray a little on my wrist and then bring it to my nose, closing my eyes as I inhale. Why I find his scent so oddly comforting when the man himself is anything but, I'll never know. To make matters even worse, I spray it onto my chest and my neck too.

When I reach to put it back, something else catches my attention. A woman's necklace. The chain is faded, and it looks like it was a well-worn piece at some point. I recognize the symbol from a yoga class I took with Sybil. The Om symbol. It seems odd to me that this would be sitting in Sebastian's cabinet, and I can't stop myself from picking it up to examine it. Who does this belong to? And more importantly, who is she to Sebastian?

A knock on the door startles me, and I quickly shove the necklace back into the cabinet, attempting to cleanse the guilty expression from my face even though they can't see me.

"Yes?"

"We need to get you back to your dorm," Sebastian says.

"Okay, I'm just changing. I'll be out in a minute."

Quickly, I throw on the sweatpants and tee shirt and smooth out the tangles in my hair, briefly pausing in horror at my reflection. I look like death warmed over. Mr. Carter saw me like this, and now I officially can't deal.

God, this whole situation has been so humiliating. But if I thought it couldn't get any worse, I'm proven wrong. Sebastian apparently chose to dismiss himself from the situation, and at his request, Dr. Jen walks me back across campus. The sun is out, and it's the middle of the afternoon on Saturday, and the campus is full of students. Students who all seem to have their attention on me. I smooth my hair back and keep my head down, trying to walk faster.

"Ignore them," Dr. Jen says.

"Does the school know what happened?" I ask.

"Not that I'm aware of," she answers. "Officially, you were signed out by your aunt yesterday. AKA me. Sebastian didn't want you to get into trouble."

I give her a funny look, and she must notice.

"I know he comes off as harsh, but he has his reasons. Just don't take anything he says too seriously, okay?"

I want to ask her more about it, but before I can think of anything else to say, we're back at my dorm. "Thank you so much for your help. I'm so sorry if I inconvenienced you."

"You didn't." She smiles, offering me a card with her phone number on it. "And I'm still available, if you do decide you need to speak with someone."

"Thanks." I shove the card into my pocket, and we say our goodbyes before I disappear into Lawrence Hall.

I can't even make it past the common room before Louisa and her lion pack push their way into my path.

"Oh, look everyone, it's the resident slut." Louisa sneers.

"You're overexposed, Louisa," I respond flatly. "It's not a good look for you."

Amusement washes over her face, and both the girls at her side start laughing too. "Last I checked, I'm not the one splashed half naked all over the LA Underground app."

I don't know what she's talking about, but I have a feeling I'm not going to like it. She knows I'm at a disadvantage, and she's getting off on it. But before she can give me any more trouble, Sybil appears, pushing them aside as she pulls me down the hall into her room.

"Oh my God, Stella." Tears well in her eyes. "I'm so sorry. I am so, so sorry. You must think I'm such a horrible friend. Are you okay?"

"It's not your fault," I assure her. "I shouldn't have taken a drink from anyone. I shouldn't have even gone."

A tear splashes against her cheek, and I feel awful that she feels so awful.

"I was so worried about you," she gulps out. "Please tell me you're okay."

"I'm okay." I sit down on her bed. "What is Louisa talking about, though?"

Sybil worries her lip between her teeth and sits down beside me. "Okay, well the first thing I think you should know is that Ethan was expelled last night."

"He was?" Some of the tension bleeds from my body as I consider the fact that I won't have to see him again.

"Yeah, they did an afterhours search of his room based on a tip. No idea where it came from, but they found a bunch of Xanax and alcohol in there, so they expelled him."

"Holy shit."

"Yeah, and then he had a meltdown," Sybil continues. "Loyola has a private social media app made by one of the students. Ethan went on there and posted pics of you in your bra and underwear last night, along with some snaps of him kissing you."

"Oh my God." My stomach drops, and I jump up. "Are they still on there?"

"No." She shakes her head quickly. "They went live this morning at like nine o clock, and within ten minutes, his account was removed from the app. Then another hour later, the entire app was gone. It was crazy. Someone in the staff must have seen. That's the only thing I can think of."

I hang my head in my hands and resist the urge to cry. I have a feeling I know exactly who saw them and exactly how they were removed. The same man who took care of me last night. The same man who got Ethan expelled. And the same man who now hates my guts.

"This is insane," I whisper.

"I'm so sorry." Sybil pulls me in for a hug. "But the good news is the photos are down."

"And the bad news is everyone saw them, and now they're calling me a slut."

"That's just Louisa and her gang of bitches," Sybil argues. "But I think you'd be surprised. Everyone knows how slimy Ethan can be, and there were a lot of people calling him out on the app before those photos got deleted. People defended you."

"This is just so embarrassing," I whisper.

"I know." She frowns. "But I think the only thing you can do at this point is own it. Who cares what anyone else thinks? You are Stella fucking LeClaire. Rockstar photographer. Badass bitch. You are gorgeous and smart and funny, and people will want to take you down. But don't let them, Cherrybomb. You're better than that."

I collapse back onto her bed and consider her words, knowing she's right. I can't let them win. And I won't.

CHAPTER FOURTEEN
STELLA

Sybil and I skip lunch on Tuesday to work on our cheer moves, like she promised. Practice is all week, and then we have tryouts. It's not really what I want to do, but it's keeping my mind off everything else, so that's something. We spend the entirety of the hour breaking down the dance moves and repeating them while stuffing our faces full of gummy bears to survive.

"You're going to do great," Sybil insists. "It will be fun. You'll see."

Secretly, I'm hoping I don't even get onto the cheer squad. Honestly, I have no idea what I'm doing anymore. I just don't want to disappoint Sybil. I don't want to disappoint anybody, but it seems like that's all I've been doing lately. And more than a few times this last week, I've wondered why I even bother. My parents still haven't returned my calls. It's not like they would even care or expect any different of me if I didn't succeed here. But still, my dad's words continue to haunt me. *I'm putting everything on the line, Stella.*

As crappy as my first week at Loyola was, there are some silver linings. I have Sybil. And my grades are good so far. Other than having detention with Mr. Carter for the foreseeable future and getting into trouble over the weekend, there's still time to turn everything around. Getting onto the cheer squad is a good way to start. That's something my mom can be proud of. Or at least, I hope it is.

"Your birthday is next Friday," Sybil reminds me. "We should do something crazy to celebrate."

I eye her wearily, and she laughs.

"I didn't mean too crazy. Just something fun and secret. Like a tattoo or a piercing. After all, you'll be legal."

I consider her idea, and it actually doesn't sound too bad. I've always wanted a cartilage piercing in my ear.

"We can do that," I agree. "But I'll have to check with my parents. I don't know if they have anything planned for the weekend or if they even remember it's my birthday."

"Okay." Her phone alarm sounds, signaling that it's time to go. "We better scram before Mr. C has a coronary."

I head over to the patch of grass where we left our bags, but right away, I notice something looks off. The zipper on my backpack is open, and I know I didn't leave it that way. I glance inside and don't see anything out of the ordinary, and there isn't time to inspect it now. Hell hath no fury like Mr. Carter when you're late to his class.

Slinging the bag over my shoulder, Sybil and I head off for Research. We even manage to arrive three minutes early, which is almost a miraculous feat for me. But just as soon as we sit down at our desks and I start to dig around inside my binder, I realize there's a problem.

I check three times just to be sure, even going so far as to look in my books just in case I stuffed my homework in there. But I can't seem to find it. And before I even have a chance to panic, Louisa arrives to gloat.

"I made you something in art class." She smirks as she sets down a paper craft letter S that looks like it's been painted with blood. "Since you're so fond of red, I figured you deserved your own scarlet letter. S for slut."

"What the hell is your problem, Louisa?" Sybil hisses.

"Did you take my homework at lunch?" I accuse.

"Is there a problem here?" Mr. Carter interrupts the hubbub, his shadow falling over all three of us. When I glance up at him, he only looks at me briefly before turning his gaze to the red S on my desk.

"The problem is Louisa is being a bitch," Sybil belts out. "And I'm sick of it."

"Sybil." Mr. Carter's voice is a warning, but his gaze is on me now. He's waiting for me to say something, but I feel like it's a trick. Either way, I can't win. If I throw Louisa under the bus, would it make any difference? She'd just come back harder next week. But I can't keep letting her get away with this either.

"Stella, is there something you'd like to say?" he asks, challenging me with his eyes.

I feel his pressure bearing down on me. He wants me to make the right choice, but what is the right choice? I can't figure it out at a moment's notice, especially not when I'm lost in the forbidden green sea of his eyes.

"Use your words, Stella."

Words. Right. I need some of those right about now because everyone is staring at me. I shift in my seat and fold my hands together beneath my desk. And then I remember Sybil's speech about owning it. Who cares what anyone here thinks? It's not like their opinions matter. Louisa certainly doesn't matter, and I refuse to let her believe she's getting to me. So instead, I take the scarlet S on my desk and secure it to my binder, displaying it for everyone to see.

"There's not a problem, Mr. Carter. I'm sorry we interrupted your class. Louisa was just giving me a present for my birthday on Friday. I'll be eighteen. Totally legal. I mean, an adult."

Oh God, why am I still talking? Now Mr. Carter is practically scowling at me, and somehow, I've only managed to irritate him even more. How is it possible this man can make me shiver with a single look from across the room?

"Louisa, take your seat." He returns to the front of the classroom. "Are there any other disruptions that can't possibly wait until school hours finish?"

Nobody volunteers for that suicide mission, so Mr. Carter walks to the door to shut it. Once he's satisfied with the tomblike state of the room, he continues. "Open your books to page sixty and retrieve your essays."

Everyone shuffles around in their bags and pulls out their things while I quietly look through my binder one more time. But there's nothing. Nada. I'm so fucked. I open my book to page sixty and hope by some miracle he won't notice, but I should know miracles in his class don't exist.

"Stella LeClaire, you're first. Stand and read your essay to the class."

A bead of sweat tickles the back of my neck as I remain in my seat, unmoving. It's bad enough that I have to say it out loud. I don't want to stand while I do it.

"Is there a problem?" He slides a pencil between his masculine fingers. Fingers that could so easily crush that frail instrument, and me.

"I don't have my assignment, sir. I'm sorry. It appears that it went missing from my bag at lunch time."

"It appears you seem to be full of excuses," he bites back. "In fact, from what I've gathered over the last week, Miss LeClaire, you don't seem ready to put in the effort required for this class. So why are you even here?"

His words sting, and I swallow down the shame I feel as I try to find an answer to that question. But the truth is, I don't know. I don't know what I'm doing in this class, or any of the others. Or where I'm supposed to go to college. Or what I'm supposed to be doing with my life. And it's all too overwhelming to think about. So instead, I remain silent. A silent participant in my life. And every day, I die a little more inside. Does Sebastian see it? Does he care?

"Take the day to consider it," he says. "And only come back again when you are prepared."

With that cold dismissal, I have my answer.

By the time detention rolls around, I'm strung tighter than a fiddle. Mr. Carter waits for me inside, silent and apathetic to my obvious emotional plight as I sit down in the desk directly facing him. I take two deep breaths and work up the courage to plead the case that I've been preparing over the last two periods.

"Mr. Carter?"

He barely acknowledges me, instead, keeping his attention on the stack of papers in front of him. "Yes, Miss LeClaire?"

"Stella," I correct. "Okay, I'm just Stella. You know this. I know this."

He drops his pen and looks up at me. "You might want to think twice about whatever you're about to say."

"You had your thumb on my lips," I tell him. "I felt your body against me. I kneeled before you. So, I think we can skip the formalities from now on, can't we?"

The corner of his lip turns up in predatory amusement. "Are you trying to blackmail me, Stella?"

"No, of course not. I just want to talk to you without feeling…" I wave my hands around, trying to convey my emotions. "Like this. I know you're still mad at me about the pond, and you're punishing me for it. That's what today in class was about, wasn't it?"

"Today in class was about you not being able to stand up for yourself." He clips the words out, and then instantly looks as if he regrets them.

"You wanted me to out Louisa in front of the entire class?" I ask in disbelief. "Why not just give her a loaded shotgun while I'm at it."

"Girls like Louisa win as long as you let them."

"And what would you have done had I outed her?" I challenge. "Humiliate me in front of the entire class?"

"I would have punished her."

The way he says punished her sends an irrational jolt of jealousy through me, and I don't like it. I don't like thinking of Mr. Carter punishing anyone else. Or touching anyone else. In my mind, those things are only for me. He can see it on my face, and he likes it. He likes my jealousy. He likes it so much I bet his cock is hard beneath his desk right now, and all I can think about is crawling to him to worship at his feet and beg for forgiveness.

"Mr. Carter." My voice breaks as I work up the courage to ask him the most dangerous question I can think of. "Would it make you feel better if you punished me?"

He sucks in a breath, and his eyes pool with darkness as he steeples his palms on the table in front of him. "And how would I do that, Stella?"

"However you want."

Our eyes lock, and silence fills the space between us. My heart is beating so hard it feels like a gunshot inside my chest cavity. I want him to touch me again. I want him to tell me how bad I am and make me pay for it. I'm pretty sure this isn't normal, but I don't care. I want him to do depraved things with me.

"You have no idea what you're asking for." He gets up, but instead of coming for me, he just stands there. "You don't even know what you want."

"Yes, I do," I whisper.

"Tell me, then," he commands. "Tell me what your place is in this school, Stella. Tell me what your future looks like. Tell me how getting onto the cheer squad is going to solve all of your problems."

My eyebrows knit together. I didn't realize we were having Research class all over again, but here we are. And he's right. I don't know the answers to those questions.

"I don't know about any of those things," I admit. "But I know what I want right now."

"Right now, you want to discuss how you're going to make up your grade for the essay you failed to turn in today," he redirects the conversation, and my frustration compounds.

"How am I going to do that?"

"You are going to turn in a three-page essay on the consequences of choices. Tomorrow morning, in my office at seven thirty."

"But I have cheer practice tonight," I protest.

"Choices and consequences," he repeats without mercy.

"Better make it a good one, Stella."

CHAPTER FIFTEEN
STELLA

When I show up to cheer practice, Sybil squeals in excitement, but I don't feel the same. I'm still not sure what I'm doing here. What Mr. Carter said was true. I have no idea what my place in this school is, or what my future looks like, and I'm almost eighteen. Shouldn't I at least have some of it figured out by now?

I fumble my way through the routine, but in the back of my mind, all I can think about is my essay and what I'm going to write. It only gets worse when I notice Mr. Carter walking across the quad after soccer practice. His eyes lock onto me, and he looks disappointed. Or angry. I can't be sure which because I can never tell with him. But either way, it's obvious he's displeased.

I feel like he's trying to tell me something about the path I'm on. Like I'm heading for disaster unless I figure it out soon. But that doesn't make any logical sense. I know from the Google stalking I did that he was raised in an affluent family, and he's the heir to a luxury resort chain. Sebastian went to the best schools, and I have no doubt he faced the same pressures I did. So why does it always seem like he's contradicting what Loyola stands for. Excellence in education. Bright futures. As I consider their motto, it also occurs to me how rigid the definition is. What exactly is a bright future? Is any job less important than another?

All of these thoughts make my head hurt, and Sybil notices when I'm not giving it my all. She isn't thrilled when we finally stop for the night.

"What is going on with you, Cherrybomb?" She studies me with concern. "You were all over the place."

"I know." I wipe my forehead with a towel. "I'm sorry. I just have a lot on my mind, I guess."

"Do you want to talk about it?" she asks. "We can go grab some dessert and have a girls' night."

"I wish I could," I groan. "But I have to write a huge essay for Mr. Carter since my assignment went missing. It's due tomorrow morning."

"What an asshole." She rolls her eyes.

"I can't figure him out," I admit. "One minute, it seems like he's pushing me because he expects more from me, and the next, he acts like he doesn't care at all."

Sybil gives me a funny look, and I wonder if I said too much. But before we can hash it out, I notice my mother waving me down.

"Mom?" I walk over to meet her. "Is everything okay?"

Her lips tighten, and she doesn't look like her usual self. Sybil seems to notice as well when she darts over to join us. "Hey, Lila. Are you feeling all right?"

"I'm fine, thank you, Sybil." My mother answers out of politeness, but I can tell something's up, and I don't like it. She would never come to visit me on her own. And especially not unless she was dressed to the nines. But right now, it almost looks like she's in disguise with a giant poncho and huge sunglasses.

"Stella, I need to speak with you in private. I thought perhaps we could go grab a bite to eat."

"I already ate dinner," I say. "It's almost eight o' clock."

"Well, dessert then. It's important."

"Is Dad here too?"

She shakes her head. It feels weird going somewhere with just my mother since we barely speak. But I know she wouldn't be here unless she had something big to tell me. I look at Sybil, wishing I could drag her along with me, but I know that's not an option. I offer her a weak smile.

"I'll catch up with you later?"

"Okay. Rain check on dessert. I'll take your stuff back to the dorm." She tosses her hair over her shoulder and flits off to grab our stuff while my mother and I head for the exit.

Silence lingers between us until we get onto the street, and she walks toward a car I don't recognize. A pre-owned Honda Civic. I can't remember her ever driving before, and to the best of my knowledge, Luis has always chauffeured her around. But here she is walking over to the car as if it's the most normal thing in the world.

"Hurry up and get in, Stella," she barks. "It's humiliating enough that I have to be seen in this. No need to linger."

I climb into the passenger seat and stare at her as she pulls out onto the street and drives aimlessly. She said we were going to dessert, but it's clear that was just another statement to keep up appearances. Instead, we end up at a public park where she parks the car and turns off the ignition.

"Mom, can you please tell me what's going on?" I ask. "Is Dad okay?"

Her fingers tighten around the steering wheel in obvious frustration before she removes the sunglasses that aren't even necessary in the evening light. To my utter shock, she isn't wearing a shred of makeup, and it's obvious from her puffy eyes she's been crying.

"I assume since your father left the country with the last of our money, he must be fine."

"What?" I stare at her in disbelief. There's no way that's true. "That doesn't even make sense. Why would he do that?"

"Because, Stella." She looks out the window. "He's been embezzling from the company for years. Apparently, he knew the house of cards was about to fall, and he didn't want to be left standing in the dust when it did."

I shake my head on autopilot, intent on denying these awful things she's trying to tell me. It can't be true. My father would never...

"He wouldn't leave me. And he wouldn't steal."

"He did leave you," Mom snarls. "And he left me. And now we have nothing. The feds have frozen our bank accounts. They are going to take the house. The cars are already gone. Do you understand, Stella? We have nothing."

Tears fill my eyes as I retrieve my phone and dial my father. But I get the shock of my life when the message on the other end tells me the number is no longer in service. I try three more times before my mother finally pries the phone from my hands and turns it off.

"You won't even have that much longer." She nods at the phone she tossed into the console. "It's only paid until the end of the month, and then I don't know."

Tears splash down my cheeks as I come to accept what she's telling me. My father abandoned me. The same man who brought me here and told me he put everything on the line for me. And that's when something else occurs to me.

"What about my tuition?"

Mom looks away again, and I know it's going to be bad.

"Your father sent them a check before he left, but it didn't go through since the last of our funds have been frozen. Honestly, Stella, I don't know what you're going to do."

"What I'm going to do?" I repeat numbly.

"Well, you're almost eighteen," she says. "Maybe you could explain the situation to the school and ask to work something out."

Oh my God. Why would I ever expect anything else? Of course, she's not going to help me.

"So I'm just on my own then?" I ask in disbelief.

"Stella, I can hardly take care of myself," she huffs. "You know I haven't worked since I got pregnant with you."

Even now, she chooses to throw that in my face. She's always been quick to remind me that I ruined her career, but at a time like this, when I need her the most, she tries to make me feel guilty for my existence.

"What are you going to do then?" I ask.

"I'm going to stay in New York for a while until I figure that out."

"With Luis?" I narrow my eyes.

"It's none of your concern who I'll be with."

"So that's just it. You came here to tell me I'm basically on my own and to figure it out?"

"If you'd like someone to blame, you can thank your father for this mess," she retorts. "I hope he enjoys his time in prison when they catch him because I'm done with him, and I think you should be too."

"There has to be a mistake," I insist.

"There is no mistake. Now, if you can't figure that out, then why don't you go speak with the school office when you return. I'm sure they can confirm your father's check bounced. He knew exactly what was going to happen, and he chose to abandon us."

My heart sinks into the pit of my stomach as I try to wrap my head around what she's telling me. I don't want it to be true, but deep in my heart, I know that it probably is. It's not like there haven't been signs. The stress on my father's face. The long hours in the city. The pressure to keep up the lifestyle my mother so desperately demanded. It all adds up to one thing, and what my mother's telling me isn't so farfetched when I piece it together. But that doesn't mean it hurts any less to hear.

"So just like that. Dad is gone, and you're leaving too, and I'm on my own."

"I'm sorry." My mother's voice cracks, and for a split second, I think she will reconsider. At least until she opens her mouth again. "For now, that's the only option we have. We both have to figure out how to make our own way now."

CHAPTER SIXTEEN
SEBASTIAN

Glancing at my watch, I check the time and note that I still have twenty minutes before Stella is due in my office. I consider what I asked her to write, and I find that I'm anxious to read her thoughts on the subject. As I'm discovering, there's a thin line between animosity and obsession when it comes to Stella. I'm having difficulty separating the two.

I see so much of myself at that age in her. An eagerness to please. Dedication and drive. She obviously doesn't get the attention she requires from her parents, so she seeks it out through other authority figures. Namely, me. At least, that's what I like to believe. Contemplating the possibility that she might be just as eager with any of her other teachers makes me feel homicidal.

Would it make you feel better if you punished me, Mr. Carter?
She has no idea how much I want to punish her. How many times over the past two weeks I've already hate fucked her in my mind. How I've imagined her crawling on her knees for me. Ass in the air. Mouth open. I would corrupt her in every possible way if morality wasn't an issue. But how moral can I really be if I'm intent on breaking her down regardless?

A knock on my door startles me, and I glance over my shoulder as I finish stuffing papers into the briefcase on the table. Nobody ever comes to my house on campus, so I can't imagine who it could be. Unless Stella got the locations mixed up. Perhaps she's intentionally trying to tempt me beyond my control by meeting with me in the sanctuary of my home. But it isn't Stella on the other side of the door when I open it. Beyond reason, I stand there, numb, as my eyes roam the length of my father's frame.

"Sebastian." He greets me with the same detached manner he's always possessed. The militant expression on his face is unchanged, even after five long years. "May I come in?"

The request is a mere formality. Being the man that my father is, he doesn't wait for a response. He pushes his way inside and makes himself at home at the kitchen table. For a minute, I can't move. I can't even blink as I study him. And as usual, it takes me longer than it should to find my voice where he's concerned.

"What are you doing here?"

He unbuttons his blazer and shrugs. "You haven't responded to my calls or letters. This is the next logical step."

"I have nothing to say to you."

"Well, I have plenty to say to you." His voice booms through the small space. "So shut the goddamned door and pour us a drink."

"I have classes today."

"Cancel them."

Bitterness uncoils in my gut in response to his selfish demands, but after all these years, I expect nothing less from him. This is the man who groomed me from a young age to be exactly the image he wanted. He sent me to all the best prep schools. Jammed my schedule so full of extracurriculars and AP courses that I never had a spare minute to think for myself. Under his dictatorship, he called the shots, and I came to him like Pavlov's dog, salivating eagerly for my next command. But I'm not the same person I was then. My days of doing his bidding ended the night he ruined both of our lives.

"I'm leaving." I reach for my briefcase, and he slams his hand down on top of it, holding it hostage.

"Goddammit, Sebastian. I need to speak with you. If you leave now, I'll be here when you get back. Either way, you can't avoid me any longer. Take a seat like a man and get it over with."

Our eyes clash, and for the first time, his betray a weakness I hadn't noticed until now. He's still the same hard-ass man who raised me. The man who designed my entire life and accepted no alternatives. But beneath that, there is a frailty I've never seen in him before. As I study him, it occurs to me that it isn't just in his eyes.

My father is tall, like me, but his usually muscular frame has diminished considerably since I last saw him. His previously well-tailored suit now hangs loose on his body, and the hands that were always hard as bricks seem weaker than before. Is it the natural evolution of time, or simply misery?

At sixty years old, it can't be merely his age responsible for the rapid decline. The last I saw him, I'd resolved to hate him until he died, and I anticipated he would live forever just to spite me. But now, it seems the opposite is true. There is no room in my heart for sympathy, not when it comes to him. He might be blood, but I owe him nothing. Not even my time. However, knowing my father as I do, I take his words as a promise. If I leave now, he will still be here when I come back. If I don't deal with it now, it will only prolong the headache.

With a sigh, I retrieve my phone and email the administration, alerting them to my absence today. It will be the only absence I've ever taken in my three years at Loyola Academy. I fetch the bottle of Japanese twelve-year whisky I keep in the cupboard, pouring us both two fingers.

"What do you want?" I take a seat across from my father and squeeze the life out of my glass.

Harrison Carter drains the whisky I poured him and then shoves it aside, his lip curling in obvious disapproval.

"It's time for you to quit this nonsense." He folds his hands together and examines me. "You've made your point. Come back to New York and take your place at the company. I have an office set up for you. An assistant, car service, a penthouse on hold ten minutes from the building. It's all yours."

"It's all mine regardless." I scoff. "Or did you forget that I'm the majority shareholder?"

The barb that was once effective at riling my father seems to fall short of even ruffling his feathers now. When my mother died, she left her family's legacy to both of us with the majority to me, specifically. It was her way of trying to bring us closer, but all it ever managed to do was drive us further apart. My father still believes he's in control while I've waited patiently for the day I can pull the rug out from under him. If or when I ever take my place at the Carter Holdings empire, it will be when my father no longer has a seat there.

"Sebastian." Harrison sighs. "What's it going to take? Do you want me to confess my sins? Is that it? Do you want to hear the words from my mouth? Will that make you feel better?"

"No." I shoot up from the table and knock my chair over in the process. "I already know what you did. I don't need to hear you say it. This was a mistake. You need to leave."

"It isn't logical," he replies, ignoring my request. "I understand that now. But I was goddamned furious with you. I spent years investing in you for you to turn around and throw it all away. Telling me you'd rather kick a ball around on a field than work where you were needed. It was a slap in the face. It was disrespectful. I was blinded by my rage, and I couldn't accept it."

"You couldn't accept that I was done being your puppet," I bite out. "You couldn't accept that I had a mind of my own, and a path that might not be yours."

"I'll give you that." He bows his head. "I never meant for anyone to get seriously hurt."

"But they did." I turn my back to him and slam my glass down on the counter. "In your desperation to end my soccer career, you ended my sister's life. Your own fucking flesh and blood. Don't try to deny it."

"I won't deny it," he echoes softly. "I hired those men to rob you and fuck up your knee. Katie wasn't supposed to be there. That was never supposed to happen."

His admission comes as no surprise. I've known for years the truth about that night, even if I couldn't prove it. I'd begged Katie to come out with the team. I wanted her to help me celebrate my decision to play soccer professionally. I was finally breaking free from our father's hold, and she was so happy for me she couldn't say no. And now, because of my request, she's gone.

Whenever I close my eyes, flashes of her death come back to me in vivid detail. They are the only fragments I remember, but they never leave my mind. We left the bar, drunk and happy. We weren't paying attention, and I should have been paying fucking attention. Katie screamed when three men cornered us. They demanded my wallet, and I handed it over, but they didn't leave. Instead, they shattered my knee with steel batons and beat me into unconsciousness while my sister fought to get to me.

Pop. Pop. Pop.

The gunshots still echo through my nightmares. I can still see her body crumpled on the ground beside me, her hair matted with blood and her face unrecognizable. It's always too late to save her when I wake up, and the pain never goes away. I just want it to fucking go away.

My pulse thrashes in my ears as I turn back to my father, and before I can stop myself, I knock him out of his chair with a solid punch to the jaw. He topples onto the floor, and I follow, each of us wrestling for dominance as we work out our anger the only way we know how.

"Fuck you!" I scream at him. "Fuck you for what you did to her! You should be rotting in a prison cell."

"Goddammit, Sebastian." He shoves me off and staggers to his feet, brushing away the blood on his lip. "Can't you see that I already am? And so are you. We are both rotting in prisons of our own making. The day Katie died, I died too. If you don't think for one second that I'm paying for my choices, I'm paying for them every time I look in the mirror. Just like you."

I rise to my feet and meet my father's blank gaze. The man has never been philosophical. He has never apologized for anything that happened that night. I wouldn't accept it if he did because he's right. This is the prison I've made for myself. As long as I continue to wake up with a pulse, I will punish myself for her death.

"It's too late for me," he says. "I'm dying, son. My body is riddled with cancer. At best, I have six months left, but realistically, I could go next week."

His impassioned declaration provokes my resentment. Of course, he's fucking dying. He's taking the easy way out while I'm left to carry on in the land of the living.

"I didn't come here to fight with you," he utters. "But if you want to punch me, then do it. If you want to beat me bloody, or shatter my knee, or shoot me in the goddamned head if it will make you feel better, then do it. I just can't sit by while you waste your life trying to prove a point to me. This isn't what you were meant for."

"This is what Katie wanted."

"For herself," he snarls. "Not for you. You aren't a fucking teacher any more than I'm a saint. You hated this place when I sent you here. Why on earth you would come back makes no logical sense to me."

"Because I refuse to watch another parent shit all over their kid's plans."

A dry laugh wheezes from his chest. "So, you're going to single-handedly save them all, are you? You're going to show them all that their parents are wrong, and they can do whatever they want, consequences be damned? Even if it means sacrificing your own life? Your own happiness?"

"What happiness?" I retort. "What the fuck is happiness? I've never known it. Neither have you."

"That isn't true." His eyes soften a fraction. "I was happy once. When I had your mother, that was all I knew. When you and your sister were born, those were the greatest moments of my life. I may have been a lousy fucking father, but I was proud to be your dad. And you deserve to have those things too. You deserve better than what you're settling for right now. Megan still loves you. You could have a real life with her. Your place is back in New York, at the company, with her by your side. Don't waste your whole fucking life trying to prove a point to a dying man, Sebastian. That's all I came to say. It's probably the last chance I'll get to say it."

He heads for the door and glances over his shoulder one last time. "It wasn't your fault, son. It was never your fault."

Chapter Seventeen
Stella

I arrive at Mr. Carter's office at exactly 7:28 AM. I'm already sweating bullets, trying to conjure up a viable excuse for why I only wrote half a page last night. He's probably going to rip me a new one, and in my current emotional state, I'm probably going to cry.

I already went to the office this morning and confirmed what my mother told me. There's still twenty thousand dollars left on my tuition bill, and it needs to be paid in one week or else I'm out. All the scholarships have already been used up for the year by other students, and I'm on my own to figure it out. In a matter of a few hours, my life has been turned on its head, and suddenly, staying at Loyola Academy isn't just a goal, it's a necessity.

While I laid in bed last night staring up at the ceiling, I considered all my options. I have an aunt in Florida on my dad's side, but she hasn't spoken to him since I was about two, and I don't even know her, so it's not as if I can ask her for help. Even if I could, from what my dad has told me, she already has three kids to support and very little money. So regardless, she's out of the equation. In just a few days, I'll be a legal adult and fully responsible for myself. I knew this day would come, but I stupidly thought I'd still have a soft place to land.

I can't believe my father would do this to me. My heart feels like it's been smashed to bits with a wrecking ball. It hurts to breathe. It hurts to think. I didn't even want to get out of bed this morning. I just keep wondering if he even thought twice before he left. Is he thinking about me at all? Does he even care?

These are questions I don't have the answers to right now. But what I do know is I don't have the luxury of time to wallow in my circumstances. I have to keep going. I have to figure something out. Starting with Mr. Carter, who is now ten minutes late. *What the hell?*

I peek inside his locked office. All the lights are off. There are no signs he's been here this morning, and I know I couldn't have missed him. But I'm going to miss my first class if I don't get going soon. I can't imagine him ever being late, and in the back of my mind, I wonder if he's okay.

I set my backpack on the floor and rip out a piece of pink paper from my notebook. My search for a pencil comes up empty, so I settle for my red lipstick instead. Scrawling a hasty note across the paper, I examine it to see if I should add any other explanation. But I think that says it all.

I was here. You weren't.
Stella

"That ought to do it," I whisper to myself as I slide it under his door. At least now he won't be able to complain about my half-assed essay. Unless he complains that I didn't leave it behind, at which point I'll have no defense.

Glancing at his door one last time, I sling my backpack over my shoulder and head off for my first class. I have a busy day ahead of me and a lot of shit to figure out.

Somehow, I manage to survive the day on autopilot, even successfully acing a pop quiz in my Computer Applications class. When I arrived at detention, I was disappointed to find that Mr. Carter wasn't there either. In his place was Mrs. Chen from the science department. And surprisingly, I wasn't the only student in detention today. There was another girl from Brentley Hall who got caught skipping class along with two boys who snuck into the science lab and blew shit up in the dryers, apparently. We made idle conversation while Mrs. Chen listened to a romance audiobook that was so loud, we could still hear it through the earbuds. The boys giggled every time they heard the word *member*, and Mrs. Chen was none the wiser.

Cheer practice comes and goes with Sybil nagging at me about my focus while she plies me with gummy bears and energy drinks. By the time we finally finish, I'm dead tired, but I know the real work is just beginning. As we traipse back toward our dorms, Sybil nudges me with her elbow.

"Hey, are you okay?"

I nod because I don't want to allow the possibility that I'm not. Sybil will inevitably find out what happened, given that her father works with mine. I wouldn't be surprised if she knows by this weekend. But right now, the wound is too raw, and I can't admit it.

"I need your help brainstorming," I say. "Do you have time?"

"Always." She smiles. "Let's grab some froyo from the cafeteria and pop a squat in the grass."

I nod and follow her into the cafeteria. Even though I haven't been hungry all day, I make myself a frozen yogurt and pile it with cookie dough before we leave to find a quiet place in the grass. Sybil makes a whole production of it, taking out her notebook and glitter pen while intermittently stuffing her face with yogurt.

"So what are we brainstorming?" she asks.

"It's for a creative writing assignment," I lie.

"In Ms. Hargrave's class?" She questions.

Since we're both seniors, we have the same teachers for almost everything, so there really isn't a logical explanation for what I'm asking.

"Extra credit," I offer, feeling awful that I'm lying to her at all. "I asked for it. And now I have to write a short story, but I need to figure out how someone would make a lot of money fast. Like in a week fast."

Sybil accepts this answer and taps her pen against the paper as she considers my question. "Well, there's always drugs." She snickers. "That's the obvious answer. Or robbing a bank."

"Yeah…" I shake my head. "Those won't work. My character isn't really the criminal type."

"Well, what is the money for?" she asks.

"College," I blurt before I can think of anything else.

"Okay. So a young woman around college age." She takes another bite of yogurt. "She could donate her eggs. I heard you can get like ten thousand dollars for that."

"Yeah, but probably not realistically in a week," I snort.

"Right." She shrugs. "Hmm… what else? Do you think strippers make that much money in a week?"

"Probably not." I dip my spoon into the yogurt and swirl it around. "Unless it's a really high-end club. And even then, she'd need to have the skills. Not likely to get those in a week."

"Ugh, this is hard," Sybil whines.

You have no idea.

We eat the rest of our dessert in silence, and I feel like all hope is lost when Sybil blurts out another idea. "Oh my God, I know. Is she a virgin?"

My stomach flips as I nod. "Yes. Why?"

"There was an article in a magazine once about a girl who auctioned off her virginity to pay for college. I remember my mother reading it in dismay, but I thought it was actually kind of genius."

"Wow," I murmur. "That is…"

"Perfect!" She declares. "It's fiction, right? And if it could happen in real life, it could totally happen in fiction. I think the whole sex thing is really overrated anyway. The first time sucks no matter who it's with."

I nod, but I can't seem to find the words I need to agree. Because the truth is, it's a legitimate option, even if it sounds horrifyingly insane. The question is, how far am I willing to go to save myself? At this point, my options are either homelessness, or Loyola Academy. And if I want to stay at Loyola, it will take extreme measures. But would anyone even pay twenty thousand dollars for my virtue? It seems so archaic. There's only one person I'd even deem worthy of giving it to. And I wonder what he would say if he knew I was considering this.

"So you like it?" Sybil interrupts my thoughts. "I think we found ourselves a winner."

"Yep." I force a smile. "It sounds like a winner."

I spend the rest of the week alternating between panic and uncertainty. After googling resources available for homeless teens, I promptly threw up and decided I don't want to go to a group home or a shelter. I've looked into every avenue, and the only thing that makes sense is staying here at Loyola. But in order to stay, I'll have to do something insane and potentially dangerous.

There is one solution that keeps circling around the drain of my mind, and his name is Sebastian Carter. My dark tormentor and secret savior. He's proven that he wants me, but his sense has kept him from crossing that invisible line. The question is, would he cross it to save me? Even as I consider it, I don't know how to feel about it. I hate that this is what it's come down to, but I want to believe he will help me. The only problem is that he hasn't been around for the past two days, and I don't know why. The administration has told us nothing, and when someone in class asked if Mr. Carter was okay, the substitute simply nodded. I need to find a way to speak with him. But how can I if he isn't showing up to class or detention?

Luckily, by Friday, I've found a friend who actually can help me. His name is Patrick, and he's the tech genius in my computer class who created the LA Underground app. When I introduced myself to him, he apologized for what happened on the app and told me to let him know if there was ever anything he could do to make up for it. I didn't hesitate to take him up on that, and now here we are, on the verge of something completely crazy.

"Is everything all set up?" I take a seat on the park bench beside him.

"Yeah." He pulls out his phone. "Let me show you how it works."

With a few taps of his finger, he pulls up the app he created just for the occasion. It's password protected and requires an invitation to join. An invitation Patrick assured me will only go out to a select number of clients from the escort database he hacked into. Technically, what we are doing is illegal in Connecticut, and although I'm sweating bullets, Patrick assures me his system is foolproof.

"The money will be untraceable by the time it gets to the school. I linked it to a fundraising campaign for your education along with a few small details about you and your goals. Payment will be made directly through that site to Loyola, and the buyer will remain anonymous. As far as the federal government is concerned, you received a bunch of random donations, and that's that."

"How can you be sure?" I ask. "If the LA Underground app got removed, isn't this a risk too?"

Patrick gives me a funny look. "The LA Underground app got taken down because Mr. Carter threatened to expel me if I didn't remove it. I thought you knew."

I suck in a breath and shake my head. "I didn't know that."

"I removed the photos Ethan posted as soon as I realized what was happening, but it was already too late. Mr. Carter was on the warpath."

Again, this is something I didn't know. It gives me hope that he will find a way to help me before I go through with this, but at this point, it's anyone's guess.

"I'm sorry Mr. Carter tore into you," I offer. "I didn't realize. But I appreciate you helping me out regardless."

"No biggie." He shrugs. "This isn't even the craziest thing I've been asked to do. When kids with huge amounts of money at their disposal figure out all the shit that's available on the dark web, the sky's the limit."

I'm just glad he isn't judging me. Patrick seems like a cool kid, albeit a little nerdy. But I'd expect nothing less from someone who's off-the-charts genius.

"So Saturday night at the charity gala," I breathe. "Unless I pull the plug before then?"

"Absolutely," he agrees. "I won't go live with it until I get the go-ahead from you."

"I just need the link for the private invitation along with the passcode," I tell him. "There's one more I want to deliver personally."

"Stella?" Sebastian blinks at me when he opens the door to find me standing there. "What are you doing here?"

I frown at his disheveled state. He doesn't look like he's slept in days, and he smells like a whiskey distillery. His shirt is rumpled, only half tucked into his trousers, and for a second, I wonder if he's got someone in there with him. The thought makes me feel sick, but one glance inside the house confirms that isn't the case. There's only one glass on the table next to the empty bottle of whiskey, and no signs of anyone else.

"Are you, uh… sick?" I ask.

"No." His gaze lingers on my lips, and I feel it deep between my thighs. "Why are you at my house?"

"I came to give you this." I offer him my essay. "I was supposed to turn it into you this week, but you've been absent."

He stares blankly at the red envelope in my hand. "So, you came here instead?"

His voice is gravelly, and I can't read his face. Something is obviously going on with him, and suddenly, I'm doubting everything. I don't want to admit how vulnerable I feel in front of him. This plan could completely backfire. For all I know, he will be happy to see me go. But I still have to try. He's the only hope I have left.

"Mr. Carter, can I talk to you?" I whisper. "In private? It's really important. I wouldn't be here if it wasn't."

He drags a hand through his hair and sighs. "You need to go, Stella."

The detachment in his voice turns my stomach, and I feel pressure building behind my eyes. *How can I make him see?*

"In that case, will you just promise to read my essay tonight?"

He snatches the envelope from my hand and shakes his head. "It's Friday night."

"Please." My voice cracks. "I need you to read it."

His eyes soften for a fraction of a second, and in that second, I can see a well of pain inside him. I forget all about my own problems as I reach out to touch him, but my hand falls short as he pulls away from my grasp.

"Good night, Stella."

Before I can answer, he slams the door in my face.

Chapter Nineteen
Sebastian

I wake up with the hangover from hell, and a glance at my clock confirms it's just after three in the afternoon. Saturday, I think. I've been on at least a three-day bender since my father's visit this week, but I'm officially out of whisky and fucks to give.

Scrubbing the sleep from my eyes, I strip off my clothes and head for the shower. The water is scalding hot when I step inside, but I don't move. It singes my nerves and washes away any emotions I may have allowed to creep back in over the past few days. It's time to pull my shit together and get back to the grind.

I don't want to think about my father dying. I want to bleach our entire conversation from my mind. And even though it's easier not to think about her, I wouldn't dishonor my sister by pretending she never existed. So, when I exit the shower and wrap a towel around my waist, I reach for her necklace in the cabinet. Sitting down at the table with her memory is how I punish myself. Every time I stare at that faded gold pendant, I force myself to remember she isn't here. If she was, she would have done a hell of a lot more with her life than I have. But she never got that chance.

Katie was one of those rare people who genuinely cared about others. She was good and kind and pure. She spent her time volunteering and brainstorming ways to solve problems and make the world a better place. It never occurred to her that the world was a better place simply for having her in it. I didn't inherit the same benevolent genetic makeup. As much as I've tried to resist the notion, there is so much of my father in me. Self-loathing is a familiar friend of mine, and I'd be lying if I said I hadn't considered ending it all as my contribution to world peace.

Except this year, I haven't. Not since Stella came into my life like a bright, burning flame. She gave me purpose. A new project. She's the one I keep telling myself I will save somehow. But how the fuck can I save her when I don't even know how to save myself?

My attention drifts to the red envelope she hand delivered yesterday. The essay on choices and consequences that at the time of my ruling, I thought was rather clever. Now, I don't know how I feel about it. But I pull it out of the envelope anyway and set the necklace and my warring thoughts aside as I begin to read.

Stella goes into great detail about the choices she has made to get to where she is. The choice to stuff down her emotions to appease her parents. The choice to fit in when she knows she was never meant to. The choice to follow her father's path only to be led astray. Her words are full of passion and emotion and an insight atypical of other students her age.

Stella is legally an adult now. Yesterday was her birthday, and I intentionally chose to disregard it like the bastard I am. I sent her away to prove how little she matters to me. My default setting is programmed to push everyone away, and that includes Stella, especially, because she's the most hazardous of all.

I want her to hate me, but worse yet, I want her complete submission and devotion. She is so pliable. So soft. She craves my guidance and attention, and that's a dangerously intoxicating feeling. I don't have as much self-control as I should when it comes to her. So many times, already, I have toed the line and even stepped over it altogether. It's only going to get harder with time. Every day, I find myself studying her, reading her expressions, and watching the way she moves. I've committed these things to memory, and I don't want to let them go.

While I read through the rest of her essay, a fleeting urge prods me to abandon this project. She doesn't have to be the one. I could pick someone easier. Someone who doesn't challenge me and make me question my methods. There's a boy in my first period class whose mother has convinced him he wants to be a doctor. Meanwhile, he spends all his free time dreaming up new video game ideas. It would be easy to set him on the right path. But would it fill the void in my soul? The end of Stella's essay draws nearer, and the escalating desperation of her words reaches a crescendo. She's being vague, but something is off. I can feel it in the hopelessness of her tone. Stella looks at the world through rose-colored glasses, and these bleakly chosen words are more suited to my personality than hers. How can someone so bright possibly be so conflicted? She speaks of being disappointed, abandoned, and completely alone, but it still isn't clear why she feels that way. At the end of the frantically written mystery, there is only one haunting final sentence.

I have to save myself now.

Below that is a link for an app and a passcode. It's written in red lipstick, and I wonder if that choice was intentional, or if she's been taking notes on her homework again. When I type it into my phone, my finger hovers over the download button as I consider what I'm doing. Moments ago, I told myself I needed to purge this infatuation with her. But the burning question in my mind won't be ignored, and there is no justification for this insanity.

I download the app and enter the code. When the information loads, horror and rage creep into every muscle fiber of my body as I read through the description. In the back of my mind, I think this must be some sort of sick joke. Stella wouldn't do this. But I recall the desperation on her face last night when she asked me to read her essay, and now I understand why. She was trying to tell me something. She was begging for my help, and I sent her away. This is the irrefutable proof that every choice has a consequence, even for me.

Stella is auctioning off her virtue, and the bids close in five minutes.

CHAPTER TWENTY
STELLA

After giving Sybil a raincheck on the birthday celebrations, she decided to head home for the weekend. I felt awful for brushing her off and used the excuse that I needed to study, but she accepted it as Sybil always does. There was no way I'd be able to pull this off with her here, and I have a feeling once she comes back, everything will implode. Her father will most likely tell her what mine has done, and things will inevitably be different between us. I just hope that once it's all said and done, she won't cast me aside too.

My phone chimes with a message from Patrick, alerting me that the bidding for the auction has closed. He's sent over some notes from the buyer, and I have never been more nervous in my life as I read over them.

We are meeting at the masquerade charity gala at the Grand Hotel, and I'm requested to wear a dress of my choice and the mask that will be held for me at the front desk along with a key card to the suite. In addition to that, the buyer requests that I enter the suite and wait for him on the bed, and that I do not turn on any of the lights. There is a small note that candles will be provided.

My stomach flips as I read the words repeatedly, wondering if it's possible that this is actually Sebastian. Did he read my essay? Did he find the code, and does he even care?

The uncertainty is bearing down on me, and I feel like I might be sick as I begin my preparations for the evening. In my mind, I've already decided I won't be able to accept any other option. If it turns out to be another buyer, I will have to turn him away, regardless of the consequences. It's the only way I can feel at peace as I prepare to sacrifice my virginity at the altar of Sebastian Carter.

Please let it be him. Please let it be him. Please let it be him.
The mantra plays on repeat in my head as I sneak off the campus at nine o' clock and meet the cab that I ordered. The ride to the Grand Hotel is short, only fifteen minutes, and not nearly enough time for me to catch my bearings. Once I'm on the curb, I hesitate again, glancing around, hoping to catch sight of the only man I've ever wanted. But he isn't here, at least that I can see, and the only way to find out for sure is to go inside.

I make my way to the reception desk, and the woman behind it eyes me curiously as I pick up my mask and key. She asks me if I'm here for the charity gala, and I tell her I am before excusing myself to the elevator.

The suite the buyer rented is all the way on the top floor, and every step I take toward it feels doomed as I consider my fate. I want so badly for it to be him, but I have no idea what's waiting for me on the other side of that door. I realize the potential dangers, but I didn't come completely unarmed. Inside my clutch is a can of mace, and I won't hesitate to use it if I need to.

With a deep breath, I tap my card against the sensor, and the door unlocks, allowing me inside. I swing it open slowly, greeted by the soft glow of flickering candles. From my vantage point, I can see the bed and lounge area, and they are both empty. It's just me here, as the note informed me it would be. Following my instructions, I walk to the bed and sit down, staring off into the void as I set my clutch beside me and smooth out my dress. The crimson floor-length gown compliments the lace mask the buyer left for me at the desk, and despite my reservations, I slip it on as requested. My vision becomes limited to what is directly in front of me, and as I'm considering that, the door to the suite opens.

Before I can use the light pollution from the hall to my advantage, the tall figure shuts the door behind him, securing us into the suite together. He's wearing a black three-piece suit and leather oxfords, but his face is obscured by a mask, and it's too dark to make out any discernable features.

"Mr. Carter?" I force the name from my dry lips.

He doesn't reply, at least not right away. I can feel his eyes on me, but I don't know what he can see. Maybe his vantage point is better than mine, or maybe he's reconsidering this whole situation too. The silence draws out for what feels like forever before he finally issues a husky command.

"Turn around."

The command itself is as precise as anything Sebastian would say, but uncertainty still lingers as I hesitantly obey. He hasn't answered me. I don't know who he is, and I won't until I smell him. Keeping the clutch in my line of sight, I wait with stuttered breaths as he draws nearer. The first thing I feel is his warmth against my back, and it sends a shiver straight down to my toes.

"Sebastian?" I whisper.

Still no response. His fingers feather over my shoulder, drawing my hair aside before he drags his nose down the length of my throat, inhaling me. Goosebumps erupt along my skin as I practically melt into the familiarity of this touch. Without a doubt, there is no other man on this planet who would breathe me in like Sebastian Carter does. And if that weren't confirmation enough, the lingering notes of his cologne hit me like a sedative.

It's him. *It's really him.*

I relax into his touch and release a lungful of anxiety as his skilled fingers begin to explore my body. His fists curl into my dress and haul me back against him as his lips assault the delicate flesh of my throat. A tortured sound escapes me when I feel the solid ridge of his erection digging into the base of my spine.

"Sebastian," I chant, this time out of certainty, not question.

He responds by unzipping my dress and sliding it down my body until it pools on the floor. I'm not wearing a bra, and I can feel his sharp intake of air behind me as he realizes that. The only barriers left between us are my red lace panties and his suit.

I don't dare move. I don't even want to breathe as he unbuttons his suit coat and tosses it aside. Anticipation thrums in my veins as I realize this is really happening. Sebastian Carter isn't just saving me; he's claiming me. When his palm slides between my thighs and cups my pussy, a thousand volts of electricity pulse through my body. I crane my neck to the side to breathe him in, leaning back into his solid frame as his teeth nip at my collarbone. I'm soaked for him, high on him, but when he paws at my breasts, it's all over.

I start to beg, and his fist tangles in my hair in a silent warning. I want to hear his voice. I want to feel his breath against me as he speaks. But he doesn't give me that. It feels like another punishment, and I have no doubt that it is. He hates me for making him do this. His resentment is written in the unyielding hardness of his body. He loathes the fact that he wants me, and even as he touches me, he wishes he could stop.

It's intoxicating to think I have this power over him. This man is ten years my senior, and everything about this relationship is the definition of reckless. But I want him to drink the Kool-Aid. I want him to drown in the chemistry he can no longer deny. I want Sebastian more than anything I've ever wanted in my life, and tonight, I don't care if he knows it.

"Sebastian." His name leaves my lips like a prayer when he kneels behind me and drags my panties over my hips and down my thighs. The thin lace material falls around my ankles as he pushes my body forward, and I collapse onto the bed, ass still in the air. His face is so close I can feel his breath between my thighs, warming me as I curl my fingers into the bedding. His hands come to rest on my ass, kneading into me as his nose grazes the seam of my sex. I cry out at the sensation and begin to tremble when his fingers dig into me and force my legs farther apart.

There is a moment of stillness in which I can only assume he's considering the strength of his resolve. Once he crosses this barrier, there's no going back. We both know it. This living, breathing animal of lust between us is as illicit as Eve's apple. But ultimately, Sebastian chooses to indulge his sinful desires when he buries his face between my thighs and lashes at me with his tongue.

I wiggle in his grasp, crying out in shock and pleasure as his tongue invades the most private part of my body. He eats me like a man who's been starving for ten thousand years, and I live for every second of it. At times, it's so intense I beg him to release me, but his torture is relentless, and it's only when my legs give out that the orgasm rips through my body like a tidal wave.

Blood rushes to my head and waves of dizziness crash over me. I'm little more than a rag doll when he flips me over and pulls me into the middle of the bed. I study his profile, wishing I could see all of him, but he turns away and removes the rest of his clothes. Stripping the articles off one by one, he lays them onto the desk and then blows out all but one of the candles in the room. It's so dark I can only see the faintest hint of his silhouette when the bed dips beside me.

His scent engulfs me as he grips my thighs and spreads them apart, opening me up for his body. Vaguely, I recall our agreement about being safe, and I trust that he's wearing a condom since I made it clear I'm not on birth control.

He kneels between my parted thighs and pauses there for a moment. I want to know his thoughts. What is going through his mind as he lingers on the threshold of no return? There isn't time to ask. In the matter of a second, his lips crash into mine with a growl that tells me he lost whatever battle he was fighting. I breathe him in. I drink from his lips and curl my fingers into the hot flesh of his back, our hips bumping against each other as we desperately try to align our bodies. He kisses with an art that only Sebastian could possess. The art of a man who knows what he wants and how he wants it. I know he will fuck me like a man too.

Between ragged breaths, he reaches down and nudges his cock against the sanctuary that could only ever belong to him. I bury my face deep in his neck and inhale. God, I will never get enough of this. He's already ruined me for anyone else. Does he know that? Does he know in my mind, I'm already his?

There are no words spoken between us when he thrusts his hips forward and shatters my virginity. There are only stuttered breaths and teeth and nails and pain. I invite the pain. I open wide for his pain. I pull his face back to mine and sob into his mouth once he's all the way inside me. Relief is all I feel. He's a part of me now, my body bending to his needs, slowly giving way. I'm soaked for him, and that helps, but it doesn't completely take the edge off. Nothing will. The only thing to do is accept it. As far as Sebastian Carter is concerned, I have no doubts there will always be pleasure and pain.

He rolls his hips, and I cling to him like the needy fiend I am, desperate for his every heartbeat, his every sound. They roll from his lips so freely, grunts and muttered curses. He pauses then starts again, then pauses, trying to rein in his control. I want him to lose it. I want him to lose his goddamned mind just like I have as he fucks me into the bed.

"Sebastian." I reach out to touch his face, and he swiftly pins my wrists above my head. A sound of protest leaves my lips, but he doesn't care. He's in control. Always in control. And he proves that as he begins to work my clit with his free hand, making me shatter all over again.

That's when the real fucking begins. It's animalistic. It's pure fire. His hips drive in and out of me, smashing against my body as our lips clash together. I can taste blood from his teeth, and the salt of our combined sweat. I savor those explosions across my tongue as I wrap my legs around him and squeeze him deeper into my body, trying to hold him forever. But nothing lasts forever, and he is testament to that when he throws his head back and roars out his release. It sounds like ten years of pent-up tension just detonated inside his body, and when he releases my hands, he's too exhausted to fight when I stroke his back and hold him against me just a little longer.

I want to stay like this for eternity. I want to fall asleep with him and wake up next to those dark green eyes, and then do this all over again. But he has other plans, just as I feared he would.

He pulls away from me and leaves me there while he disappears into the bathroom. I can hear him cleaning himself up, and when he returns, he uses a hand towel to wipe between my legs. I allow him to do this even though it feels like the first step to a dreaded goodbye.

Tension has returned to his body, and the deafening silence is almost crippling when he retreats and begins to dress. I wait for something from his lips. *Anything.* But the only thing he leaves is a card on the desk. My pride won't let me ask him to stay, and his already has him walking out the door.

After I managed to put myself back together again, I took the car service, courtesy of the card he left on the desk. Back at the dorms, I curl up in my bed and don't leave again until Sybil comes bounding in on Sunday afternoon.

"Are you okay?" she demands, eyeballing the mess that is my hair.

"I'm good," I lie.

She sighs and sits down beside me. "Stella, I know about your dad."

"Your parents told you?"

She nods. "I'm so sorry. I can't believe he would just leave you like that."

She doesn't say anything about the crime he committed, and for that, at least, I can be grateful.

"I guess I'm pretty much on my own now," I say.

"You aren't on your own." She offers me a sad smile. "You have me. And I can always help you with whatever you need."

"Thanks." I force a smile in return. "I appreciate that."

Silence descends over us, and she seems to consider something for a moment. "When you said you were doing that creative writing assignment, that wasn't really about you, was it?"

The shame I feel inside is too awful to bear, and as much as I want to, I can't lie to Sybil again. But it turns out I don't need to because it's written all over my face.

"Oh my God, Stella. You didn't do something crazy, did you? Is that why you wanted to stay behind this weekend?"

Emotion bubbles up my throat as I consider how much to tell her. I trust Sybil, and I know she would never, ever, ever spill a secret. But at the same time, I don't think Sebastian would be too happy with me if I told her. Regardless, she's my best friend, and right now, I'm not too happy with him either. So, we're even, I guess.

I drag my body upright and gesture for the pack of gummy bears in Sybil's hand as I offer her the only explanation I have. "I'm pretty sure I sold myself to Mr. Carter this weekend."

After Sybil's freak-out and the hours-long discussion that ensued, I feel a lot better about facing Monday, if only to have it off my chest. She promised me she wouldn't say anything after I assured her I was okay, and that as crazy as it sounds, I wanted it. Then Sybil pointed out that she felt this weird sexual tension between me and Mr. Carter but didn't want to say anything in case she was wrong. She also went on to tell me how numerous girls at this school have tried to seduce the hot devil teacher, and I have been the only one on record to succeed. That doesn't make me feel any better.

The financial office confirmed receipt of my tuition, plus a little extra for expenses. I'm officially safe to stay at Loyola for the remainder of the school year as long as I don't screw up. I should feel relieved, but I don't. Especially when I get to class on Monday, and Sebastian won't even look at me. Today, he's wearing a Prussian blue suit with a pale blue undershirt and black cap-toe derby shoes. He looks good enough to die for, and I don't know how I'm supposed to concentrate when I can still taste him on my lips. When he asks Louisa to shut the door this time, the green-eyed monster in me glares at her as she skips across the room.

Almost immediately, Mr. Carter launches into a discussion on QUEST framework and our end of year presentations, which we need to start planning now. I'm struggling to keep up as I cave into my baser needs, studying every line and curve of his face.

"You might want to be a little less obvious." Sybil elbows me in the side.

His eyes snap to us, and I force my attention to my journal as I pretend to jot down notes. What I'm really doing is doodling his name a thousand different ways. Is he just going to act as if Saturday night never happened and carry on with the rest of the school year giving me the cold shoulder? Sybil's thoughts seem to echo my own as the class draws to an end, and we leave together. Sebastian never addressed me or bothered to look my way again after he caught us whispering.

"Mr. Carter was in fine form today." She points out.

"I know." I sigh.

"No offense, Stella. The dude might be hot, but he seems colder than ice. What was it even like, anyway?"

Pieces of Saturday night flash through my mind, and my entire body turns feverish. Sebastian might be cold, but what happened between us was anything but.

"I think there's a reason he's that way," I remark. "I don't think he intentionally wants to be so detached. Who would?"

"We all have our crosses to bear, I guess." She shrugs. "I'm sure you're right, but still. It just seems to me like you don't deserve his cold front. If you're going to have a rendezvous with a teacher, it needs to be worth it. Just be careful, okay? I don't want to see you get hurt."

When I swallow, it feels like I'm choking on a lie. Or maybe the truth. Either way, it leaves a bitter taste in my mouth. "It doesn't matter. I doubt anything will happen between us again. He's made it pretty clear where he stands."

"I guess so." She nods. "Will I see you at cheer tryouts this afternoon?"

I chew on my lip as I consider it. Now that my parents have both disappeared, it seems pretty dumb to keep up this charade. They were the only reason I applied for cheer squad to begin with. My mother would have loved adding that to the list of things she actually liked about me. But that ship has sailed now.

"I don't know if I'm the cheer type," I admit.

Sybil's lip tilts up at the corner. "Yeah, I kind of figured your heart wasn't in it. But that's okay. You can just come and watch me steal the show."

"Sounds like a deal." I laugh.

To my disappointment, Mr. Carter didn't show up to detention today either. Instead, I was stuck with Mrs. Chen and the never-ending saga of her romance audiobook. At least I still had some company from the boys who got in trouble in the science lab. It appears they'll be in detention for a while too. And while I'm pretty sure that I've served my sentence, I keep showing up regardless, and I will until Sebastian tells me otherwise.

Cheer tryouts are this evening, and I help Sybil practice on the quad before they call her in. She makes me wear one of her old uniforms to make the experience authentic, whatever that means. We've studied the routine so many times that she's not nervous about it, and I already know she's a shoo-in, but she won't know for sure until next week.

"I have to go put in some studio time," she tells me as we leave. "You going to be okay?"

"Always." I bump her hip with mine. "I'm just going to take a walk around campus to burn off some of this excess energy."

"Okay," she chirps. "Have fun. I'll be back in my dorm before curfew if you want to chat."

I nod, and she skips away while I consider going back to the dorm to change. It's cool outside, but I'm still burning up from practice, so I opt to keep the cheer uniform on for my evening stroll. I haven't really had a chance to explore the entire campus yet, and I really need to do something to clear my head. It's a good plan until I realize that the seasons are quickly changing, and the light is fading a lot faster than it normally would. At seven o'clock, the campus is already swallowed up by darkness, apart from the occasional lights around the buildings.

Regardless, I keep moving along the fence line on the east side because the cool air is refreshing and I'm feeling rebellious. Secretly, I hope that if I exhaust myself, I'll be able to put Sebastian out of my mind and get some sleep tonight. But that notion falls to pieces when I hear his voice behind me.

"What the hell are you doing?"

The biting sharpness in his tone makes me jump before I turn around and glance in his direction. The blue suit is gone, and now he's in a black T-shirt and gray sweats. The sheen of sweat across his forehead seems like an indication he's been running off his own pent-up frustration. And it looks like he's been at it for a while. My tongue darts out to wet my lips, and I force myself to remember how much I hate him as I toss out my reply and turn away.

"Walking, obviously."

I don't get what his problem is. It's not even curfew yet, and technically, I'm not doing anything wrong. But Sebastian doesn't seem to agree, and he makes that clear when he catches up with me and grabs me by the arm.

"Stella." His voice is a warning, and the silhouette of his face in the shadows reminds me so much of Saturday night my entire body comes alive for him.

"What?" I croak.

"It isn't safe for you to be out here," he snaps.

The severity of his tone irritates me to no end, and I yank away from him. "Don't act like you care."

I try to move, but he corners me against the brick border wall that acts as a fence line, caging me in with his arms. We are completely alone out here, and he knows it.

"Goddammit, Stella." He pinches my face between his warm fingers. "I'm not fucking around. What the hell are you thinking walking alone out here?"

"I'm thinking that it's a nice fucking night, and I wanted to go for a walk," I bite back.

His nostrils flare, and even now, fireworks are flying between us. His face is only inches from mine, and his body even less. But he's still trying to act like a teacher, and he doesn't want to acknowledge any other truth.

"I know it was you," I tell him.

His grip on my face tightens as he leans closer, his words laced with venom. "Do you even realize what could have happened to you if it wasn't me?"

My rebellion falls apart under the weight of his angry confession. He just admitted it was him, and that feels huge to me. There's still a lot to be said, but right now, I don't care. I curl my fingers into his shirt and lean up on my toes to kiss him.

Sebastian doesn't allow me for one second to think I'm in control. As soon as our lips come together, his hand fists in my hair, and he starts to devour me. This time isn't like Saturday night. This kiss is one hundred percent venom, and it's clear that Mr. Carter is all out of patience as far as I'm concerned.

I'm left gasping for air when he whirls me around and slaps my hands down onto the brick wall, commanding me not to move. He flips my skirt up behind me and tugs the spankies and my panties down around my knees. The cold air hits me between my thighs, followed by his warm palm sliding over me.

"You look fucking ridiculous in this outfit," he grunts.

"Yet here we are," I whisper. "With your hand between my legs, regardless."

"You're soaked for me, you little deviant." He nips at my ear. "Because you haven't stopped thinking about it, have you?"

I don't want to be so transparent, but there's no denying the truth between my legs. The evidence is there on his fingers, sticky and sweet and wanting.

"This time isn't going to be tender," he threatens as he yanks down his sweatpants. I feel his hard cock poking against my ass before he slides it down between my thighs and kicks my legs farther apart.

"Don't even think about moving." His fingers dig into my hips.

I don't see why I would, at least until he thrusts deep inside me, bottoming out with a groan. The urge to wiggle in his grasp is real, but I hold my breath and wait for him to use me like his own personal fuck toy. And tonight, that's exactly what he does.

He thrusts against me and claws at my body, slamming his hips forward so they slap against the skin of my ass. I don't move a muscle, even as my legs tremble and threaten to give out. It's the single most erotic game we could play, bending over for Mr. Carter in a dark corner of the campus while he fucks me like an animal. Our sweaty bodies collide, his scent soaking into my skin. But I want so much more. I want to taste him. I want to melt him in a spoon and inject him into my veins.

Somewhere in the back of my mind, it occurs to me that he's fucking me raw. Just like he fucked me raw on Saturday. That wasn't the agreement, but after he wiped me down and left, there was still traces of him on my skin. Even now, as his grip on me tightens and his breath grows ragged, I can't find it in me to care. I want to feel his come dripping down my thighs. I want him without any barriers or restrictions.

But he doesn't give me the satisfaction. When my body surrenders to him with an orgasm so violent I can barely breathe, he withdraws his cock and pumps it in his fist, releasing himself directly into my panties. And then he pulls them back up over my hips, rubbing the soaked material into my pussy.

"Something to remember me by," he growls into my ear.

"Go ahead. Try to forget me." I yank down my skirt and turn to face him. "You and I both know you aren't going to stop. Face it, Mr. Carter, you're balls deep in this situation now. And I think you like it."

CHAPTER TWENTY-TWO
SEBASTIAN

A full week has come and gone, and I've successfully managed to avoid all contact with Stella. No small feat, considering she's been plaguing my mind every godforsaken second of every day. When she's not in my class, I'm wondering what she's doing. And at night, as I stare at my wall when I should be sleeping, I wonder if she's safe. On more occasions than I care to admit, I've found myself slipping on my Nikes only to run past her dorm to check for her light. This problem is becoming a fucking nuisance, and I don't have the first clue how I'm going to purge her from my system.

Shame and self-loathing eat at me as I jerk off in my fist every night thinking about her pussy. The tight, untouched pussy that I fucked and claimed. The towel I used to wipe away her blood in the hotel room is still sitting on my bathroom counter, and my head is so fucked up I can't even bring myself to throw it away.

Initially, I thought Stella had created the whole elaborate tuition charade to force my hand. It wouldn't be the first time one of my students had tested their powers of seduction on me. In my time at Loyola, I'd seen every trick in the book — requests for office hours, batting eyelashes, cloyingly sweet perfume, short skirts and blouses too low to be decent — and I'd never had an issue turning them away. I've never considered myself a weak man, and immaturity doesn't fall on my list of desirable attributes in a partner. But Stella is neither immature nor is she the type to willfully pursue an illicit affair for the sake of boredom. What Stella craves is security and attention, and for that reason, I should have known there was more to the story.

As a teacher, I don't typically have access to the financial records at Loyola, but I do have access to Stella's file, and when I saw a note regarding her father leaving the country, it prompted me to do a little digging. That digging turned into a complete archeological excavation into her family. And one by one, the skeletons presented themselves, completing a shattered picture of Stella's not so perfect family. It seems father dearest ran into some financial difficulties and decided to help himself to the company pot at the Arthur Group before skipping town and abandoning his wife and daughter. The word sleazebag doesn't do him justice.

So far, I haven't been able to gather any information on Lila Monroe's whereabouts in the aftermath. According to the notes in Stella's file, the school's calls to her have also gone unreturned. There is also the small matter of the family's assets and bank accounts being caught up in the scandal, which means it's unlikely Lila is still in Greenwich. She probably left town in the wake of her humiliation, but regardless, Stella is eighteen now, and therefore, she's legally responsible for herself. Which would explain why it would fall upon her to come up with the remainder of the tuition on her account. A fact I only became privy to after schmoozing Marcy in the office with my concerns over Stella's family situation.

Marcy was all too happy to divulge that Lila Monroe is a gold-digging social climber and Stella's father is no better. She laid bare her opinions for a solid twenty minutes, adding in tidbits of gossip she'd picked up from other faculty members along the way. She also speculated on how Stella came up with the tuition, adding that a federal agent had been poking around in her files as well but had ultimately found nothing useful. They asked about the fundraising campaign for tuition, of which the school had no knowledge, and determined it was legitimate. Though Marcy couldn't fathom who would want to help a girl like Stella, which was where our conversation came to an abrupt end. She immediately retracted her statement once she realized we were, in fact, not on the same side. But thanks to Marcy's big mouth and nosy ways, I have a much better understanding of Stella's actions last week. That being said, it doesn't make it any easier to swallow what happened between us.

She sold herself to the highest bidder to keep a roof over her head. And being the prick that I am, I exploited that opportunity under the guise of keeping her safe. There was no other man in this world who could take what she was offering. I never would have allowed her to put herself in real danger. It would be a noble justification, if I hadn't fucked her and blown my load in her like a goddamn caveman without a single logical thought in his head. What's worse is now that I know Stella's situation, I still want to do it again and again. I want to manipulate and degrade her and use her for the high that she gives me. A high I haven't experienced since my soccer career ended. When I'm inside her, or toying with her, or even stalking her like a fiend, it makes me feel alive again. And while I don't claim to be a morally superior man, there are some things that even I take issue with. Without a doubt, fucking Stella again is out of the question.

Routine is the death of joy.

Katie once told me that while she was drunk on wine coolers and high on life. She could be oddly prophetic when she drank, and I lost track of how many times she rattled off something that made perfect sense. They were always simple but enlightened truths. I wonder what she'd have to say to me now, watching as I repeat the same sequence every week with little chance of deviation.

I am a creature of habit. Shopping at the same stores, eating at the same restaurants, summers in Nantucket, and winters at Loyola. I sleep very little and maintain my fitness by running, even though it hurts like a motherfucker with my reconstructed knee. I enjoy the pain, and up until now, I have enjoyed the comfort of my routine. But when Friday rolls around, I know that if I spend one more goddamned day around Stella, I'm going to do something stupid, like shove my cock down her throat.

So instead, I leave after third period and venture into the city. I don't particularly know why. It isn't a place I'm fond of visiting, and I have no good memories here. But at one point in time, this was my routine. Walking down the streets of New York. Staring up at the steel and glass monstrosity of Carter Holdings as I considered what my future would be like. Now, I can just imagine my father up there, ruling his empire with an iron fist even as the cancer eats away at his body.

I don't step inside. That was never the intent of my trip. My father and I said everything we had to say to each other during his last visit. We both know I'll never forgive him for what happened to Katie, just as I'll never forgive myself. There will be no Kumbaya moments between us, and I accept that as I move along to one of my favorite haunts a few blocks away. It's a specialty bar where rich douchebags like me drink exquisitely overpriced and exotic whiskys. In particular, I'm fond their Japanese selection, and I used to sample them often when I lived here.

Like everything else in New York, the place is already crowded, but I manage to find a secluded booth in the back. It isn't taken because it's not trendy to sit alone and drink, which is evident by the number of patrons standing at the bar, scanning the sea of potential for the night. Among them, I'm not even really surprised to see a familiar face. He recognizes me too before I can look away, and I immediately regret my decision to come here as he cuts through the crowd. The waitress appears before he does, offering me a disinterested glance as she requests my order.

"He'll take a double Yamazaki 12," Remington answers for me as he slides into the opposite seat. "And so will I."

Efficiently, she files away the order in her memory and leaves, and then I'm left alone with Remington Moncrief. He's now widely known as the goalkeeper for MLS New England, but at one stretch of time, he was a friend and fellow teammate at Harvard.

"Sebastian Carter." He shakes his head and grins. "Has it been a minute or what?"

"Indeed, it has," I answer dryly.

Remington is up to speed on my past, my family, and even my current situation. I can only assume that he's keeping the atmosphere neutral because I've been anything but welcoming to his presence over the past five years. It has nothing do with him and everything to do with the reminder of the night I lost everything. I've always been too chicken shit to tell him that, but then again, I've never needed to.

"How are you, friend?" He leans back against the booth and scrubs a hand over his chin as he examines me.

"Surviving." I shrug. "I would ask how you are, but I already know from reading about you in the papers."

His lips tilt up at the corners and he shakes his head. "Can't believe everything you read in those."

"Never do," I answer. "But regardless, I'm glad that life is treating you well."

Silence descends over us, and I regret the bitterness that still colors my voice. Remington deserves everything he's accomplished and more, and I don't begrudge him for that. But this was never how things were supposed to play out. We weren't supposed to meet in a bar and discuss our lives like two strangers. I was meant to be right there beside him, chasing a ball across the field and living my dream while Katie cheered us on in the stands.

Life is a bitch.

"I heard about your father." Remington waits until the waitress delivers our drinks to drop the bomb. "I'm sorry, Sebastian."

"I'm not." I take a long pull of the smooth whisky. "I think that's what the new age types like to call Karma doing her job."

Remington sighs, and I'm certain he's probably second-guessing his decision to come sit down here with me. But he doesn't leave.

"He said you're still teaching at Loyola," he adds. "I hear you're even coaching the soccer team up there. They're lucky to have you."

"It's more of a recreational sport at the Academy," I reply. "They enjoy it, but it's all about competitive resume stuffing."

"Ahh, yes." He nods. "I remember those days."

My eyes drift to his hand, noting the ringless finger. "I see one of your crazy fans hasn't tied you down yet."

Tension creeps into his face, an obvious sign this is a conversation he'd rather avoid, but he answers, nonetheless. Remington has always been honest to a fault. "No, but I am dating someone. It's starting to get serious."

He waits for my rebuttal, probably expecting that I'll leap across the table and bust his kneecaps. But I've lost the will to make anyone else suffer in misery beside me. "That's good, Rem. Katie would have wanted you to move on."

He visibly flinches at the reference, even though it was meant sincerely. His fingers tighten around the glass and he stares into the amber liquid, swirling it around in circles.

"It's been hard. I'm not going to say otherwise. It's taken me a long time to get to a place where I felt like I could really date again. And this might sound weird, but I think Katie would actually like her."

"No, she wouldn't." I snort. "She would have ripped her throat out."

Remington laughs, and the humor helps to dissolve some of the lingering tension between us, but only a little. For a split second, it feels good to be around him again. To laugh and talk about the good old days like both of our lives weren't torn apart.

"She probably would have," he agrees. "You Carters always did run hot tempered."

"Fire and ice," I correct. That's what Katie used to say.

"That's right." He smirks. "She was the fire, and you were the ice."

"At least some things don't change." I shrug.

The waitress returns with two more drinks, which quickly turns into three. Remington and I fall into comfortable conversation, bullshitting about life and skirting around anything too delicate. Eventually, he checks his watch and calls time on our blast from the past.

"My girl's meeting me here soon," he says. "But I'd love to catch up again."

"Sure." I nod in my half-intoxicated haze. "We can make that happen."

He arches an eyebrow at me. "You know, in order for that to work, you actually need to return my phone calls."

"Oh, right. That's how it works."

He leans back and pulls out his wallet, unaware that I already slipped the waitress my card. "That is how it works." When he looks up at me again, his eyes are cloudy and emotional. A trait that hasn't changed over time. "I get why you avoid me, Sebastian, and I know what you're doing. Withdrawing from life, taking yourself out of the game. It all makes sense. But maybe it's time to stop and consider how long you can reasonably stay on this path of self-destruction."

"Why change what works?" I challenge bitterly.

"Because Katie wouldn't want this for you." He stares into the vacant void of my soul. "This isn't you, man. You're better than this. I know you wanted to play soccer. I know you had a dream. But you can do so much more with your life, and she would want that for you."

"She isn't here to tell me what she wants," I remind him. "So, I think I have to call bullshit on your theories."

He shakes his head, but luckily, his girlfriend has arrived to save me from the therapy session. When she approaches the table, I notice that she's the opposite of Katie, and I wonder if that was intentional. I already know nobody will ever compare to her. Rem knows it too, but I meant it when I said I was happy for him. I just wish she wasn't looking at me right now with that pitiful expression on her face when he introduces us.

"Carrie, this is Sebastian Carter."

"Right," she murmurs as if she isn't quite sure how to act around me. "Nice to meet you, Sebastian."

"Uh-huh." I dismiss her with a nod and gesture to Remington's wallet. "I already squared us up. Go enjoy the rest of your evening."

He hesitates before he gets up and slaps me on the shoulder. "Thanks, man. And just think about what I said, okay?"

"Sure."

He takes his leave with his girlfriend in tow, and I drain the rest of my drink, trying to wipe that entire conversation from my mind. As I'm seeking out a distraction, I notice the hot blonde at the bar sizing me up. She's reed thin and stick straight with bleached hair and fake tits. Stella's opposite in every way. And maybe for tonight, that's exactly what the doctor ordered.

I gesture her over because I look exactly like the rest of these douchebags, and she'd expect nothing less from our kind. She toddles over on sky-high heels that probably cost more than her monthly rent and sits down across from me.

"Hey there." She offers me a dazzling smiling with perfect veneers. "I was hoping you might call me over. I've had my eye on you all night."

I'll bet she did. It doesn't take a genius to deduce that whoever she is, she's in the market of give and take. It wouldn't be the first time I ran across a woman like her, and it certainly won't be the last. But I decide to humor myself and ask a few probing questions just to see if I'm right.

"What's your name?"

"Alana," she answers coyly. "And you?"

"Sebastian."

"Sebastian." She drags a polished finger across the edge of the table, trying to draw my attention toward her cleavage. "You look like a Sebastian."

"Do I?" I ask dumbly.

"You have a certain… *je ne sais quoi* about you," she answers, and I have to admit, she knows how to play the game. She's well acquainted with men and their fragile egos.

"May I ask, Sebastian, what you do for a living?"

What she's really asking is how much I make. Am I worth her time? I pause for dramatic effect before I offer a vague answer, just to make her work a little harder.

"I have eggs in a few baskets. What about you, Alana?"

"I do some modeling," she replies, and by modeling, she probably means webcam. She's got the sweetheart act down, anyway. "But can I tell you a secret, Sebastian?"

"Only if you trust me to keep it."

She leans forward with a predatory smile and slides her fingers over to stroke mine. "What I really like is sex. And excuse me for being blunt, but how would you like to take me to a hotel and fuck my brains out tonight? I can make you forget all of your problems."

Her claim is bold. Not so much the sex, but the promise to make me forget my problems. Though I highly suspect that nothing will cleanse Stella from my mind at this point, I consider it anyway. Then I wonder dryly if there's a money back guarantee.

I imagine myself shoving Alana face down onto a bed and squeezing her hips while I jam my dick inside her. But try as I might, Stella manages to pollute this fantasy for me too. Because it's her face in my dream. Her body. Her sounds. But I already decided Stella is off-limits. And Alana is right here, willing and ready. She would be the appropriate choice, and the best part is, I won't give a fuck when it's done. I could fuck her into oblivion all night long with no qualms about it.

The only problem is… that isn't what I want.

CHAPTER TWENTY-THREE
STELLA

"Are you sure you want to stay in tonight?" Sybil asks for the third time. "I know the last gathering didn't exactly go as planned—"

"I'll be fine," I assure her. "I have chocolate and Netflix. I promise I'll survive."

She doesn't look so sure, but I'm really not in the mood to be the third wheel. As much as she wants to convince me the small group will be different this time, I have no desire to join the festivities. Maybe I'm just ancient for my time, or maybe it's everything that's been happening in my life, but those things don't hold the same appeal for me as they used to.

"Go have fun with your boyfriend." I shoo her toward the door. "Just be safe."

"I will," she promises. "You too, okay?"

I nod, and she tiptoes down the hall toward freedom. It's already past midnight, and it will likely be morning before she sneaks back in. While I told Sybil that I had a date with some chocolate and Netflix, the truth is, I really just want to curl up in my bed and sleep. So, after I brush my teeth and throw on my pajamas, that's exactly what I try to do. But sleep doesn't come.

As I stare up at the ceiling, green eyes continue to haunt me. Ironic, considering Sebastian managed to avoid direct eye contact all week. Maybe he took what I said to him as a personal challenge. He keeps telling himself he doesn't want this to happen while he pushes me away, and I guess he's a lot stronger than I am.

The truth is, I've never felt more alone in my life. I have no idea where my father is or even my mother, for that matter. Apart from Sybil, Sebastian is the only constant in my life. And if the only thing I have to rely on are his mercurial mood changes, then at least I can count on those.

What Sebastian doesn't know is that he doesn't have to be an active participant in my obsession. When I close my eyes, he's right here with me. I've studied his lines and curves. The way he moves. I've committed them all to memory, and I recall them every chance I get. To make matters worse, I'm wearing his stolen tee shirt to bed every night, just so I can smell him on my skin. I wonder if he thinks of me too, while he's so busy trying to avoid me.

Something scrapes against my door, distracting me from my thoughts, and I sit up in my bed, wondering if one of the boys snuck into the dorm again. But when the door opens, and my room floods with light from the hall, it's the last person I'm expecting standing there in the frame.

Sebastian looks… odd, and I can't quite figure out why. My favorite plaid wool blazer from his wardrobe is slung haphazardly over his arm, and his hair is mussed. It isn't until he shuts the door behind him and steps closer that I can smell the whiskey on his breath. He's been drinking.

"Sebastian, are you okay?"

He stalks toward my bed and unfolds his large body next to me, the weight causing me to dip closer to him. My leg bumps against his, and I leave it there as I try to get a read on him. I want him to feel my presence. I want him to acknowledge me, and for once, he does. His fingers feather over my jaw and down the sensitive flesh of my throat. A shiver crawls up my spine as I consider whether he's going to strangle me or fuck me. Sebastian puts an end to those thoughts when he leans in and brushes his lips against mine.

"Make me better, Stella."

My heart fractures under the weight of his sorrow. I always suspected this pain lurked inside him, but I never thought for one second he'd ever show it to me. I don't know what to do. Dealing with something this enormous is overwhelming, but for him, I would move mountains if he asked me to.

My natural inclination is to crawl into his lap and eat him alive, so that's what I do. Sebastian groans into my mouth as I drag my fingers through the silky locks of his hair down to the base of his skull. I can keep him here, just like this. Hold him and never let him go. My body is already moving, grinding on his cock while his hands come to rest on my ass. If we keep up this pace, it will be over before it even begins. He asked me to make him better, and I want to do that. I want to please him. Releasing him from my grasp, I sink down onto my knees before him and frantically unzip his trousers. Secretly, I'm still terrified he might change his mind. If he were going to fail me for anything, it would be convincing him how right this is. When I'm drunk on this chemistry between us, nothing else matters. At these moments, he's worth losing everything for. And when I peek up at him, he isn't protesting as I slide my palm over the bulging cock beneath his black briefs. Nobody's attention has ever tasted so sweet.

His fingers tangle in my hair as I withdraw his cock, but he doesn't force it. For once, I'm in control, and it feels so goddamned good. My tongue darts out and swirls around the head, and he groans like he's in physical pain as his grip on my hair tightens.

Slowly, I gather my wits and start to lick at him, sucking and nibbling and squeezing the head of his cock into my mouth. It doesn't matter that I don't really know what I'm doing because Sebastian's sounds tell me everything is just right.

My freedom is short lived, and soon he's got me on a leash again. His giant palms slide to the base of my skull, cupping me there as he thrusts up into my mouth. I cough and choke and sputter on his cock every time he forces it into my throat, and he growls out his approval. He can't get enough of it, and by default, neither can I. My fingers dig into his thighs, and I hum a pleasurable chorus against him as warmth spreads through my core.

"I like you on your knees for me, Stella." His grip on my hair tightens along with the muscle in his forearm. "My little deepthroat princess."

To prove his point, Sebastian tips his head back and thrusts as deep as I can take him, groaning in agony as his come spills into the back of my throat. I swallow everything, but it isn't enough. I don't want it to be over, so I keep licking him, sucking him, silently worshipping at his feet. He strokes my hair, and I can feel his approval radiating through my body. For a blissful moment, nothing else exists outside of us. It's the most intimate moment I've ever shared with anyone. So naturally, he has to ruin it.

He pulls his soft cock from my lips and smears some of the come left behind onto the beating pulse in my throat. A moment later, he's hauling me up against his body, dragging his thumb over my lips.

"I'm a sick fuck," he growls. "And so are you, Stella. I put you through hell to amuse myself, and yet you keep crawling through the coals for just one more second of my attention. It's goddamned pathetic."

His words slice through my starving heart like a machete. He may as well have gut punched me. And it occurs to me now that it's too late to protect myself. This man already has the power to hurt me, and not only does he know that, he takes pleasure in it.

"Fuck you." My voice cracks, betraying my emotion. "You think I don't know who you're really talking about—"

My tirade is cut short when his lips clash with mine, hot and fierce and possessive. Against all rational thought, I melt into him. He's a broken shell of a man. I knew it the first time I saw him, and regardless of his cruelty, I still want to take his pain away. But what about me? What about my pain?

He kisses me until I'm breathless and my lips are bruised. I kiss him back because he's right. I am fucked up.

"I hate you," I murmur against him.

"Say it like you mean it," he chastises. "You think I haven't noticed you're wearing one of my tee shirts you dirty little pervert? You're obsessed with me."

My lips remain sealed despite my self-preservation screaming at me to deny the obvious.

"That's what I thought," he says. "Now quit faking it and tell me you want to please me."

My head is telling me to say no, but my heart blurts out the answer before I can even think about it.

"I do."

"Come to my house at noon tomorrow," he tells me. "And be ready to spread your legs for me."

It's two minutes before noon when I arrive at Sebastian's door. Though it was an adrenaline rush to sneak across campus, knocking on his door is an entirely different beast. I have no doubt that he chose this time because the majority of the school is at the football game, but even so, there's always the possibility of getting caught.

Located on the far northeast corner of campus, his house is the most secluded in the teacher's village. I catalogued most of the details inside from my last visit, but I wonder if anything has changed. Focusing on that simple thought calms the raging beat of my heart when Sebastian opens the door.

Today, he's wearing dark wash jeans, a black polo shirt, and a downright predatory gaze. His eyes sweep over my crushed red velvet skirt and thin cream-colored blouse. I wonder if he can tell that I'm wearing nothing else beneath it. He opens the door wider, wordlessly cocking his head to the side to gesture me in. I follow his silent command and pause on the threshold of his living room, waiting for his next instruction. Sebastian seems to sense my uncertainty, and he makes a point to let me know.

"This is your last chance to back out, Stella. You can still run away, and from now on, we will be nothing more than strangers."

"We'll never be strangers, Sebastian." I meet his gaze head on. "You've been inside me."

His eyes pool with an undeniable hunger, but as bad as I think he wants this, I'm also certain he wishes I would set him free. He'll never admit that he's just as fucked as I am. I came here today with the understanding that he will do everything in his power to push me away. Logically, I'm prepared for it, but emotionally, I think Sebastian Carter might be the death of me.

"So you've made your choice then?" he asks. "You want to continue down this path with the understanding that it can only end in catastrophe?"

"I'm handing you the loaded gun," I reply. "Now what are you going to do with it?"

"Shoot, Stella," he answers mournfully. "I always shoot."

"All good love stories end in tragedy." I swallow.

His eyes flare, and his features turn to stone. "This isn't a love story, baby. It's just a tragedy. Now take off your clothes or leave."

Piece by piece, I remove every shred of clothing I have on until I'm standing before him naked and vulnerable, just how he likes me. This is his game, and I am his perfect little doll.

"Kneel." He points at the floor. "Spread your legs so I can see your pussy."

The position is awkward and exposing, but I do as he bids, never breaking eye contact. For every challenge he issues, I will rise to the occasion. For every harsh command, I will work to prove myself to him. And until he sees that, I'm not giving up on Sebastian Carter.

"Do you think it wise?" He circles me like a shark in bloody waters, slowly removing his leather belt from his jeans. "To walk across campus with your tits chafing against that white blouse for any pre-pubescent motherfucker to see?"

"It wasn't for them." I crane my neck to look up at him. "Nobody saw."

"Those tits are mine, Stella," he growls as he lowers himself onto his knees in front of me. "They are for my eyes only. Understand?"

"I understand," I whisper as he loops his belt around my neck and pulls the end taut in his hand. I really am at his mercy now, and he wants me to know it.

"Bend over," he growls. "Onto your forearms. Keep your ass in the air."

I do as he requests, staring at a spot on the wall while I hold my breath. What's he going to do with me now? His palm slides over the curve of my ass, stroking me and warming the skin beneath his solid fingers. And then, without warning, he slaps my ass so hard my entire body lurches forward as I cry out in shock.

"You can scream if you want to," he tells me. "Nobody will hear you."

Before I can process the weight of his statement, he slaps my ass again. It shouldn't please me, but it does. I know this is a test. He's trying to scare me. He wants me to run. But Sebastian doesn't understand how resilient I am. A secret smile curves my lips as he smacks me again and again, leaving red handprints all over the flesh of my ass and against the back of my thighs. He's nearly breathless when he finally stops, and I'm soaked.

"Fucking Christ," he murmurs as he dips two fingers inside me from behind. "You are a little deviant, aren't you?"

I don't answer because he slaps my clit next and then starts to finger fuck me. It's all I can do to stay upright on my hands and knees, and in this position, so exposed, it feels insanely good. It's rougher than he's ever been, and holy fuck, I feel like I'm going to explode. I don't even know what's happening, but when he pulls the belt tight around my throat, I welcome the uncertainty and pain. And then Sebastian surprises me yet again when he leans down and bites my ass so hard, I will undoubtedly be marked for days.

My scream gets swallowed back down my throat as the belt cinches tighter and tighter, and his fingers fuck me harder and harder. And then, against all control, it's happening. My orgasm rips through my entire body and splashes against his fingers as I collapse on the floor. Blood rushes between my ears like a freight train, and I'm fairly certain I can't hear or see anything. It takes me several long, deep breaths to pull myself back together, and that's when I realize he let go of the belt at some point. Now he's leaning back on his knees, wearing a satisfied smirk on his lips as he points at the hardwood beneath me.

"You made a mess on my floor."

"Holy shit." My cheeks flame when I notice the puddle there. Is that from me? It isn't just his floor. His arm is wet too. And his shirt.

"You squirted all over me," he answers darkly. "Now it's my turn."

I don't know what that means, but I watch him as he stalks across the room and takes a seat in his oversized chair.

"Crawl to me," he orders.

Pivoting up onto my hands and knees, I crawl to him, stopping only when my knees bump against his bare feet. He grabs the bulge in his jeans and stares down at me.

"What will you do for this?" he asks.

My tongue darts out to wet my lips. "Whatever you tell me to."

For a moment, there's a hint of softness in his features as he reaches down to stroke my face beneath his palm.

"To what length will you debase yourself to prove your loyalty to me?"

"To whatever length it takes to make you understand that I'm not going anywhere."

"Why?" he asks. "Why would you want this?"

"Because you make me better too," I whisper.

"Unzip my jeans," he rasps, refusing to acknowledge that he ever uttered those words last night.

I lean between his parted thighs and gently stroke the bulge along the seam of his jeans before I unzip them and tug down his briefs. Mr. Carter's cock is a thing of beauty, if ever I saw one. Right now, I want to worship him, but I know better. Waiting for my next instruction, I continue to trace the bulbous head beneath my fingers, taking immense satisfaction in the way his eyes grow heavier with my execution.

"Come up here," he demands.

I rise on trembling legs and force my thighs apart as I straddle him. I'm still a mess for him, and Sebastian feels it when I rub against his cock. I reach out and try to touch him, but he grabs my hands and forces them behind my back.

"This is my show, Stella. Now sit on my cock, you little pervert."

I ease my hips forward, and he pushes his swollen flesh against me until my body begins to sink over him. Taking him all the way inside, I feel so incredibly full in this position. Sebastian reaches up and grabs me by the throat, lightly squeezing as he drags my face to his. He kisses me as if he's starving for me, all the while insisting he's still in control.

I draw in a ragged breath as his fingers dig into my hip, guiding my movements to show me what he wants. He turns my face away from him, squeezing my body against his chest so I can't look at him. But regardless, I catch a glimpse of our reflection in the window. His tall, muscular body draped in the chair while I bounce up and down on his cock like he's my favorite toy. He's still fully dressed, and I'm completely naked, yet I suspect he's the one who feels stripped bare. His body is unyielding, and I know if he really wanted to, he could easily crush me. He knows how to push me to the edge but never over it. And even if it's illogical, I trust that I will always be safe in his presence. My eyes drift shut as I let that tranquility wash over me, soaking up the sounds of Sebastian. The pressure inside me builds again, and my thighs squeeze together, pinning him inside me as I get lost in the feeling. It's like climbing up a roller coaster and then free-falling at a hundred miles per hour when I drop. And when I come for him, it leaves me just as breathless too.

"Sebastian." I collapse onto his chest, and he flips the script, pounding his cock in and out of me at a frantic pace.

"Motherfuck." He swears as his orgasm passes the point of no return. At the last second, he pulls out, his come shooting across the creamy skin of my abdomen. He milks his cock dry and collapses back into the chair, his eyes colliding with mine as he catches his breath. Using his thumb, he drags it through the remnants of his come, and then brings it to my lips. I suck his flesh clean and possession stirs inside those deep green irises.

"Go clean yourself up," he orders. "I'm not finished with you yet."

CHAPTER TWENTY-FOUR
SEBASTIAN

After fucking Stella three times, I'm not entirely sure what to do in the aftermath. Her auburn hair spills across my white sheets, her dewy skin flushed from exertion, and her lips swollen and bruised from mine. I would bet my entire bank account that if I were to part her thighs, she'd be swollen there too. Over the past three hours, I've given her pussy more of a workout than an entire month's worth of my nightly runs.

We are playing a dangerous game, and every time I fuck her, I'm tempted to bury myself balls deep and unload in her one more time. But for now, I'm trying not to completely implode both of our lives. A task that, so far, is coming up short.

I don't know what the fuck I'm doing, and that becomes apparent every time I look at her. Stella has been abandoned by her family, and now she's seeking out comfort from the worst possible source. A man with no morals and no heart. She looks up at me with eyes so warm they could be mistaken for melted caramel. She's a fucking viper with a kitten's heart, and she doesn't even know it. She has no idea what she does to me, taunting me with those eyes. I know what she needs from me. I know what she wants. It's written all over her face. Nothing would make Stella happier than to have me crawl in behind her and pull her body against mine. But the sooner she learns that I'm the last thing she needs, the better off she'll be.

That's what I tell myself as I turn away and reach for a towel.

"Sebastian?" She calls out to me in question.

"You need to leave. I'm done with you now."

Silence lingers in the wake of my destruction, and being the coward that I am, I can't bring myself to look at her face. I don't want to see the damage there. If I cave on this, I'll do something even worse than fuck her. I'll let her in.

I opt for the safety of the bathroom, shutting the door behind me and locking myself away from her. As I wash, I remind myself that this is how it has to be. Stella will learn to stand on her own. She will come to understand she doesn't need anyone, least of all me, and it's best she doesn't become any more invested in this than she already is. Because, without a doubt, I will destroy her. I will fail her. And I'll never be able to look at myself again.

Those assurances do nothing for the shotgun-sized hole in my chest when I step into the bedroom and find that she has gone. Not a single trace of her remains except for her scent. Tension seeps into every muscle fiber in my body, and it isn't logical. This is what I asked her to do. This is the only thing that's right. So why does it feel like she's betrayed me?

The remainder of the weekend passes in a blur. Squashing every urge to stalk her and fuck her again, I resolve that this will be the week I let her go for good. When Monday rolls around, I take relief in the fact that she doesn't have class that day. But when the time for after school detention comes and she doesn't show, it feels like a slap in the face. Of course, she doesn't actually have detention. She's served her sentence, and there is no logical reason she should be here. But that hasn't stopped her from showing up every day regardless. Until today.

My irritation only compounds when on Tuesday, she doesn't show for class either. When I ask Sybil where she's at, she tells me that Stella is sick, which I already know from the attendance logs, but that isn't the explanation I want to hear. Stella isn't sick. This much I know. But I suspect her absence has everything to do with the fact that news of her father has just gone public, and now the entire school knows. I wonder how she's handling it, and then I berate myself for thinking I could ever care. I am a Carter, after all.

By Thursday, I'm strung so tight it's inevitable that I'm going to snap. And when she finally shows her face in my class, it's the first time I feel like I can breathe again. I don't know what the fuck is wrong with me, or what I'm even supposed to be doing for the lesson plan today, which becomes apparent to the entire class as I fumble around with my paperwork. It's at this point the chatter starts, and Louisa makes a point to let her voice be heard above all the rest when my back is turned.

"Hey Stella, nice outfit. Did your daddy steal that too? Maybe you should consider changing your signature color to prison orange so you guys can match."

Her friends start to snicker before joining in on the witch hunt with their own remarks. "Will you have to do sexual favors to spring him?" Libby adds.

"I'm sure she'll see him again soon. She can work off some of his time," Louisa retorts. "On her back."

Slowly, I turn and meet Stella's gaze. Her cheeks are red, and it's painfully obvious she's on the verge of tears as Sybil turns around to defend her. But I interject before she can say anything.

"Louisa." Her name snaps from my mouth like a whip, and she jumps before swiveling her head in my direction. She thinks she's untouchable because her father donates sizable contributions to the school every year to make up for her hellish behavior. But today, she will come to understand that unlike the rest of the staff, my willful ignorance is not for sale. "I'd like to see you and Libby in the hallway. Now. Gather your things, you won't be coming back here today."

The classroom falls silent as Louisa and Libby gather their things with wide-eyed expressions and follow me into the hall. I had the best of intentions to remain professional, but Louisa is already opening her mouth, armed with an excuse for her behavior.

"It was just a joke, Mr. Carter," she says sourly. "We didn't mean anything by it."

"Do you think it's a joke to Stella?" I ask. "Do you think for one second she found your ignorant and cliched commentary funny?"

Louisa's mouth falls open in dismay, and her face mottles with the anger of a teenager who's never heard the word no in her life. "You know this is how things work, Mr. Carter. She doesn't belong here. And I'm sorry that I'm the one who has to point out the obvious, but she's the daughter of a criminal."

"Oh?" I fold my arms over my chest and examine her. "And you've never done anything illegal or immoral, Louisa?"

Her lip trembles as she attempts to hide her surprise. "I don't know what you're talking about."

"I believe there were several shoplifting incidents your father took great care to keep off your record. There was also the matter of the pills the headmistress found in your locker. And then there was the time you seduced a teacher your freshman year in exchange for a better grade. Mr. Norman, if I remember correctly. I'm not certain if that was before or after you were caught in a compromising position with two boys in the library."

"What is your point?" she snaps.

"My point is that you should be very careful who you throw stones at, considering the skeletons in your own closet. Regardless of how much your father pays, nothing is a secret here at Loyola."

"You can't say those things to me," she protests. "You're a teacher."

"I can, and I just did. Now take your things and leave. You will not receive a grade for the test today, and you won't have a chance to make up for it either. Perhaps next time you consider opening your mouth in my class, you'll have something educational to add to the conversation."

"You can't do that." Libby pales. "Our grades for this class go on our college applications, Mr. Carter. Please—"

"Then you might consider keeping better company." I shrug. "Or learning to pick your battles. Regardless, it makes no difference to me if you want to implode your futures to prove a petty point. Now I have a class to teach. Goodbye, ladies."

I leave them standing there, slack mouthed and dumbfounded, with no doubts they'll be running straight to the headmistress to demand my termination. But if I'm being honest, I give zero fucks about whatever storm they bring my way. When I re-enter the classroom, my eyes fall on Stella, her face hidden by the veil of hair around her as she scribbles in her journal.

I rattle off my instructions for the class to read silently amongst themselves, adding their essay assignment to the whiteboard before I dust off my hands.

"Miss LeClaire, I'd like to see you in my office."

Her head snaps up as everyone else opens their books and begins to read quietly. I don't wait for her response. Instead, I walk into the hall and unlock my office door. Stella isn't far behind, and when she joins me inside, the silence swallows us whole when I shut her into the small space with me.

Our eyes meet, and I have no fucking clue what I want to say to her. But I find that words aren't what I need right now. Instead, I stalk toward her and pin her against the wall with my body as my fingers tangle in her hair and my mouth crashes into hers.

Stella is too stunned to put up a fight, and for that, I'm grateful. I know how I left things with her, but I also know what she needs right now. I kiss the hell out of her until neither of us can breathe, and then I drag her to the desk like a caveman and spread her out on top of it. Prying her legs apart, I yank her panties down and tear them off, stuffing them into my pocket.

She watches me with a dazed expression as my lips ghost over the creamy skin of her thigh, all the way up to the paradise between her legs. When I lash at her with my tongue, she whimpers and curls her fingers into my hair.

"Sebastian." It sounds like a protest, but there is no heart in it. I eat at her pussy and fuck her with my tongue until she trembles around me and shatters into a million pieces beneath my hands.

My dick is so hard I could fuck her for hours and never be satisfied, but this was never about me. Once she is satisfied, I rise to my feet and kiss her again, softer this time. A kiss I hope conveys the words I can never bring myself to say.

I'm sorry. I'm so fucking sorry that everyone has let you down.

She melts beneath my touch, and I don't want to let her go. Finding my voice is a challenge, but somehow, I manage.

"Time to return to class, Stella."

CHAPTER TWENTY-FIVE
STELLA

When Sybil and I arrive back at the dorms after dinner, neither of us are in the least surprised to find that my wardrobe has been ransacked and all my clothes are in the middle of the floor, covered in flour.

"You know this is probably just the beginning," Sybil groans. "She's going to be after you like a dog with a bone now. Nobody humiliates Louisa."

"I didn't even humiliate her," I growl as I gather up some of my things and begin to shove them into the laundry basket. "She did it to herself."

"Yes, but in her mind, she can't let you get away with that. Same with Mr. Carter. Guaranteed he has a target on his back now too. But I gotta give the guy mad props for calling her out like that. It's about time someone finally did it."

"Well, she'd have to be insane to go after him," I remark absently.

"I think you mean that the other way around." Sybil stoops down to help me gather my clothes.

"What do you mean?" I glance up at her.

"Louisa thinks she owns this school because she practically does. Her father donates a shitload of money every year for Loyola to put up with her. They even bought the new science building, which I figure must be worth at least a million. That's why everybody turns a blind eye to her catty little comments. The staff are all secretly aware that if it comes down to them or the money, it's always going to be the money. Mr. Carter wouldn't be the first teacher that Louisa got fired."

"Are you serious?" A knot forms in my throat. "She can really do that?"

Sybil shrugs. "I'm just saying it's happened before. I don't know what will happen this time, but he really stuck his neck on the chopping block today."

Clothes forgotten, I flop down onto my bed and worry my lip between my teeth. Up until now, Louisa has just been a thorn in my side. But it's an entirely different matter if she's messing with Sebastian.

"What can I do?" I ask Sybil. "She's not going to stop."

"Honestly, I have no idea." She shakes her head. "You could fight fire with fire, but that means stooping to her level."

"I don't have time for that." As it stands, my schedule is already overwhelming enough. And I don't want to resort to immature antics to deal with Louisa.

"I know." Sybil offers me an apologetic smile. "In the meantime, I think you just need to be cautious. The last thing you want to do is give her more ammunition. So, be careful if you're sneaking around with a certain teacher. She would call you both out so fast your head would spin."

My chest squeezes as I imagine the possible fallout. "You're right. We need to be careful."

Between dealing with the public shame of my father's crime and Sebastian's constant mood swings, I'm exhausted. I spent the entirety of the day deflecting questions about my family from other students and trying to keep my head down. The headmistress even took it upon herself to address me privately, asking if I was okay.

I told her that I am, but that really isn't true. I'm hanging on by a thread and pretending that I'm not is harder than I thought it would be. Despite what my dad has done, I miss him. And even though my mother told me she wouldn't be around, it still hurts that I haven't heard a single thing from her. The only silver lining is that my phone was officially disconnected today, so at least I can't readily search out the news articles.

My entire future is up in the air, and it's all so overwhelming. Right now, I'm supposed to be planning for college and what I'm going to do once I no longer have the safety of Loyola to fall back on. But how can I do that if I'm barely managing to handle the current circumstances?

I curl up in my bed and try to sleep, but it doesn't come. I have this horrifying notion that Louisa will come crashing through my door at any moment like the Kool-Aid man and try to ruin what little sanity I have left. But when my door opens tonight, it isn't Louisa standing there. It's my other tormentor. The one I can't seem to make sense of no matter how hard I try. And stupidly, I take comfort in the fact that he's here. I feel slightly less crazy whenever he proves that he's thinking of me too.

"Hi," I murmur, though all I really want to do is blurt out a million questions. What is he doing here? Is he going to use me and leave again? Because tonight, I really can't handle it. I will break for real, and I'm so terrified he doesn't care.

"Shh." He closes the door behind him and slips off his coat, and then his shoes. It's an unexpected move, and I watch him in nervous anticipation to see what he will do next. I have no idea what to think when he slips into the tiny bed beside me.

"What are you doing here?" I whisper, too afraid to move for fear he might disappear like some figment of my imagination. His response is to stroke my hair and kiss my forehead. A gesture I wouldn't even believe Sebastian Carter was capable of if I hadn't witnessed it myself. He pulls me against him and wraps his arm around me.

"I'm here, Stella. Just go to sleep now."

CHAPTER TWENTY-SIX
SEBASTIAN

As the next week comes and goes, I harness my self-control and do my best to avoid Stella. After spending the night in her room and leaving her asleep the next day, we have not exchanged a single word. She comes to class, and I dutifully ignore her while Louisa and her minions shoot daggers into the back of my head.

The headmistress called me into her office to discuss the situation, as I knew she would. She made a point to say that perhaps I was too hard on Louisa, but what she really meant was she didn't want to lose her father's funding for the school year. I contended that Louisa is a senior, and the money will dry up eventually, regardless. After that blunt statement, I was dismissed without further argument.

In an attempt to take the edge off my frustrations, I've been logging extra time at soccer practice and taking longer runs than I typically would. If I'm not fucking my pent-up energy into Stella, I need to find other ways to manage it. And right now, she needs to come to terms with her family situation. But when the weekend comes and I discover she isn't on campus, her casual disappearance sends me over the edge.

"She isn't here," Sybil informs me when she catches me lurking around outside of Lawrence Hall.

Her face confirms everything I already suspected, and if I were a smart or even a rational man, I would deny her unspoken accusation. But I've never been smart or rational when it comes to Stella, and right now, I can't be bothered to give a fuck that Sybil knows.

"Where is she?" I demand.

"She left me a note that said she was going into the city." Sybil explains. "That's all I know."

My jaw clenches, and I'm forced to temper the hostility in my tone before I give myself away. "The city as in… New York?"

"I'm assuming so." Sybil shrugs. "If I had to guess, I'd bet she was looking for her mom."

It occurs to me that I don't have Stella's contact information, and why the fuck didn't I think to get that? When I ask Sybil for the phone number, she gives me a puzzled look.

"She doesn't have a phone anymore. At least not one that works. Her service was cut off, and I offered to pay for it, but she said no."

"Of course, she did." Blackness seeps into the edges of my vision as I consider Stella's current circumstances. "So she's gone to New York City without a phone and no way to contact anyone."

"It would appear that way." Sybil blinks at the sudden darkness in my expression. "Do you think she'll be okay?"

Ignoring any possibility that she won't, I move on to what's important. "Do you have any idea where her mother might be?"

Sybil considers it for a moment before she nods. "She mentioned something once about her mother having an affair with their driver, Luis. Maybe if you could find him, you'd find Stella."

Thanking her for her help, I leave Sybil behind as I dial an old friend from Harvard. At one point in time, he was my roommate, but now he runs a multi-billion-dollar security corporation. He helped me with my investigation into Katie's death, and I'm hoping he'll do the same for my current situation.

Three hours later, I'm banging on Luis Furtados's door like the SWAT team. When Stella's mother answers, she appears stunned as I push my way inside.

"Is she here?" I demand.

"Who?" Lila barks, staring at me as if I'm a peasant beneath her shoe. All while she's living in a shoebox of an apartment with little more than a single suitcase to call her own. I take in the sad state of her affairs and realize this is a lost cause. The entire apartment can be seen from where I'm standing, and there's no sign that Stella was ever here.

"Have you spoken to your daughter?" I ask through gritted teeth.

"No, I haven't." Her lips pucker as if she's sucked on a lemon. "Are you from the school?"

She tilts her head to the side, examining me in a new light, and I realize my fuck up about the same time she does. It isn't normal behavior for teachers to chase their students into the city, even if the tuition at Loyola costs a small fortune. Lila certainly knows that, and I've sparked her curiosity. I have a feeling this isn't going bode well for me.

"Sorry for the intrusion." I turn on my heel and leave before she can ask any more probing questions, but in my gut, I'm certain this won't be the last I hear from Lila Monroe.

With my only lead crumbling in my hands, a thousand different scenarios play through my mind. Stella could be injured, alone, hungry, lost, or any number of the above things, and I can't get to her. Why didn't I think of something so goddamned simple as getting her a cell phone? And why didn't she stop to think how this would affect me?

Because she doesn't know. Stella has no idea why something like this would make me worry. When she looks at me, she thinks I'm her savior, but she's blissfully unaware that I've already failed to protect someone else I cared about. Now I feel like I'm failing her too.

Without any other leads to fall back on, I drive to the only other place I can think of, hoping the address will be worth something. The apartment doesn't belong to Stella's father anymore, but maybe she went looking for him. It's a long shot, but when I walk up to the sixth floor and find her sitting outside the door, I can finally fucking breathe again.

"Goddammit, Stella." She blinks up at me through tear-filled eyes before I drag her up into my arms and examine her. "Are you okay?"

"How did you find me?" she croaks.

"That doesn't matter," I tell her, refusing to divulge the level of insanity she provokes in me. "What are you doing? What are you thinking coming here alone? Do you even realize what could happen to you?"

She looks up at me like I'm certifiable, and I don't blame her. She doesn't understand, but to me it makes perfect sense. And I need her to understand. I need her to understand so badly I just want to shake her.

"You can't ever do this to me again." I glare at her. "Do you get that? You are never to run off without telling me where you're going."

"Why?" she fires back. "How am I supposed to keep up with what you want? One minute you're there, and the next you're ignoring me."

"That doesn't matter," I argue. "This isn't acceptable. I need to know where you are at all times. If you want to get my attention, there are better ways of doing it."

"Not everything is about you." She pins me with her gaze. "Tell me why you're here. Is this a Loyola rule, or is it yours?"

"You already know the answer to that. Don't ask stupid questions."

"I want to hear it from your mouth," she insists. "Admit it, Sebastian. Just fucking admit it. You can't live without this, so why are you still fighting it?"

"Let's go home," I deflect.

"Home?" She shoves me away from her and folds her arms across her chest. "What home? I don't have a fucking home." I don't know what to say to make this better for her. And even worse, she's right. She doesn't have a home, but she should know that I would never allow her to go without. Maybe I can't offer her solace, but I could buy her anything she might possibly need. It just sounds so shallow to say it out loud, so I try again to reach for her, but she refuses me.

"Lie to me," she pleads.

"What?"

"Tell me something nice." Her lip trembles, and she tries so hard not to let it show. "Just one nice thing, Sebastian. And then I will go with you."

I stuff my hands into my pockets, conceding that she's cornered me. She knows I won't leave here without her, and she also knows I'm not a man to bow to anyone else's demands. But this isn't about me. This is about Stella and what she needs from me right now, even if she can't say it.

"You are so goddamned pretty, it defies my willpower."

It isn't a lie. And this time, when I reach out for her, she doesn't pull away. I drag her against my body and kiss the top of her head because I'm weak, and then I whisper another not-lie in her ear.

"I'm trying to protect you from me because I will leave you empty, baby. It's just who I am."

Her chest deflates, and she accepts the worst of me without a fight. "My father isn't here. So you can take me back, I guess." Wordlessly, I lead her to my car and make the hour-long drive back to Connecticut in silence. Stella stares out the window, and it's only when I stop at the cell phone store that she looks over at me. "What are we doing?"

"We're getting you a phone."

"I don't have enough money to maintain a phone bill," she protests.

"I'm aware of that. But I do, and I want you to have one."

"Sebastian, no—"

"This is non-negotiable." I open the door and gesture for her to follow. "I need a way to communicate with you."

After another five-minute argument about whether I should or should not buy her a phone, she gives up and follows me inside the store. Twenty minutes later, she has a brand-new iPhone on my plan with my number programmed on speed dial. Once we have that sorted, I pull a handful of hundred-dollar bills from my wallet along with a credit card and toss them into her lap.

"What is that?" She glares at me.

"Pocket money." I start the car and drive back toward Loyola. "Use the card for whatever you need throughout the year."

"I'm not your responsibility," she reminds me. "I don't need you to take care of me."

"I know you don't." My voice softens. "But it makes me feel better, so just take it and don't say another word about it."

She looks like she isn't finished arguing, but I'm fucking exhausted, so I reach over and squeeze her knee in my palm. "So help me, Stella, if another protest comes out of that mouth, I will pull over and smack your ass until you remember your manners. If you really want to thank me, you can do it tonight. After I fuck you until you can't walk."

Chapter Twenty-Seven
Stella

As the seasons begin to change, so does my growing addiction for Sebastian. He's still the same moody asshole he was at the beginning of the school year—hot one minute and cold the next—but this volatile obsession inside me has morphed into something else now. I'm chemically dependent. Jonesing for every secret look or touch. Nothing in my brain feels right until he gives me my next fix. Enjoying him in moderation is never enough. I'm only content when he lets me overdose, and he's a lousy enabler.

This nuclear love affair doesn't get any easier with time. As my feelings deepen, so do my fears. I was so cocky in the beginning, priding myself on my resilience. I swore that I would do whatever it took to prove my loyalty to him, but Sebastian has taken that point literally. He still pushes me away every chance he gets, and I'm still here, battered and hanging onto my sanity by a thread. Because even when he's cruel, he's still mine. Or at least, that's what I want to believe. Sebastian is always quick to remind me this isn't a relationship. He tells me once I graduate, our time will come to an end. Yet even as he makes those threats, he's contradicting himself with demands to know where I am and if I'm safe at all times. It's the dying flicker of hope I cling to. As long as he's worried about me, he isn't abandoning me. While I'm certain Freud could have a field day with our relationship, I'm too emotionally taxed to consider the dysfunctionality. After all, my parents didn't set the best example, and I haven't a clue what's actually good for me. After weeks of searching for my father, I've all but given up hope. I haven't heard a peep from Lila, and I don't expect to, so when she shows up at my dorm on a Friday evening, I get the shock of my life.

"What are you doing here?" I stare at the woman I almost don't recognize. She's gained some weight, and the circles under her eyes are too dark to hide even with the best concealer.

"We need to talk." She barges in. "Let me take you out to dinner."

"Mom, it's nine o' clock." I stare at her like she's from another planet. "I ate three hours ago."

"Fine." She glances around the space as if it's beneath her, but it will have to do. "Then we'll talk here."

After shutting my door and taking a seat at my desk, she examines me from head to toe, her nose turning up in disapproval over my red tartan skirt and fishnets.

"I told you to throw out those tights," she says. "They make you look like a common whore."

"Thanks, Mom." I roll my eyes. "Missed you too. So nice to see you. How have I been? Oh, just great, thanks for asking."

"Stella." Her eyes cut into me. "Are you having an affair with your teacher?"

"What?" My face blanches, and I have the sudden urge to vomit. "Why the hell would you ask me that?"

"Because he came to my apartment looking for you."

"He did?"

My mind drifts back to the night Sebastian followed me into the city. It's the only time he would have gone looking for me there, and oddly enough, he failed to mention that he spoke with my mother.

"Yes, Stella, he did," she replies sourly. "And I've been doing some investigating on this man."

"Why?" A flush crawls over my throat, and I'm terrified that she can see the lies all over my face.

"If he's been carrying on an affair with you, you need to tell me right now."

"He isn't," I deny. "Stop saying affair like that. Why don't you focus on your own life with Luis instead of coming here to sling accusations at me?"

"Did you know that your teacher is the majority shareholder for Carter Holdings?" She arches an eyebrow as if this is the most important news in the world.

"So?" I swallow. "What does that have to do with anything?"

"He's wealthy and powerful," she answers. "And you know how those men are. If they think they can get away with something, they will. So if he's done something with you, sweetie, you need to tell me so we can make it right."

Suddenly, the pieces start to fall together. And when I look at my mother, plotting how she can singlehandedly destroy Sebastian's career while she steals his money, I've never been more disgusted with her in my life. I always knew that she never truly cared about me. I was just someone to dress up and use as one of the stage actors in her life. But to come here and drag me into this scheme of hers under the guise of caring about me is a whole new level of sick.

I walk to the door and open it for her. "I want you to leave."

"What?" She blinks at me.

"You heard me. It's time to go. And please don't ever show your face here again. You and I are done."

"Who do you think you are speaking to me that way?" she demands.

"Well, I'm certainly not your daughter," I answer bitterly. "Because it's obvious the only trait we share is DNA."

"I don't need you," she threatens as she heads for the door. "There are other ways to find out, you know."

"Just leave me alone," I tell her. "Leave me alone and don't ever come back."

"Do you want to hang out tonight?" Sybil tosses a gummy bear into her mouth and then does a ballet trick in the middle of the quad.

"What about Micah?" I ask. "I was beginning to think you two were permanently attached at the hip."

"Ha-ha." She pokes her tongue out. "Micah has a thing with his parents this weekend. I want to party."

"As appealing as that sounds, I think I'll have to pass," I say.

"C'mon," she begs. "We haven't done something fun in ages."

"Something fun is an entirely different concept than sneaking into the boys' dorms to get drunk on cheap liquor while they try to molest you."

"Ugh, when you say it like that, it does sound lame," she agrees. "What about your secret lover? Why aren't you over at his place getting your jollies off?"

"He's busy." I deflect the question and check my phone for the hundredth time. Sebastian read my texts over two hours ago, and he still hasn't bothered to reply. I'm trying not to overthink it, but the same thought keeps playing on repeat in my head.

He's abandoning you, just like everyone else.

"What is he busy doing exactly?" Sybil pries. "Or should I say who?"

I flinch at her question, shaking my head on autopilot. "He isn't sleeping with anyone else."

"How do you know that for sure?" she presses.

"Why would you say that?" I narrow my eyes in her direction, and Sybil flops back onto the grass with a dramatic sigh.

"Ugh, I'm sorry. I don't know what's wrong with me. It's just that men are dogs, and you can't trust them."

"Did Micah do something?" I ask.

"He told me he was going home for the weekend." She squints up at the stars. "But I saw him sneaking off campus with Bethany Lind."

"No way." My lips pinch together. "Why would he do that to you?"

"Because that's what guys do, Stella," she answers as though it should be obvious. "Look at our parents. Your mom was having an affair with Luis. Who knows what your dad was doing. And I'm pretty sure my dad's banging his secretary. So, if you ever wonder what Mr. Carter is doing on the weekends when he's not with you, I'm just saying, don't be surprised if you catch him dogging around too."

Her words cut right through the last thread of my sanity as I check my phone again and type out yet another message. I'm aware that I'm starting to sound needy, but that's because I am. Sebastian should know this by now.

"He isn't texting you back, is he?" Sybil asks quietly.

"What?"

"You've been staring at that stupid phone all night. If you want to know what he's up to, then let's just go see."

"You mean like… spy on him?"

"Duh." She leans up on her elbow and studies me. "Besides, it will give us something to do."

I want to say no, but for some reason, I find myself stumbling to my feet as Sybil hops up too. Even though this seems like the dumbest idea ever, I also want to prove to Sybil and myself that Sebastian isn't like her boyfriends. He wouldn't do that. But it occurs to me as we trample across the quad that Sebastian isn't my boyfriend. I don't know what we are, but he would never allow me to grace him with such a title.

Sybil and I sneak across campus and into the thicket of trees surrounding his house. Already, I'm making silent bets on what we'll find. Sebastian grading papers. Sebastian drinking Japanese whisky. Sebastian getting ready to go for a long run or watching a soccer game. These are all viable options. What I don't expect to find when we peek inside his window is Sebastian sitting at the kitchen table with a beautiful brunette.

"What the actual fuck?" Sybil hisses beside me. "I didn't really think he'd be with anyone, Stella. I'm so sorry. This was a stupid idea. We should go."

But I can't go. I can't move, and I can't look away. The interloper glances at Sebastian with an expression of warmth and familiarity. She knows him well, and she looks like she's close to his age. Suddenly, she tosses her head back in laughter as if he's said something funny, but Sebastian never jokes, and I don't get it. As if that weren't bad enough, her arm brushes against his, and he doesn't even move.

I want to rip her throat out. I want to cry. And worst of all, I want to beat myself up for allowing my stupid heart to catch feelings.

"It just looks like they're having a conversation," Sybil says, trying her best to make me feel better. "Maybe she's an old friend."

"Maybe." I swallow, but it doesn't feel true.

For five minutes, we watch them talk, and what hurts the most is knowing that I reached out to him. I texted him, and he saw my messages, and he chose to ignore them because he's with her.

"We should go," Sybil urges again. "You can ask him about it later."

"You can go," I tell her. "I don't want to."

"Stella," she pleads. "Don't do this to yourself. If anything goes down with her tonight, then he's a dog for real, and you don't need to see it. Please don't overthink this."

It's too late for that. I'm already overthinking it.

"What the hell are you two doing?"

My head snaps up at the shrill sound of Louisa's voice, and the better question is, what the hell is she doing here?

"Are you following us?" Sybil hisses. "Seriously?"

"Why are you spying on Mr. Carter's house?" Louisa cocks her head to the side like she already knows, but she wants to toy with me.

I'm too numb to think of a clever response, and I know this is bad. Really, really bad.

"We were going to break in and steal his whisky," Sybil offers smoothly. "But it looks like he's home, so there's no point."

"You could just buy whiskey from Charles," Louisa challenges. "Why would you go to all the trouble of coming up here?"

"Why would you go to all the trouble of following us?" Sybil bites back.

"Because I saw you two creeping around, and I wanted to see what you were up to. Obviously, it's nothing good."

"Well, you would know." I finally find my voice.

"We were just leaving." Sybil grabs my arm and tugs me away from the window. "Just in case you'd care to follow us over to the boys' dorms, that's where we'll be."

Louisa eyes Mr. Carter's house and then turns on her heel, stomping off in the direction she came from as Sybil drags me down the hill. Numbly, I follow her down to the border wall, and she pulls me aside with a panicked expression on her face.

"Holy shit. Do you think she knows?"

"I don't know." I bite my lip. "She seems like she knows something. If not, she definitely suspects."

"This is crazy." Her eyes bulge, and her fear only manages to inflame mine. "If the academy finds out, Mr. Carter could lose his job, like for real. His career would be over. And then… I don't know. They might kick you out too. That can't happen."

"I know." I pace back and forth as I consider the worst-case scenario, but even as I'm trying to be rational, I'm thinking about the mystery brunette. Logically, I understand that my house of cards is teetering dangerously right now. Sebastian could lose everything because of me. And I could lose the only home I have.

But is he with her right now?

The thought echoes in my mind, and I wish I could forget I ever saw them tonight.

"I think my mom knows too," I blurt. "She came here and vaguely threatened his job. She wants his money."

"Oh my God." Sybil looks disgusted on my behalf. "What the hell?"

I fall quiet, trying to make sense of the jumbled-up thoughts in my head, but I can't.

"Hey." Sybil pokes my arm and offers me a soft smile. "I have an idea. Why don't we get out of here this weekend? We can go check into a hotel room and have a spa day. I have my dad's credit card."

Normally, I would never even consider doing something so luxurious that I can't pay for. But right now, I can't think of anything else to save me from this black hole.

Our weekend spa date turned into a chocolate and Netflix binging session, and by the time we return to campus on Monday morning, I feel five pounds heavier but a whole lot lighter too. After talking things through with Sybil, I've come to the decision that I need to avoid Sebastian until things calm down. And maybe, realistically, I just need to avoid him altogether.

That's easier said than done when he won't stop texting me. After hours of silence, I finally received a message from him just after midnight on Friday. He asked me where I was, and I didn't respond. Then after about five minutes, I got another text. And another. The barrage of questions and demands started, and not only did I find them hypocritical, but I was too hurt to reply.

It seems childish now, but I can't let go of this feeling of betrayal. He never mentioned who he was with or offered an excuse for not replying sooner. Yet he expects that courtesy from me if he doesn't hear from me within minutes.

I turned off my phone that night and thought long and hard about our situation. Every time it feels like I've come to a decision, a different emotion comes up and drags me back to one unfaltering truth. I need him. I need Sebastian like I need air to breathe, and I don't know how I can reasonably let him go. But I also don't know how I can hold onto him with Louisa and my mother hot on our trail.

Winter break is fast approaching, and I need to focus on my studies. Next semester will be all about college applications and meet and greets and all the expectations that have been laid out before me. I'm already light years behind, considering half of my peers have applied for early admissions. But even as I panic about that, I don't know why I'm still going down this path. I have nothing to prove to anyone anymore, yet I'm as lost as I've ever been.

When I get back to my dorm, I'm greeted by a glaring red note on my mirror, written in my lipstick.

What the fuck, Stella.

Immediately, my stomach flips as I consider that he was here, looking for me. And from the scattered contents of my book bag on the bed, it looks like he was here for a while. Did he go through my things? Was he trying to figure out where I was?

There isn't time to debate it now. I only have twenty minutes to change and get to my first class. But I have an awful feeling as I plug my phone in and leave it to charge that I'll definitely be facing Sebastian's wrath today.

Chapter Twenty-Nine
Sebastian

After an entire weekend of radio silence from Stella, she has the audacity to trot into my class and sit down on Monday afternoon like nothing ever happened. With no regard to the fact that I've been losing my goddamned mind, she sits down at her desk and pulls out her journal and doesn't even spare a single glance in my direction. Little does she know, her cold front is about to meet my desert storm.

"Stella LeClaire." My voice slices through the classroom with the subtlety of a machete. "Why don't you begin today. Tell us the implications of your findings on wealth inequality."

She blinks up at me, clearly startled by my command, but rushes to retrieve her essay from the pink binder she carries in her backpack. Only, that assignment is missing, and I know this because it's sitting on the desk in my office.

Her cheeks flush with color as she flips through the scattered mess of papers that she has never bothered to organize, another annoying fucking trait that has touched my last nerve.

"I'm so sorry," she blurts. "I... I can't seem to find it. But it was in here—"

"What did I tell you about coming to class prepared?" I snap. Her eyes meet mine, and finally, she understands the gravity of what she's done. "Don't bother coming at all?" she answers hesitantly.

"That's right." I gesture to the door. "Now pack your things and go. There will be a seat in detention for you over the next two weeks."

"Wait, Mr. Carter," Sybil interjects. "It's my fault."

"This has nothing to do with you." I dismiss her with a tone that warrants no argument and watch Stella sneak toward the door with a shadow of humiliation behind her. "Now is there anyone else who couldn't be bothered to show up to class with their assignment today?"

"You're late."
Stella offers me a defiant glare as she flings her backpack onto the desk in front of her. "So what are you going to do about it? Give me detention? Oh, wait, you already did that."
I shut the classroom door, and with what wits I still have intact, I turn the lock and close the blinds. When I stalk toward her, she loses her attitude as she stumbles back into the desk with wide, nervous eyes.
"Where were you, Stella?" My fingers come to rest on the beating pulse in her throat before I whirl her around. She shrieks in surprise as I bend her over the desk and kick her legs apart, flipping up her skirt. To my satisfaction, the one thing she could do right today is wear a thong beneath her tights. I jam my fingers against the seam and split them down the middle, leaving a gaping hole between her thighs. With a quick yank, her thong is out of the way too, and when I slap her clit, she jumps.
"Where were you?" I repeat the question as I force her head down against the desk with one hand while unzipping my trousers with the other.
"I went to a hotel with Sybil," she clips out, as if this is a perfectly reasonable explanation for her absence.
"You went to a fucking hotel with Sybil," I mock. "To do what, exactly?"
"We had a spa day."

She says this while I spread her ass apart to get a good look at her tight pink pussy, soaked with want for me even as she continues to flaunt her rebellion.

"I hope it was worth it." The darkness of my tone is only equal to the venom in my heart as I jam my throbbing cock balls deep inside her. To my satisfaction, Stella cries out, and I twist my fingers in her hair, forcing her to arch back as I retreat and slam into her all over again.

I fuck her into the desk, closing my eyes and trying not to focus on the relief I feel. After spending the entirety of the weekend assuming the worst, she deserves this much from me. I want her to feel the pain that I felt. The pain she caused when she left me to wonder about her safety.

"Sebastian." She cries out as I drive into her. The little deviant is practically begging me to let her come, but why should I? I tell her as much when I lean forward and drag my teeth over the shell of her ear.

"This is for me, baby. How does it feel to be left out in the cold?"

I thrust into her again and again, pinching her flesh in my fingers while I brand her throat with my teeth. It's a reckless move, but I'm well past giving a fuck. All I can think about right now is proving my point. She fucking belongs to me, and if she didn't know it before, she's going to know it now.

I bury my dick as deep as her body can reasonably take me and squeeze her hips as my cock explodes inside her. Warm come leaks into her womb, and I don't do anything to stop it. Stella realizes it when she turns back over her shoulder and meets my gaze.

"Sebastian—"

Someone knocks on the door, and I blink, startled.

"Christ." I drag my wet dick out of Stella and secure it back into my trousers while she flips her skirt down and takes a seat. Her eyes drift to me, full of silent terror, and I swallow my own dread as I walk to the door, adopting a neutral expression.

When I open it, Louisa, of all people, is standing there, a smirk playing across her lips. I can't tell if she heard us, or if she's just being her devious self.

"Can I help you, Louisa?" I ask flatly.

"I just came to ask you a question about the project for class," she says. "Is it all right if I come in?"

Shielding Stella from her view, I cross my arms. "You know when my office hours are. You can schedule a time to meet with me to discuss homework."

"But the dance team has a trip this week, and I really want to get started. I can't come during office hours since we'll be away."

For fuck's sake. She's right, and I know she's right. I can't reasonably turn her away, but I also suspect that she's not really here for an assignment. Louisa has had a target on my back since the day I sent her packing in class.

"Fine, come in." I gesture her inside. "Make it quick."

She sashays into the room and waits next to my desk, her eyes cutting over Stella with a scrutiny too keen for my liking. Stella dutifully ignores her as she flips through the pages of her binder with a bored expression on her face.

I take a seat at the desk and stare at Louisa. "What issue have you taken with the assignment?"

"It's not an issue, per se." She bends forward and slides her notes across the desk, making a point to let me know her blouse is unbuttoned at the top. Just a few inches short of being school appropriate. This is a new move on her part, and one that immediately raises my hackles. "I just needed some clarification."

"On what?" I ask, unable to temper the irritation in my tone.

"You said we could choose our own topics. But what if it's controversial?"

"That is the point of the class, Louisa. I don't expect you of all people to pick something that wouldn't be controversial."

A slow smile bleeds across her face as she wraps a strand of hair around her finger. "So the dynamic of taboo relationships wouldn't be off the table?"

Her words feel like a threat, and I'm curious if she knows something, or if I'm just being paranoid. "If that's what you wish to write about, I have no objections. Just keep it class appropriate."

"Swell." She snatches her notebook back. "That's so helpful, Mr. Carter. I'm really looking forward to this assignment." She toddles off in the direction of the door and then turns around as if she forgot something. "By the way, this might not be the appropriate time to tell you this, but as I said, I'm leaving on a class trip."

"What is it, Louisa?" I bite.

"I caught your pal Stella over there spying on you through your window Friday night. Just thought you should know. Toodles!"

Chapter Thirty
Stella

Holy fucking shit.

Sebastian whips his head in my direction just as soon as Louisa leaves, and while I'm busy panicking about her vague threats, his thoughts seem to be in a different place entirely. He stands up and drags a hand through his hair, studying me. "You saw me with Megan."

I make a lame attempt to choke back my obvious emotion, but I know he can see right through me. "Yes, I saw you with her. And it wasn't how Louisa described it. I mean, I was looking in the window, but Sybil's boyfriend had just cheated, and —"

"Christ, Stella." He comes to sit on the desk in front of me. "You should have told me. That's why you ran off and ignored my calls?"

"Yes." I force myself to acknowledge how stupid that sounds now. "But you ignored my texts."

"Again, there are better ways to get my attention," he scolds. "You had me thinking the worst all weekend."

"How do you think I felt?" I protest. "I saw you with her, and you wouldn't reply. Who is she to you?"

"She's an... ex-girlfriend," he admits. "She came to visit after I ran into an old friend last week, and he told her where I was. Nothing happened between us."

"But she wanted it to," I press.

"Yes," he acknowledges. "Maybe. I don't know what she wanted. But at the very least, I owed her an explanation."

"For what?"

The muscle in his throat works, and it looks as though he's recalling something painful, but I can't be certain. "For kicking her out of my life without an explanation five years ago."

I nearly choke on that statement. Without intending to, Sebastian has just confirmed that he's capable of what I fear most. At some point, he could do the same to me. All the while, we're both staring down a double barrel shotgun that is Louisa and my mother. Logically, I know the smart thing to do is call this thing off. But in my heart, I don't know if I can, even if it means saving us both.

"Is that how things will end between us too?" I squeeze my hands together in my lap because all I really want to do is reach out and touch him. "Someday, I'll just be another Megan?"

I want him to tell me it will be okay. I want his assurances that just because things are messy right now, it doesn't change anything. We can find a way to be together, regardless. But the truth is, I still don't know how he feels, and I desperately need him to throw me a life preserver.

"What do you want me to say?" He stands up and paces back to his desk as if this is the last thing he can be bothered to discuss at the moment.

"Say something." I raise my voice. "Do you feel anything for me at all, or am I really just a toy?"

He doesn't cave. Instead, he just stands there, leaning against his desk while I'm left to wait on the edge of a cliff. If I'm going to jump off it, I need to know he's right there beside me.

"Fine." I open my mouth and lay it all out for him. "I'll go first. You want me to say it?"

"Stella, don't," he warns.

"I'm in love with you, asshole," I shout.

"Love?" He throws the word back in my face with such contempt, it steals the breath from my lungs. "You don't know what love is. You don't even know who you are."

"I know what love is." Tears prick at my eyes, but I refuse to let them fall. "I'm not as ignorant as you'd like to believe."

"Call me in ten years and tell me if you still feel that way," he says. "Someday, you will look back on this while you're sitting at your desk at a job you hate, and you will barely remember a thing about me."

"What the hell is that supposed to mean?" I demand.

"You don't know what you want." He throws his hands up, exasperated. "I saw the notes in your journal. The neat little path to Cornell that your mother paved for you. And in the face of everything that's happened, you're still chasing that bone. Cheer squad, fashion PR… who are you kidding with that bullshit? That isn't your dream. You can't figure out what you want five minutes from now, let alone what you want to do with the rest of your life."

Anger bubbles up inside me, but mostly because I know he's right. I'm still following the path Lila picked for me, and I have no idea why, but I'm not about to admit that to him.

"You were the one who took my assignment out of the binder," I accuse. "Weren't you?"

He looks away, and at that moment, I know I'm right.

"Seriously?" I stare at him in disbelief. "What the actual fuck?"

"Watch your mouth," he snaps.

"No." I start to gather my things, even though I still have fifteen minutes left. "You crossed the line. You got pissed at me and took it out on my grades. How is that fair?"

For once, he doesn't have a rebuttal. Our eyes lock, and I realize I'm going to have to be the stronger person here. He'll never admit his feelings for me, and I'm finally beginning to understand why. Beneath that iron heart with a lock I'll never crack, there's a motive, and I can't believe I'm just now seeing it.

"You knew from the beginning this wouldn't go anywhere," I whisper. "You just wanted to teach me a lesson."

He doesn't deny it.

"Have you learned, Stella?" He cocks his head to the side. "Have you figured it out yet? Will you ever?"

"What exactly was it that you thought you were teaching me?" I ask. "That love is horrible and one-sided and worse than I ever thought it could be?"

"No," he bites out. "It was never about love. It was about you learning to stand on your own. Figuring out your own goddamned path instead of trying to please everyone else. But you still don't get it. Even in the face of constant cruelty, you will literally break your back trying to prove your loyalty to me. And for what? What have I ever done to deserve that?"

Silence settles between us, and his words crush me like quicksand. "Nothing," I rasp. "You've done nothing to deserve it. But that doesn't change how I feel. So don't tell me I don't know what love is. I'm not asking you to say it back. I know you won't, and I'm far past accepting that. But don't ever assume you know how I feel just because you don't have a heart."

CHAPTER THIRTY-ONE
STELLA

As a winter storm ravages Connecticut, the ice around my heart metastasizes too. It's been nearly three weeks since my standoff with Sebastian, and I'm so miserable I feel like I'm dying every time I see him. Meanwhile, he continues to ignore me as if nothing ever happened.

"Don't be so dramatic," Sybil tells me.

"What?"

"That sigh." She mimics as we leave our last class of the semester.

"Sorry," I murmur. "I don't know what's wrong with me."

"You've been in the funk of all funks," she says. "I'm worried about you, babe."

I assure her that she has no reason to be, but honestly, I'm not so certain of that myself. I've been so exhausted. Everything just feels unsettled, and despite the adage that things get better with time, I only feel worse with every passing day.

"I know this isn't what you want to hear." She loops her arm through mine as we walk across the quad. "But it's probably for the best. At least for right now. With Louisa and your mother breathing down your necks, it was only a matter of time before you were discovered anyway."

"I know," I admit. "Logically, I get that. But I just... I miss him so much. It doesn't even make sense. He acts like he's fine, and—"

"Stella, he isn't fine." Sybil stops and stares at me as if I've sprouted another head. "Have you not noticed the dark circles beneath his eyes? Or the way he keeps staring at you in class when he thinks you won't notice?"

"He does that?" Against my better judgment, my heart does a little flip.

"Yes, he does that. Regardless of whatever he told you, I think Mr. Carter does care for you. But he's just fucked up, and you can't fix that for him."

"What do you think made him so bitter?" I ask.

"I don't know." She leads me into the cafeteria, where we proceed to get a snack and sit down at a quiet table. "What came up in your Google searches?"

"Nothing too much." I shrug. "Just his biography. Things about soccer, Harvard, his family's company. Run of the mill stuff."

"Hmm…" She takes a dainty bite of her cookie and sets it back on the napkin in front of her. "It's weird that he doesn't play soccer anymore. There has to be a reason for it, especially if he was supposed to be drafted into the Major Leagues."

"True." I dunk my potato chip into a cup of ice cream, and Sybil cringes at the concoction in front of me.

"I don't know how you can eat that."

"I don't know either." I laugh. "But it sounded good."

"So this is what you plan to do all winter break?" She stares at me incredulously. "Sit around eating crap like this when you could be picking up hot snowboarders in Aspen with me?"

"I need to figure out my plan for next semester," I tell her, which is only partly true. While I haven't stopped thinking about Sebastian's words and trying to figure out what I really want to do with my life, I also don't want to impose on Sybil's family. She swears it wouldn't be awkward with her dad even though he worked with mine and has been affected by the scandal, but the last thing I want is her family spending another dime on me. I don't think I'll ever be rid of the shadow my father cast over our family when he stole that money, and it's important to me that nobody thinks I'm mooching off them too.

"I already told you what your plan should be." Sybil wipes off her hands and shrugs. "You love taking photos, and you are so good at it. Why not follow your dream?"

"Because it isn't realistic," I answer bitterly. Or at least, that's what my father always told me.

"How is it not realistic?" She presses. "You can find plenty of jobs as a photographer. Especially with your talent. It might mean accepting a different vision for yourself than the one your family mapped out, but do you really need all the trappings of a fancy life?"

"No," I admit. "I don't."

I never wanted any of those things. That was just my mother's plan, and I let her talk me into it. But Sybil is right. How much money do I really need to be happy? And just because photography is a risky career, it doesn't mean I'm any less successful than the next person.

"Well, if you're so hell-bent on staying behind this winter break, then chew on that while you're taking photos," she suggests. "Look into schools and give it some thought."

"I will," I assure her.

"And please reconsider coming to spend Christmas with me," she says. "I can't stand thinking of you here all alone."

"I'll think about it," I lie.

With only a few faculty members left behind, an eerie quiet has settled over the campus. Surprisingly, I'm not the only student still here. There are some other stragglers who are either hard-core into their schoolwork, or their families are overseas and the students can't be bothered to make such a long trip back home. Either way, I use the opportunity to do as Sybil suggested.

When I'm not taking photos, I'm making lists and researching schools and internships. On a whim, I even apply for a couple next semester that might work with my current schedule. And for the first time in a long time, the future looks a lot brighter.

There's still a crushing weight on my chest whenever I think of Sebastian, and I don't think that's going to go away. But at least now I have something else to look forward to. Something I can be proud of.

Still, as the holidays get closer, the isolation threatens to swallow me whole. I wonder what my father is doing. Is he on a beach somewhere enjoying a beer, and does he even think of me at all? To my relief, my mother has honored my request to leave me alone, at least for the interim. If she's celebrating Christmas with Luis, I'm glad I'm not there to witness it. In fact, I'm glad I'm not with either of my parents.

Christmas with my family was never really Christmas at all. Mom would be drunk, trying to impress whoever showed up, and Dad would be counting down the minutes on his watch until he could escape. This year, I have a choice how I want to spend the holiday, and nobody can tell me otherwise. I don't have to put on a show or wear a fake smile. I don't have to pretend to be anything. If I want, I can just sit right here in my pajamas and eat cookies all night long. Which, if I'm being honest, that's probably what I'll end up doing. In any case, I still have a few days to figure it out.

As I lay in bed tonight, I count my blessings instead of my fears. And when the door creaks open, I'm only a little surprised to see Sebastian standing there. Somehow, I sensed he would come to me like this. Looking weathered and worn, exhausted and defeated, he shuts the door behind him and meets my gaze.

"Stella." He breathes my name like it's the answer to all his troubles, and the frosty wall I've built up over the past three weeks is already starting to thaw. How does he do that? How can one man have such a hold over me?

"What are you doing here?" I ask wearily.

"What do you think?" He comes to sit on the bed beside me, and it isn't fair. Just his presence makes me feel better. His scent comforts me in a way nothing else can, and I hate that he is my ultimate weakness.

He feathers his fingers over my jaw and looks down at me. "Do you need me to say it? Do you need me to tell you that you've gotten under my skin? Because I should think that would be obvious by now."

"It's not so obvious to me," I murmur.

"I'm here, aren't I?"

"For now. But for how long? I could freeze to death waiting for your warmth."

"I won't let you," he says, and for a second, I believe him. "I'm ready to crash and burn, Stella. Just don't give up on me."

His words, spoken so softly, hit me like bullets. And the worst part is that I still want him. My God, I still want him.

"What made you like this?" My voice cracks. "What made you so bitter? So cruel?"

His fingers fall away from my face, and I almost regret the words, but I need to know. I can't keep doing this with him. Hot, cold, hot, cold. Either he gives me all of himself or leaves with nothing.

"It's complicated," he answers.

"More complicated than this?" I challenge. "Go ahead. Mindfuck me."

Despite the gravity of the situation, his lips tilt up at the corners, and for a second, I could almost swear he's proud of me.

"I was raised in an emotionally harsh environment." He sighs. "My father was practically militant in his expectations, and anything outside of those was not acceptable. He was domineering and obstinate and unyielding in his demands."

"Sounds like someone else I know," I say lightly.

Sebastian shrugs, and his self-contempt is evident in that moment. "I suppose I developed some of those same traits over time. I had no desire to be like him, but time and circumstances made me cruel."

"Cruelty is just pain's gatekeeper." My fingers reach out for his, and for once, he accepts without protest. "Tell me what happened."

"Believe it or not, this isn't what I had planned for my life."

"That isn't hard to believe." I smile. "No offense, but you're like the worst teacher ever, considering you hate almost everyone."

He smirks, and it lightens the mood between us, at least for a moment.

"So what did you want to do?" I question. "Play soccer?"

He turns away, his spine rigid, but despite his obvious discomfort, he answers me anyway. "Yes. I wanted to play soccer, but I had a career-ending injury before I ever really got the chance. My knee was shattered in a mugging outside of a bar, and after that night, everything just... went away."

"I'm so sorry," I whisper. "I had no idea."

"So now you know the gist of it." He studies our intertwined fingers. "I'm a fucking asshole, Stella. I'm not going to lie. I'm a miserable bastard, and I don't deserve you. But I want you, and I haven't wanted anything in a very long time."

The rawness of his confession is difficult to ignore. I wanted Sebastian to open up to me, and he has. I wanted him to admit his feelings for me, and this is the closest he's ever come. As much as I'd like to pretend I have a choice, there isn't one. My heart rules when it comes to him, and right now, I'm as good as his.

"I don't even know why I like you," I tell him. "I knew you were poison the first time I saw you, but I wanted to drink you anyway."

He leans down and brushes his lips against mine. After everything, I know with unwavering certainty that Sebastian's kisses are worth dying for. His lips are warm and sweet and addictive. And what starts as soft and quiet soon becomes a thief in the night. A soul-shattering cataclysm that leaves us tearing at each other's clothes, desperate to obliterate every obstacle between us.

Five minutes later, Sebastian Carter is naked in my room. Fucking me in my bed. Breathing into my neck, he's inhaling me like I'm his favorite drug.

"Take me to paradise, Stella."

I curl my fingers into his back and wrap my legs around him, and we take each other to paradise, coming violently at nearly the same time. And again, he finishes inside me, raw. Something else that neither of us has bothered to address. This risky little game we are playing is intoxicating, but soon, it could become a harsh reality.

Sebastian kisses me, and I kiss him back, and then he drags me against his body like he'll never let me go. I want to believe him. *God, do I ever want to believe him.*

CHAPTER THIRTY-TWO
SEBASTIAN

Stella bolts upright and glances around the room in a panic, but the moment her eyes find mine, the tension in her body bleeds away. I feel it too, in the beating pulse of my throat. This quixotic connection between us. How can something so simple affect me so profoundly? I'm suffocating when I'm not near her, and now I know she feels it too. It's a fucking nightmare.

Nobody has ever managed to punch a gaping hole in my chest the way she can with a single glance. Not any of my short-term flings or even my long-term girlfriend, Megan. Stella unravels me. She makes me forget who I'm supposed to be and reminds me of the man I could have been. In short, she terrifies me. If life has taught me anything, it's that the things we want can only be ours for a little while.

Stella expects me to leave like everyone else in her life, and it would be the smart and sane thing to do. But I've never been smart or sane when it comes to her.

"Come away with me," I murmur.

She scrubs the sleep from her eyes as if she wants to be sure this isn't a dream. "What do you mean?"

"It's almost Christmas. We can spend the rest of the holiday at my cottage in Nantucket."

"You have a cottage in Nantucket?"

I nod, leaving out the part that I also have a Georgian estate on Connecticut's Gold Coast and millions of dollars in my bank account. Divulging those facts to Stella seems arrogant, considering she has nothing. But right now, if she'd let me, I'd sign everything over to her if I knew it would make her happy.

"When would we leave?" she asks.

"Today. Right now. After you get ready."

I don't want to waste any time. I've already wasted too much, and at least in Nantucket, we won't have to sneak around. I can fuck her and taste her and feed my obsession for her as much as I want, for as long as I want.

Stella seems to consider it for a minute, and I hate that she's even thinking about it. Rightfully so, I wouldn't be surprised if she turned me down. It's what I deserve.

Instead, she crawls out of bed and stares at the mess that is her closet. "What should I bring?"

"Bring whatever's easiest to take off you."

Stella falls asleep in the passenger seat on the drive up to Hyannis and remains that way for much of the ferry ride to Nantucket. Briefly, I wonder if she's coming down with something, but I chalk it up to her being exhausted from the night before. When the car comes to a stop in front of the cottage, she perks right up.

"This is your place?" She studies the quaint white structure with a mixture of curiosity and nerves.

"This is it." I grab our bags from the back seat, and she follows me to the door. Admittedly, I'm a little nervous too. I want her to like it here, and I don't want to delve too deep into the motivation for that desire.

Despite her family's obsession with money and material things, Stella doesn't seem like she's been plagued with the same sickness. In any case, this cottage might be small and unassuming, but the real estate is prime, being only steps from the beach, and it costs more than most average homes.

"Wow." Her eyes sweep over the space as I open the door and let her inside. She surveys the open living area with floor-to-ceiling windows and makes herself at home, examining my furnishings and touching a few knickknacks as if to leave her mark.

"Do you spend a lot of time here?" She parks herself in front of the window, studying the waves in the ocean.

"Every summer." I set down our bags and start my preparations for a fire while she reapplies her lipstick.

Now that I have her here, I'm not exactly sure what to do with her. Stella and I are good at sex. We are good at fighting. But we aren't so good at everyday conversation. Probably because I've never given her the opportunity, but there's a first time for everything.

She sits down on the sofa, looking a little unsure of herself as I light the fire. Once I have it going, I join her there, and she laughs.

"What's so funny?" I ask.

"We've never just hung out like this," she remarks. "We've had a lot of sex. We've even slept together. But we haven't ever just… talked."

"So, talk." I remove the tube of lipstick from her fingers and flip the cap off, examining the shade of red I've come to know well.

She studies me with a curious expression. "What do you want me to talk about?"

"Whatever you want."

The room falls silent while she considers it, and then she leans back into the sofa, curling her feet up beneath her. I know we're supposed to be talking, but I can't stop myself from reaching out to trace my finger along the lines of her fishnet tights. Stella shivers and then scoots a little closer, and the next thing I know, she's tucked securely against my body with my arm wrapped around her. Cuddling, I think normal people like to call it.

I need a distraction from the war inside my head, so I use the lipstick to draw inside the blank squares of her tights. Stella smirks as I add more letters, completing the game of tic tac toe on her skin.

"I changed my mind about Cornell," she volunteers.

Tension blooms in my chest, but I adopt a neutral tone as I push for her to explain. "You did?"

"Yes." She looks up at me. "You were right. I don't know what I was doing with that stupid plan my mom came up with. I didn't want any of it."

And just like that, I've finally accomplished the thing I set out to. Out of all my projects, Stella has been the only one I could ever say was a success. She opened her eyes, and now she's ready to walk her own path. It's what I've been working toward for the entirety of my career at Loyola. I kept telling myself that once I reached this goal, I would be satisfied. As if I would magically feel better about Katie's death and she would be proud of me. But when I look at Stella and remember the hell I've put her through, I know I'm dead wrong about that. Katie would be disgusted by the person I've become.

"So that's it?" My voice is too rough for my own liking. "You aren't going to Cornell. What will you do then?"

And do those plans include me? That's the question I can't bring myself to ask. I told Stella she doesn't love me, and deep down, a part of me still wishes she didn't. I'm the worst possible thing for her. In the end, it's inevitable that I will fail her, just as I failed Katie.

"I know it might sound crazy," she answers, oblivious to the current war raging on in my mind. "But I think I want to do photography."

"It's not crazy if that's what you want."

She looks at me as if she doesn't quite believe me. As if it can't be that easy, and why should it? I've given her a hard time about everything else.

"You really think so?" she asks.

"I wouldn't say it if I didn't think so. You love photography. I think it's the appropriate choice to pursue."

"But what if it's a mistake?" She frowns. "What if years from now, I'm broke and miserable, wishing I had gone to Cornell?"

"Nothing in life is certain," I tell her. "Except that we all have limited time. You should make the most of it while you're here. You only get one chance, Stella. Don't make decisions based on fear. Go after what you want and don't look back."

"That's the most passionate speech I've ever heard you give." Her lips tilt up into a beautiful smile. "And a little hypocritical, I might add."

I knew that was coming, and I don't deny it.

"What would make you happy?" She turns the question around on me.

For once, I don't know how to answer to that. Any real chance at happiness died the day Katie did too. After that, I didn't feel like I deserved to be alive, let alone happy. And for the past five years, I've done a damn good job reminding myself of that. But as I consider Stella's question, I know what would make me happy, and it's so simple it's terrifying. My second chance is sitting right in front of me.

"Remind me again why we aren't having sex right now," I say.

"Wet paint." Stella points to her lips with a mischievous smile. "Do you want to be the kind of man who ruins my lipstick?"

I drag her into my lap and force her to arch back as I bite at her throat. "If I'm not, then I'm not doing my job properly."

CHAPTER THIRTY-THREE
STELLA

For five blissful days, Sebastian and I live in our own little bubble where nothing else can touch us. We wake up, have sex, eat breakfast, and then repeat. In the afternoons, we've taken to lying by the fire and napping, which I can't seem to get enough of lately.

Sebastian asks me several times if I'm okay, but I assure him it's just the school year catching up with me. I'm exhausted, but I'm content.

On Christmas morning, he surprises me with a gift, and I feel like an asshole because I have nothing for him. When I tell him so, he doesn't look like he cares in the least.

"Your pussy is my gift," he says crudely. "And I'll be enjoying it several times today. Now open it."

I take the box from him and gently pry off the lid to find a white gold bar necklace with an engraving that couldn't be more fitting from Sebastian. *Owned* is scrawled across the back in elegant calligraphy font. It's beautiful, and it looks like it cost more than any other piece of jewelry I've ever worn.

"Wear it always," he commands in a gravelly voice. "And remember who you belong to."

The attention whore in me claps gleefully as I hand it over to him. "Can you help me put it on?"

He secures the chain around my neck and brushes my hair to the side before his lips are on me. "Do you like it?"

"I love it," I whisper. *And you.* "Thank you."

"Good." He bites into my neck. "You can love it on your knees while you deep throat my cock."

As it turns out, he means that quite literally. After taking my clothes off, Sebastian gets into the holiday spirit by face-fucking me on my knees. Once that's out of his system, he takes me against the floor-to-ceiling windows and makes love to me in front of the fire. It's no small wonder that I'm exhausted, but I wouldn't have it any other way. I want to feel his pulse inside of me until I turn to dust.

We spend the rest of the afternoon naked with my head against his chest while he drapes his arm over me casually. It feels comfortable. It almost feels too perfect, and when his phone shatters the silence between us, it turns out that I'm right.

At first, he ignores it, humming his frustration as he traces the lines of my body, which is admittedly a little softer than I'd like it to be. If my mother saw me now, she'd probably accuse me of stress eating and make arrangements to send me to fat camp on the first available bus. But Sebastian doesn't seem to mind, or even notice, as far as I can tell.

His phone rings again, and this time, he reluctantly staggers to his feet and glares at the screen.

"Yes?" he answers briskly, glancing back at me before he disappears down the hall, shutting the bedroom door behind him.

I try not to let it bother me, but I'm curious who's on the line. While he's busy with his conversation, I help myself to his bag, poking around for one of his tee shirts I can throw on. Preferably something that already smells like him. I hit the jackpot at the bottom, but his tee shirt isn't the only thing I find. The same necklace from his medicine cabinet is in there too. And this time, when I pick it up, I notice a small engraving on the side that I missed before. *Katherine Carter.*

My stomach flips as I stuff the evidence back into the bag and glance at the door down the hall. It's still closed, and I can't hear Sebastian. I don't know how long I reasonably have before he comes back, but now that I have this information, I'm dying to Google that name. I scramble for my phone and pull up an incognito browser, but before I can even click enter, the door opens, and Sebastian appears. He stares right through me, and I don't know what's changed, but it's obvious from his posture that something has.

"Are you okay?" I ask hesitantly.

He doesn't respond. Instead, he gathers his discarded clothing from the couch and begins to dress. In a matter of a few minutes, everything has completely changed. His face is a wall of apathy, and I don't like it. Already, I can feel him slipping away, out of my grasp, and back into the dark hole he's exiled himself to.

"Tell me about the necklace," I blurt recklessly. Desperation has taken the wheel now, and I'm merely a passenger on this train heading for disaster. As soon as Sebastian turns his gaze on me, I know I've made a fatal mistake. With one simple statement, I've woken the lumbering beast inside of him.

"What?" he snarls.

My hand trembles as I point toward his bag. "The necklace you brought. The one with Katherine Carter's name on it."

"What were you doing in my bag?" Vacant eyes cut through me, and it's too late. I've already lost him.

"Please, Sebastian. You can't do this to me again. Talk to me."

"Talk to you?" he mocks. "There's nothing to talk about, Stella. Don't you get that? This was a mistake. You need to go back to Loyola. Call a taxi and take the afternoon ferry."

He completes his cruel tirade by yanking cash from his wallet and tossing it onto the couch like I'm a common whore. I want to say something, but I can't. I can't even breathe. I'm pretty sure this time, Sebastian Carter has finally broken me.

For three miserable days, I take shelter at Sebastian's house on campus. I'm not proud to admit that I resorted to sneaking in through an unlocked window, but I just know this is where I need to be. He won't answer my texts or calls, and I'm determined to speak with him when he returns. When he finally does, it's late, and he catches me asleep in his bed.

"What are you doing?"

The sound of his voice jolts me awake, and I scramble to my feet, wracking my sleep-addled brain for the speech I prepared.

"Hi." I take a tentative step toward him, hopeful that he's in a better place than he was three days ago.

He doesn't look as happy to see me. In fact, it appears he's completely re-erected the ice fortress around himself. But I know if I had a chisel, beneath all that anger, I would find nothing but raw pain.

"I know about your father," I blurt. "I'm so sorry, Sebastian. I read the news, and I understand now that's why you disappeared that morning."

"What the fuck are you doing in my house?" His words hit me like shrapnel, and even though I told myself I'd be prepared for this, I'm definitely not.

"Seriously?" I fold my arms across my chest to hide my nerves. "You've just spent an entire week inside me. Don't act like I'm crossing some invisible fucking line now. I want you to talk to me. I need you to talk to me."

He turns his back on me, and my determination begins to crack. As much as I want to believe we can get past this, I don't know if I'll ever completely break down his walls.

"Detention, Miss LeClaire," he barks with the authority of my teacher. "Now."

His words stun me into silence. He's resorted to treating me as if I'm nothing more than a student, and I can't help wondering if this is another test. If I stay here, I fail. If I go, maybe there's still hope. So even though I'm fully aware he can't rightfully give me detention on winter break, I turn on my heel and head for the building anyway.

The classroom is unlocked, and I take a seat at my usual desk, waiting for him to come. Ten minutes pass. Then twenty. Then thirty. After an hour, he does show up, only to open the door, look at me, and leave again. Another two hours later, he returns and takes a seat at the desk. His face is a mask of indifference and it feels like we're back to the beginning all over again. Every hard-won ounce of progress has imploded, and I'm at a loss. Silence fills the space between us, and I hold out for as long as I can. But after the five-hour mark, I'm no longer able to hold my bodily functions.

To my utter humiliation, my bladder empties itself all over the seat and drips down onto the floor. Sebastian glances up with a bored expression on his face, and it's at this point, he finally speaks.

"Now you are free to go, Miss LeClaire."

CHAPTER THIRTY-FOUR
STELLA

"You look like hell." Sybil flops down onto the bed beside me.
"I feel like hell," I reply.
"Have you spoken with him?"
"No." I shake my head. "As far as I know, he hasn't returned to campus. There's been no texts, no phone calls, but these arrived today. There wasn't a note though."
She examines the box of burgundy eternity roses from *Fleurs De Paris* with the same level of scrutiny I had when I checked them over. "It seems like something he would do. Is he trying to send you a message without actually saying it?"
"He's toying with me. That's what it feels like anyway. He made it pretty clear before he left where I stood. So why the cryptic flowers?"
"He doesn't strike me as the type who likes the taste of an apology on his lips," Sybil observes. "Maybe this is his way of trying to convey something along those lines."
"I don't know." I glare at the flowers.
"So, he never told you about his father?" she asks.
"No." The school announced his absence today due to a death in the family. There was no indication of how long he'd be gone for, or if he'd even be coming back.
"How did it go down exactly?" She offers me a gummy bear, and I decline.
"Everything was fine, and then it wasn't." I shrug. "He took me to Nantucket, and then he told me to leave. A few days later, he showed up to get some of his things, I assume, and left again."

I leave out the part about detention, which I now understand was a message from Sebastian. *How far will you go to prove yourself to me, Stella? Why are you even here, Stella? Now that you understand your loyalty means nothing, you are free to go, Stella.*

"I'm sure it was just the grief talking," she says, trying her best to make me feel better about the situation.

"I'm sure it was," I agree. "But I just don't think I have anything left to give."

"I don't blame you." She shakes her head. "He's been a major prick. I mean most men are at times, but Sebastian could give the worst of them a run for their money."

Sybil's disparaging analysis doesn't make me feel any better. "He is an asshole, but I think I've finally figured out why."

She quirks an eyebrow and turns toward me, bumping my knee with hers. "Do tell."

"You know how you mentioned that it was odd he didn't play soccer?"

"Yeah?" She nods.

"Well, he told me it was because he had a career-ending injury. He was pretty vague about the whole incident, but then I found this necklace in his bag. It had someone else's name on it, and when I looked it up, I found out it was his sister."

"Why would he carry around his sister's necklace?" Sybil asks.

"I think he carries it around to punish himself." I pull my phone off the dresser and scroll through my bookmarks. "Or maybe to remember her. I'm not really sure, but I found this, and it explains a lot."

Once I have the article pulled up, I hand the phone to Sybil, and she reads in silence while I wait. Her expression morphs from one of curiosity to horror in the matter of a few moments.

"Holy shit," she whispers. "His sister was murdered, and he watched it go down? No wonder he's so fucked up."

"They attacked him too," I point out. "That was the career-ending injury he mentioned. But the whole thing seems odd. The article says Sebastian willingly handed over his wallet, but they still beat him and killed his sister."

"Well, people are insane." She hands me back the phone. "Who knows why they did it. But that explains why he's always freaking out about your safety."

"At least, why he used to." I shrug. The truth is, I haven't heard from Sebastian in weeks, and I have a horrible feeling in my gut I never will again. From what I've gathered, he and his father weren't close, but it's obvious his death has shaken him, nonetheless.

"You never know." Sybil rubs my back. "Things could get better."

"They could." I offer her a watery smile. "But honestly, my well of hope has run dry. I think I just need to be done now."

CHAPTER THIRTY-FIVE
STELLA

"Are you okay?" Sybil rubs my back as I vomit into the toilet for the second time this evening.

"I'm fine." I wave her away. "Go have fun. I just need to rest."

"I'm not leaving you here like this." She kneels beside me and worries her lip between her teeth. "You've been sick since I got back. I think you need to see the doctor."

"I don't," I protest. "It's just the stress of everything."

She props her hip against the sink and waits for me while I wash my face and rinse out my mouth. "Stella, I don't want to ask this, but I think I have to."

"What?" I stare at my empty reflection in the mirror.

"Did Mr. Carter... you know, wrap it before he tapped it?"

My hollow stomach rumbles, and I shake my head as I confirm what I've already suspected. The thing I've been too terrified to admit to myself.

"Oh my God," she shrieks. "We have to go get a pregnancy test."

"Could you say that any louder?" I narrow my eyes at her.

"I'm sorry, but this is crazy. I can't believe you haven't even thought to—"

"I have thought," I cut her off. "But I'm already pretty sure, Sybil. I don't know what to do."

Fat teardrops splash against my cheeks, and she pulls me in for a hug with a promise that everything is going to be okay.

"No matter what, I'll always be here for you," she assures me.

"You're all I have." I hang my head and slip a palm over my growing belly. It's already March. It's been three months since I've seen or heard from Sebastian. Pretty soon, I won't be able to hide it anymore, and I've never been so scared in my life.

"Let's go." Sybil loops her arm through mine and tugs me out of the bathroom.

"Where?" I ask.

"I have a doctor on speed dial," she tells me. "My dad says I can see her anytime I want. I'm taking you to her."

I almost hit the brakes, but I know Sybil is right. I can't put this off any longer. I need to bite the bullet, and then I have to figure out what the hell I'm going to do.

"Say something," Sybil pleads.

I stare numbly at the paperwork I brought back to the dorm with me. "Like what?"

"Anything. You're making me nervous."

I gaze out the window, imagining what would happen if I saw Sebastian running by right now. What would he say if he knew that in five months, I'd be having his baby?

"Do you think I can make it to graduation without anyone finding out?" I ask.

She eyeballs my belly. "You can hardly tell right now. I think if you wear cardigans and sweaters during the cold months, you'll be fine. But I don't know about when it gets warmer. Regardless, we'll figure it out."

"I have to find a place to live," I blurt. "And get a job. And buy things. So many things. Do you know how much stuff babies need?"

"What you need to do is tell Sebastian." Sybil yanks out her phone, and I watch as she types his name into the Google search bar. Something I haven't dared to do since I found out about his father. A flood of articles comes up, and when Sybil clicks on the photos, her face scrunches up in anger.

"What is it?" I try to see what she's looking at, but she pulls the phone out of my reach and hides it behind her back.

"Nothing. You don't need to see."

"Sybil." I reach around her and pry the phone from her fingers. "Quit hiding shit from me. If there's something I need to see…"

I choke on my words as an image of Sebastian and Megan pops up next to a news article.

Sebastian Carter of Carter Holdings pictured with Megan Hill at a dinner to honor his late father's memory.

Unable to stop myself, I read on about the hotel tycoon's unexpected return to New York City, and how he has taken his rightful seat in the business upon his father's death.

"Stella." Sybil's voice cracks as the phone falls from my hand. "I'm so sorry."

CHAPTER THIRTY-SIX
SEBASTIAN

"Have you made a decision?" My father's advisor, Edward Hanson, stares down his nose over his wire-rimmed glasses as he studies the paperwork on my desk.

I barely spare a second glance at the empty signature field before I turn my attention to the New York City Skyline. From up here, the whole world still looks like it's wide-awake, even though it's well after midnight. I'd forgotten in my time at Loyola just how noisy living in the city can be. But now, the constant noise is all I hear.

"This was your father's legacy," Edward says. "He wanted you here, Sebastian."

"He wanted to control me," I reply coldly. "And this company was just another way to do that. It was never his legacy. My mother was the true Carter, and my father was just along for the ride."

In the reflection of the glass, Edward scratches at his beard, obviously at a loss with this truth bomb. He's only worked for my father for the past three years, so he wouldn't have any knowledge on the subject.

"Elena Carter was the heiress to the Carter fortune," I explain. "This company, the hotels, everything belonged to her. They were never my father's. After they married, he changed his name. He wanted everyone to believe he built this empire, but he inherited it, same as me."

"I'm sorry," Edward replies. "I wasn't aware."

I don't answer him because there's nothing left to say. I already made my decision, but I know Edward will try to talk me out of it. He's a business minded man, and I can't fault him for that.

"You could let the board run the company," he suggests. "There's very little you'd have to do. But that way, the legacy will remain intact."

"I don't want the legacy to remain intact, Edward," I answer dryly. "That's the problem."

For this, he has no rebuttal. He probably assumes that I've lost my goddamned mind. And who wouldn't? Why would anyone give up a sure thing?

Walking back to the desk, I reach for a pen and scribble my signature across the paperwork while Edward watches with certain disappointment.

"How long will it take?" I ask.

"As it stands in the current market?" He shrugs. "Not long at all. As soon as knowledge goes public, you'll have offers rolling in."

I nod and leave the pen, and the memories of this place, on the desk.

"Let's get the process started then."

Megan meets me at my father's penthouse in Manhattan, efficient as ever as she greets me with a glass of my favorite whisky.

"How did it go?" she asks.

"About how I expected it." I drain the whisky from my glass and study the woman I dated for three years in college. She looks the same. In fact, her face hasn't seemed to age a day at all. She's still the tall, gorgeous brunette who caught my eye in my soccer playing days. But we're both different people now, and I don't know if she realizes that.

There's still a spark in her eyes for me, and though she offered this favor out of the kindness of her heart, she has another motivation. For reasons I can't fathom, she still sees something worth salvaging in me. Even after I dropped her cold when Katie died. No phone call, no text, no explanation. I ghosted her and never looked back.

"I've donated most of the items to charity as you asked," she informs me. "But there were a few things I found you may want to look through."

"There's nothing of his that I want."

"Sebastian, they aren't his things," she says softly. "They were your mother's."

I choke back the rest of the whisky in my glass and pour another one while she retrieves a file box and sets it on the counter. I'd be lying if I said I wasn't even tempted to look, but I owe my mother that much. After she died, my father locked away every visible reminder of her. At the time, I thought he'd done it to punish us, but now I know that as heartless as he was, he did it because he missed her so much. Inside the box, I find one of her scarves, her favorite book, and a ring. My grandmother's ring. I'd completely forgotten about its existence until now. My mother always loved this piece, and for whatever reason, my father wouldn't allow her to use it as her wedding ring. He insisted on buying her something new because he had something to prove. *Always something to prove.*

"Thank you, Megan." I place the items back into the box and seal the lid. "I will take these after all."

"I thought you'd like them." She smiles at me warmly as her fingers graze my arm. "I'm so glad, Sebastian."

During our last few meetings, Megan has used every opportunity to touch me. And the way she's looking at me right now, I don't doubt for a second she'd let me bend her over right here and fuck her. That's what she wants, and she probably thinks it's what I need. But Megan doesn't get it. Stella ruined me for anyone else. She's the only one who can make me well again.

"How long do you think it will take to sell?" I redirect her attention back to the only business we have between us.

Her lips pinch together, but she remains as professional as ever. "Not long at all. This place is gorgeous, and the location is prime."

"Good." I polish off my drink. "Let's get rid of it as soon as possible."

Chapter Thirty-Seven
Stella

"Finally!" Sybil flops onto my bed and sighs dramatically. "I feel like I've hardly seen you lately."

"I know." I offer her an apologetic smile. "But check this out." She props her head up on my pillow as I retrieve the cash box from my nightstand drawer. When I fork it over and she opens it up, her eyes bulge with excitement.

"Holy shit, Cherrybomb. You've been making some bank."

"It's a good start," I agree. "I have enough for an apartment and at least some baby stuff. I'm still working on it, but it's hard to keep up."

"Patrick told me the site he made for you has really taken off," she says.

"It has. Between the custom Instagram photos, student headshots, and event shoots, I have something going every weekend and at least a few nights of the week. I've also been selling some stock photos, so that helps too."

"And who said photography wouldn't pay off?" she smirks.

"I'll have to get another job after the baby comes." I shrug. "Something with a more consistent paycheck. But at least I'll have a launching pad this way."

"You are simply amazing." She smiles at me with genuine pride, and it hits me right in the feels. "I can't believe you're juggling school and all of this too. I don't know how you do it."

"I'm exhausted." I laugh. "But it makes me happy. I think everything will be okay."

But even as I say it, I can't help noticing the pain that still lingers in my voice. Focusing on photography has been a good distraction, but in the back of my mind, Sebastian is always in my thoughts. Sybil notices it too, and though she's tried to talk me into contacting him, I haven't caved yet. I'm determined to do this on my own if that's what it comes down to. Whether Sebastian will ever be a part of this baby's life is still yet to be determined.

"Tell me what's going on with you." I change the subject.

She wiggles her brows and bolts upright, and already, I can tell she has big news. "I wanted to wait to tell you, but since you asked…"

"What is it?" I prod.

"I got into Juilliard!" She screams and then throws herself back with such abandon I can't help but laugh.

"Oh my God, Sybil!" I blink. "I can't believe it. That's… incredible. You should have told me!"

The excitement slowly dissipates from her features as she turns serious and rolls onto her side to study me. "I don't want to leave you."

Sadness washes over me when I consider that in just a few short months, we will no longer be here together. Emotion chokes the assurances from my lips.

"You could come with me," she proposes. "We could get an apartment together."

"New York is crazy expensive." I offer her a sad smile. "And you're going to need to focus on school. I think a crying baby might make that more of a challenge than you need."

"Then what will you do?" She pouts. "Where are you going to live?"

"I haven't quite figured that out yet," I admit. "Maybe I'll stay in Connecticut."

"I guess that makes sense." She chews on her nail and nods. "Sebastian will be here. And eventually, you'll have to tell him. He'll want to spend time with the baby too."

"Yeah," I choke out even though it feels like a lie. "We'll need to work all that out."

"Sooner rather than later?" she asks hopefully.

"I don't know when." I close my eyes and blow out a breath. "I know I need to tell him, but I just don't know how he's going to handle this. For all I know, he's already working on a baby with Megan in New York."

"He isn't." Sybil shakes her head emphatically. "I don't believe that for one second, Cherrybomb. I know I said all men are dogs, but things are different between the two of you. It's like magic, or fate, or something. What you had was real, and that doesn't just go away."

I nod because I don't have the energy to argue, and while I know Sybil's trying to be helpful, I just need to not think about him for a minute.

"Hey, I have a free day next weekend," I tell her. "Want to go baby shopping with me?"

"Um… hell yes!" she squeals. "It's a date. No take backs."

"Did you hear?" Sybil bounds into my room with wide eyes and a breathlessness that indicates she ran across campus to get here.

"Hear what?" I sit up and glance out the window, wondering if the pyro kids blew up the whole science building this time.

"Mr. Carter is back," she hisses.

"Holy shit." I squeeze my hands together in my lap. "Are you sure?"

"Yes, I'm sure." She bobs her head theatrically. "I just saw him heading into the cafeteria. So I asked Ms. Hargrave, and she told me that he's back for the rest of the year."

"Oh my God." I curl my knees into my chest and try to process this information.

"Do you think you're going to talk to him?" she asks.

"I don't know." I blink. "It's been a long time. A lot of stuff has happened."

"Stella." Sybil lays her hand on mine. "I know you're scared, but I think you have to do this. If for no other reason than he can and should help you. And he will. When he finds out, he'll do the right thing. He'll make sure you're taken care of." I don't like the way she says *taken care of* because it reminds me of Lila. "I don't want to be like my mother. I don't want to be someone he just sends a check to every month."

Sybil shakes her head. "I know. You aren't like your mother. You're nothing like her. But he got you into this mess and he can at least share the burden with you."

"We both got ourselves into this mess." I laugh half-heartedly. "I'm not an idiot. I knew the risks we were taking, and I took them anyway."

"Just promise me you'll think about talking to him," she pleads.

"I'll think about it," I concede.

But honestly, I'm more worried about seeing him than talking to him right now. It's been months, and I don't think I'll ever get Sebastian out of my system.

As I lurk outside of Sebastian's class the next day, I conjure up a million different reasons I should skip. I think I feel a cold coming on. Or a headache. Or, more accurately, a heartache. Sybil reaches for my hand and laces her fingers through mine. "It's going to be fine. Deep breaths. Most likely, he won't even call on you during class. It's been too long, I really don't think that will be your first interaction together."

"I know." I glance at the door, noting we only have two minutes left to get inside, and I don't want Sybil to be late over my fears. "Let's just go."

I follow her inside with my head down, refusing to look at Sebastian. At least for three whole minutes. But that doesn't stop Sybil from offering me reports of his every movement. "He just looked at you," she whispers. "Now he's wiping off the board. Okay, he's going to shut the door."

"All right, Sybil." A smile curves over my face, despite my resolve to remain serious. "I get it."

"Welcome back, Mr. Carter," Louisa purrs from the back of the classroom.

"Thank you, Louisa," he answers gruffly.

I sneak a glance in his direction, noting that he looks sharper than ever in his Prussian blue suit. He's wearing the jacket open today with a crisp white shirt and matching pocket square. He's been ruling the Carter empire, and it shows. The only thing that doesn't make sense is what Sebastian is doing back here when he has an entire corporation to lord over. By his own admission, he isn't happy at Loyola. He could have stayed in New York with his cushy new title at Carter Holdings and Megan by his side. Together, they look catalogue perfect. Nothing about his return adds up.

"Take out your workbooks and turn to page two-sixty." Sebastian commands the attention of the room with the same authority that first caught my eye. "Today, we will review your progress on ethical research practices, which I'm told you've become well acquainted with in my absence. Note that there will be a quiz before the end of class, so pay attention."

A collective groan resounds through the room while I sink into my seat and attempt to harness the power of blending into inanimate objects. But as it turns out, it isn't necessary. Sebastian clips over the material at breakneck speed, only pausing to ask a few questions along the way. He never glances in my direction, and I don't bother to volunteer any answers.

The quiz is a challenge, mostly because my head is fuzzy and I wasn't exactly paying attention, but luckily, we've gone over the material so many times I'm satisfied that I'll pass. After we hand in our papers, Sebastian doles out the next homework assignment—heavy reading on interpreting qualitative data—and then sends us on our way.

"See, you survived." Sybil pokes me in the ribs as we exit the building. "That wasn't so bad, was it?"

"No." I shrug, but inside, I don't feel any better that our interaction was nonexistent. Sebastian has laid out his cards, and it's clear he's moved on.

CHAPTER THIRTY-EIGHT
SEBASTIAN

After running circles around campus for over an hour, I've managed to pass her dorm three times without going inside. But I'd be lying if I said I wasn't still considering it, even after everything. Going inside would be the selfish thing to do. Caving to my needs with no regard for hers is a pattern I'm not eager to repeat, and Stella needs to learn what's good for her.

In my absence, it seems like maybe she has. When I came home to find the roses I'd sent her crushed and torn all over my bedroom, I was only a little surprised. But it was the accompanying lipstick note on my dresser mirror that nearly brought me to my knees.

One for every time you broke my heart.

It was simple and to the point, and it completely fucking gutted me. I want to believe I did the right thing by pushing her away. She still has a chance at a future without me. One where she can figure out what she wants in life and find a nice sensible man to settle down with. But even as I tell myself that's the best thing for her, I can't accept it.

Coming to a dead halt, I pitch forward and nearly vomit from the pain radiating down my shin. This agony is the constant reminder that I'm not the man I once was. It's a grief I still haven't shaken, and at this point, it's fucking pathetic. Stella was right to call me a hypocrite. For years, I've exiled myself to this colorless reality with the belief I was doing something worthwhile with my time. But the only thing I've done in five years is exist. And still I saw fit to challenge her at every turn, pushing her to make choices I'm too stubborn to make myself. How she fell in love with a miserable bastard like me, I'll never know.

I wouldn't be surprised if she needs years of therapy after crossing paths with me. I really am the devil reincarnate, and if Katie could see me now, she would be horrified by the man I've become.

I leave Stella's dorm and my twisted thoughts behind and trudge back to my own house. It feels empty without her. The scent that once lingered here has disappeared, and this place is no longer a sanctuary, but a prison. If I'm being honest, I have no idea why I even bothered to come back. Once Carter Holdings is gone, I could go anywhere, do anything. I'll have more money than I could ever spend in one lifetime. But I won't have her.

I towel myself off and take a seat at the kitchen table, staring down the necklace that has haunted me for so long. It occurs to me at that moment how much Katie would abhor my self-flagellation. She wouldn't want this life for me, and I know it. But letting go of what happened has been the most difficult thing I've ever had to do.

It starts with a single step.

That's what she would have told me if she were here right now. And in a way, as crazy as it seems, it feels like she is. It's Katie who guides me to the box of my mother's belongings, where I deposit the memento that has suffocated me for so long.

My family is dead, but I'm not. As long as I have a pulse, I owe it to them to make the most of it. My time at Loyola is coming to an end, and where I go from here is wide open. But first, I need to see this year through. *I need to make sure Stella will be all right.*

An unsettling knock disturbs me from my restless sleep, and I sit upright, glancing at the clock. It's after two in the morning, and there's only one person I can imagine knocking on my door at this hour.

Stella.

My lungs expand with the first full breath I've drawn in months as I wind my way through the house and open the door. But to my displeasure, it isn't Stella standing on my doorstep. It's her mother.

"Lila?" I eye her wearily, and she pushes her way into my kitchen without waiting for an invitation.

"I know what you did." She glares at me. "I know about you and my daughter."

As horrified as I should be by her statement, the only thing I feel is relief. Self-preservation dictates that I should deny it, but I've never been the type of man to cling to a life preserver.

"Why don't you have a seat." I gesture to the table. "Perhaps we can try for a civilized conversation?"

"Civilized?" Lila scoffs. "I have nothing civilized to say to a man who would take advantage of a young woman."

The pulse in my throat beats a violent staccato as I stare at the woman who birthed Stella. They might share DNA, but she has never been a mother, and that is painstakingly obvious.

"Don't pretend you give a fuck about Stella," I bite out.

"Where were you this year during the parents' weekends? Or her birthday? What about Christmas? She doesn't even know how to reach you."

"I'm going to sue the pants off you." Lila tosses a stack of photos onto the table. "I will bleed you dry, Sebastian Carter."

I glance at the photos and spread them apart with my hands. They are grainy, which is a good indication they were taken on a cell phone. That isn't what concerns me. What concerns me is that these were taken by someone who knows Stella's routine on campus. The snapshots of me sneaking in and out of Lawrence Hall are a far cry from proof of my nocturnal visits to her room, but Lila is obviously desperate, grasping at anything she can to benefit herself in this situation.

I consider telling her to fuck off, consequences be damned, but then I think of Stella. If ever there was anything her mother could do to prove that she doesn't care for her daughter, it would be pursuing this. One glance at Lila Monroe, and I can tell exactly the type of woman she is. The fact that she's here proves she'd take no issue with dragging her own daughter into the spotlight of public humiliation to satisfy her pocketbook.

"How much will it take to make you go away?" I ask point blank.

Lila has the nerve to act offended for all of two seconds. Then she takes a seat at the table and folds her hands together as if she still possesses an ounce of class. "One million should do it."

I gather my briefcase from the counter and remove my pocketbook, scribbling out a check in her name. When I return, she makes a weak attempt at humility before she tries to snatch it from my fingers. I pull it back before she can grab it and study her with contempt.

"If I give you this, I want your word that you will leave Stella alone. You won't poison her life any more than you already have."

Her eyes dart from me to the check, and in a single second, she trades her soul and her daughter for a million dollars. "Fine, done. Just give me the damn check, and I'll be on my way."

Oh, Lila, if only it were that simple.

"Who took the photos?" I ask.

"Another student," she answers tersely. "Louisa Davenport. I used to play tennis with her mother at the club."

"I meant what I said." I drop the check onto the table, and Lila nearly knocks her chair over in her hurry to retrieve it. "Leave Stella alone."

She offers a stiff nod before she scrambles for the door and disappears. As happy as I am to watch her go, her confirmation of Louisa's participation in this scheme makes it evident I've only managed to put out one fire. Protecting Stella from Louisa's wrath is another matter entirely.

CHAPTER THIRTY-NINE
STELLA

With the arrival of spring, my growing belly is a constant reminder there will be another arrival soon too. Only two of the skirts from my closet still fit me, and now that the weather is warmer, my window of hiding behind chunky knit sweaters will soon draw to an end. When I'm not choking on my panic, I'm trying my best to manage my energy. I've already cut out any extracurriculars that might be too taxing, but regardless, it's still difficult to concentrate. Pregnancy sucks the life out of you, and now all I want to do is simultaneously eat and vomit. The wall of silence remains between Sebastian and me while Sybil relentlessly pursues her agenda to get me to talk to him. She's worried about me, and I get that because I'm terrified too. While everyone else is making plans for college and focusing on their test scores and applications, I'm making plans to start raising a baby after graduation. For now, it's all I can do to survive one day at a time.

It's a sunny April morning when everything changes. I wake up to find a note that's been slipped under my door, and when I peel it open, I get the shock of my life when I read the contents.

Meet me outside at noon.

Without a doubt, I recognize that handwriting as my father's. But how is it possible? Did he really come back? This information feels like way too much to process right now, so I shove the note into my backpack and head for first period. That turns out to be a stupid idea, considering I have zero ability to focus. For the entirety of the class, my mind races as I try to figure out what's going on. The only thing I know for certain is that my father is here, and he wants to see me.

Somehow, I manage to survive class without completely making a fool of myself. But there are still three hours before lunch when I meet Sybil on the quad at break.

"Hey," she chirps. "Everything okay? You look a little pale this morning."

"It's all good," I lie, not wanting to involve her in my family's drama. I don't even know if it's safe to see my father, or if I could get into trouble for talking to him. The last thing I want to do is involve Sybil too.

"I'll walk you to class," she says.

We head for English Lit, and Sybil shares her gummy bears with me along the way while she chats about her upcoming dance competition. I'm trying to listen to her and not be a jerk, but it's hard to focus, especially when Mrs. Chen catches us in the hall with an apparent mission.

"Stella." Mrs. Chen regards me blandly. "The headmistress would like a word with you in her office. Please report immediately."

The headmistress? Sybil and I glance at each other, and my fears are only confirmed in the matching expression on her face.

"What do you think this is about?" she whispers as we walk back down the hall.

"I don't know, but it can't be good."

She chews on her lip, and I swallow. "You should go, I don't want you to be late."

"Text me asap," she demands. "Or I'll be freaking out."

"I will," I promise.

We part ways at the entrance of the main building. I've been in this office before to meet with my student advisor, but I've never been summoned here. Am I in trouble? Do they know my father was here this morning?

I step inside and give my name to the administration staff, advising them of Headmistress Gilbert's request to meet with me. Almost immediately, they nod as if they are expecting me and shuttle me toward the office. But when the door swings open and I see who's waiting for me on the other side, I'm tempted to run.

Headmistress Gilbert, Louisa, and the school nurse are all sitting inside, and this is beginning to feel more like a firing squad than a meeting.

"What's going on?" I ask as the nurse ushers me in and shuts the door behind me.

"Stella, please take a seat." Headmistress Gilbert gestures to the open chair in front of her desk. "Louisa has come to me with some rather troubling accusations this morning, and I'd like to address these issues."

My legs feel like wooden pegs as I force myself into the seat, and right now, I'm not entirely certain I shouldn't just bolt. In my gut, I already know what this is about, and I feel like I might lose my breakfast.

"Louisa claims to have found these in your room." Headmistress Gilbert slides some familiar paperwork across the desk, and my stomach somersaults as I examine the pre-natal care instructions I received from Sybil's doctor. Denial isn't an option when my name is printed on the top.

"What were you doing in my room?" I glare at Louisa.

"I assure you, we will deal with that matter," Headmaster Gilbert interjects. "But I need to know if this is true, Stella. Are you pregnant?"

"Obviously, she is." Louisa smirks. "Look at all those heavy sweaters she's been wearing. And she's gained like twenty pounds from constantly stuffing her face."

"That's enough." Headmistress Gilbert sighs and points at the door. "Louisa, you are excused. Go back to class now. I will meet with you again later."

I fold my arms and watch Louisa skip from the office with a gleeful expression as Headmaster Gilbert turns her watchful gaze on me.

"Is it true?" she asks again.

"This isn't fair," I protest weakly. "She has been rummaging through my room for months, and you just let her get away with it."

"Nobody is getting away with anything," she says. "But Stella, we have more important issues at hand. A pregnant student on campus is a big concern for obvious reasons. It's our responsibility to ensure your health and safety. Is there any way to reach either of your parents? I don't have a working number for your mother."

"My parents have nothing to do with this," I tell her. "I'm eighteen. Legally, I'm an adult, and I'm responsible for myself."

"That may be true, but in any case, I think they would like to know."

"Again, that's my decision," I inform her. "And even if it weren't, you wouldn't be able to track them down. I don't even know where they are."

She offers me a blank stare and then gestures to the nurse. "Elizabeth would like to examine you with your permission."

"And if I say no?"

"Then I'm afraid we will have no choice but to ask you to leave," she says.

My heart jumps into my throat as the walls close in around me. This is it. My house of cards is caving in. I consider the consequences of going through with the exam. Can they force me to leave once they find out I'm pregnant? I don't know, but right now, it feels like I have no choice.

"Fine," I croak. "You have my permission to examine me."

"Please unbutton your cardigan," the nurse instructs as she steps forward.

I do as she requests, shielding the small bump that comes into view with my palm. Both women glance at each other with worried expressions before the nurse gently feels around my belly and uses her stethoscope to confirm the baby's heartbeat. With a solemn expression, she steps back and nods.

"She's definitely pregnant."

"Stella." Headmistress Gilbert's tone takes on a seriousness I can't ignore as she folds her hands across the desk. "I need to know who did this to you. I need a name."

"What does that matter?" I argue.

"Louisa has also informed us that you and Mr. Carter have become rather close this year." She slides some photos across the desk as she speaks. They're not the best quality, but it's obvious that Louisa caught Sebastian sneaking into the dorm several times. Still, I try to deny it.

"He's my teacher." I swallow.

"Well, if these photos are any indication, it looks as if that line has been blurred."

"He helped me through some issues." Panic causes my voice to rise. I don't want Sebastian to lose his job because of me. And worse yet, I hate the way the headmistress is looking at me as if I just don't know any better.

"Stella, I understand this may be personal," she continues. "But I need to know when this affair started. Your birthday was near the beginning of the school year. Was it before or after this?"

"It wasn't Sebastian," I lie through my teeth.

"It was." His voice spills into the office as he pushes open the cracked door behind me. My head whips around, our eyes clashing as he steps inside. I don't know how long he was standing there listening to the conversation, but when his gaze falls to my belly, there's no denying what he sees there. A heart-wrenching pain bleeds into his features as he stumbles forward and places his hands on the back of my chair as if he's protecting me somehow. I look up at him, silently pleading for him not to throw himself in front of this oncoming train.

"Everything that happened between us is my fault," he tells the headmistress. "And nothing inappropriate occurred before her birthday, but regardless, I take full responsibility. Stella is not to blame."

"Don't you think I know that?" Headmistress Gilbert stares at him in disbelief. "She's a young woman who doesn't know any better."

"I'm not stupid," I fire back. "I knew exactly what I was doing, and regardless of how you feel, I don't think it was wrong."

Sebastian squeezes my shoulder with a reassurance that I desperately need as Headmistress Gilbert's eyes narrow in on me.

"No laws have been broken here," he says. "And other than breaching school policy, Stella has not done anything that would warrant you holding her hostage. Stella, you are free to go. The headmistress and I will discuss the consequences of my actions in private."

I want to protest, but I know it's pointless. There's nothing I can say to save Sebastian now, and regardless, he doesn't want my help. He can take care of himself. He always has. But where that leaves me in the equation, I have no idea.

He helps me from the chair and brazenly pulls me toward him, his lips grazing the shell of my ear. "Don't worry about anything. I'm going to take care of it."

Whatever that means, I don't know, but I close my eyes and shiver when he kisses my forehead right in front of the headmistress. I don't want him to fight this battle on his own, but he ushers me toward the door and tells me to wait outside. As soon as I'm on the steps, I find Sybil waiting for me there.

"Oh my God." She practically flings herself at me. "What is going on, Cherrybomb?"

"She knows," I answer grimly. "She's talking to Sebastian now."

"Don't be mad." She squeezes me in a bear hug. "I told him you were here. I didn't want to, but I had a horrible feeling about this."

I'm too exhausted to be angry with her, and when I sneak a glance at my watch, I realize I'm also running late.

"Crap. I have to go." I hurriedly secure the buttons of my cardigan and ditch my backpack on the steps.

"Where?" she asks.

I don't have enough energy to keep lying to her, and I just hope she doesn't try to talk me out of it. "I think my dad is here. I know it sounds crazy, but there was a note under my door this morning. He wants me to meet him out front."

"Seriously?" Her eyes flare. "Why do I feel like my head is about to explode right now?"

"Tell me about it," I groan.

"What if it's a trick?" she asks.

"How would it be a trick? It was his handwriting."

"I don't know." She frowns. "But I'm not letting you go alone. I need to make sure you're safe."

"Only if you promise to wait at the entrance," I insist. "I need to talk to my dad alone, and I don't want anything scaring him off."

"Okay." She wraps her pinky in mine, and we head for the front entrance together. When we reach it, I turn and point at the brick column.

"Just wait there. I'll be back in ten minutes at most."

Sybil nods and keeps a lookout for me as I scan the street. My father didn't say where he'd be or what to look for. But as I'm walking, a low whistle grabs my attention from one of the cars. Sure enough, when I peek inside, it's my father. He looks different than what I'm used to. His facial hair is grown out, and he's wearing a ball cap, but he's definitely the same man who raised me.

I toss a secret thumbs-up in Sybil's direction and reach for the door.

"Get in," my father says. "We need to talk."

I sink into the passenger seat of a Kia, wondering if it's a rental car. I'm not sure I even want to ask how he got it, considering the circumstances.

"Dad, what is going on?" I demand.

He doesn't reply right away. Instead, he turns the key in the ignition and shifts the car into drive.

"Wait, what are you doing?" I screech as he whips out of the parking space. "I can't go with you."

"I know I owe you an explanation." His fingers tighten around the steering wheel as he accelerates down the street. "I screwed up. I should have just told you, but I couldn't."

"Okay, well right now, that doesn't matter," I tell him. "You're neck deep in some serious shit, Dad. So why did you even bother coming back now?"

"They're onto me." He glances in the rearview mirror. "Mexico isn't going to work out. I thought maybe I could go to Canada, and this time, you could come with me."

"Are you kidding me?" I stare at the man who has obviously lost his goddamned mind. "You just left me. You abandoned me and ran off without so much as a goodbye, and now you think I'm going to leave the country with you?"

"I'm sorry." He checks the mirrors again and hammers down on the accelerator. "It was the only thing I could do."

"This is crazy." I swallow my fear and try to reason with him. "You need to pull over and let me out. And then you need to go turn yourself in."

Before he can even respond, a siren blares behind us, and sure enough, when I turn, there's an undercover car following us.

"Fuck!" My father glances over at me. "Put your seat belt on." With trembling fingers, I reach for my seat belt and jam it into the buckle as he picks up speed again. This time, he starts dodging cars and swerving into oncoming traffic, and my fear rises with the needle on the speedometer. "Dad, please! You need to stop!"

He doesn't seem to be listening to me anymore. His focus shifts from the traffic to the mirrors and back. The midday congestion is hampering his getaway efforts, and at most, I think we've only made it two miles from the school. Squinting at the flashing lights in the mirror, I consider my options. Clearly, my father has gone insane. But without pulling some sort of stunt maneuver and safely ejecting myself from the car, my only hope is to appeal to him.

"Please pull over," I beg, shrieking as he narrowly avoids a garbage truck. "You're going to hurt someone."

"Stella, I can't go to prison!" he shouts over the racket. The sirens continue to multiply around us, and now it sounds like they are coming from every direction. Surely, he must realize that too.

"You have no choice!" I yell. "Please don't take me down with you."

"I love you, honey." His voice fractures. "I just want you to come with me. We can make a whole new life. I promise, I'll make it all up to you."

"If you love me, then let me go," I sob. "Please, Dad. I'm pregnant."

His head whips in my direction, and in a split second, something slams into us from the side. My head bounces off the passenger window and glass explodes into the car, raining down like shrapnel. Everything happens so fast there isn't even time to process it. I'm dazed and disoriented, coughing from the smoke as my ears ring so loud everything sounds like it's underwater. The car isn't moving anymore, I realize, as my father's voice breaks through my haze.

"Stella, honey. Are you okay?"

"I don't know." I dab at my temple, and when I pull my fingers back to examine them, they're coated in blood.

"Put your hands up and step out of the vehicle now," a command blares from a megaphone behind us, and when I look out the broken window, the car is completely surrounded by federal agents. I reach for the door handle, but my father grabs my arm.

"No. Wait."

"We can't wait." Terror chokes me as I stare down at least a dozen agents with their weapons drawn. "Please just let me go."

"Are you really pregnant?" he asks.

"Yes!"

He glances down the street, and then behind us like he's searching for another way out. Clearly, he's delusional. That's the only logical explanation for his behavior. And when I look at him, I realize that I don't recognize him at all anymore. He isn't the same man who used to make me pancakes and read me bedtime stories. Now, he's just a criminal who cares more about himself than his own daughter. As if that wasn't clear enough, he makes it painfully so when he reaches beneath the seat and retrieves a pistol.

"Dad!" I scream as he frantically waves it at the cops and shouts out the window.

"Let us go, or I'll shoot!" he tells them.

"You're going to get us both killed!" I try the door handle again, but this time he waves the gun at me.

"Don't even think about it, Stella. They'll never shoot a pregnant woman. You're the only bargaining chip I have left now."

CHAPTER FORTY
SEBASTIAN

"You don't have a leg to stand on here, Sebastian." Savannah Gilbert glares at me as if I'm little more than a piece of rotten gum stuck beneath her shoe. "I'll have your job for this."

"Take it." I shrug. "Do you think I'd even be here if I didn't know the consequences of my actions?"

Her lips pinch into a tight line, betraying her obvious disappointment that I'm not cowering before her, but she should know me better by now.

"I do have one stipulation, though." I take a seat in the chair Stella vacated.

Her eyes bulge as she snorts unattractively. "What could you possibly think I would do for you after what you've just admitted?"

"I want Stella to complete her studies through correspondence."

"Not a chance." She shakes her head without a second thought. "We can't have a pregnant student on our records. If anyone gets wind of this—"

"She will receive a diploma from Loyola Academy." I retrieve my phone and set it on her desk. "Or I will go to the board and tell everyone that your miserable, deadbeat excuse for a son has been distributing drugs and alcohol to the students right under your nose for years."

Her eyes widen as she examines the audio recording taunting her from my iPhone. And when she presses play, just as I knew she would, the color drains from her face as she comes to an understanding that, in this scenario, I have her by the balls.

"How long do you think your job will last when they find out?" I ask.

"Fine." She stabs at the button on my phone, effectively cutting off her son's doped up admission. "You've made your point, Sebastian."

"Stella gets a diploma from Loyola," I reiterate.

"As long as she completes her courses with passing scores, she can graduate with her classmates. But she will not remain on campus. That is non-negotiable."

"Mr. Carter!" Sybil flings open the door, breathless and eyes wide with panic.

A familiar dread creeps into my veins as I force the words from my throat. "What is it?"

"It's Stella," she pants. "Please, you have to come right now!"

Without hesitation, I follow her out of the building, and she ushers me toward the entrance. "What's going on?" I demand. "Where's Stella?"

"It's her dad." She points to the street as she tries to explain. "She met him outside to talk, but then he took off. Now the cops are after them, and there's a huge barricade…"

My legs break into a run before she can finish, and Sybil tries to keep up the pace beside me. Between breaths, she yells something about a crash, and I feel like I can't fucking breathe. Every word she utters is another crushing blow. *Standoff. Weapons. Hostage.* The worst-case scenario echoes through my mind to the tune of a broken record.

It's happening again. I'm going to lose her.

Adrenaline drives me straight into the heart of the chaos. Leaping over a cop car, I scream for Stella as two officers come at me. Diving to the left, I narrowly avoid their grasp and bulldoze my way onto the scene. That's when I find the silver Kia at the center of the commotion. The driver's rear side is smashed in, and glass litters the asphalt beneath it. *Stella is in that car.* The car that at least a dozen agents are aiming their weapons at while they bark out their orders.

"Stella!" I bellow.

Vaguely, I hear them ordering me to stop, along with their threats to shoot, but the only thing I can think about is getting to her.

"Sebastian!" She peeks out the shattered window with wide, terrified eyes. That fear on her face punches me in the gut, but it's the blood-soaked hair that sucks the life from me. I'm not thinking clearly when I yank the door open to get to her.

"Get back!" her father yells over the ruckus. "I'll shoot you if I have to!"

"Sebastian, please!" Stella begs. "It will be okay, just go."

"I'm not leaving you." I turn my gaze on her father. "Your daughter is coming with me."

"She isn't going anywhere with you." He squeezes Stella's arm in his grasp, and when she winces in pain, I fucking lose it. I lunge across the seat and pop him in the face, momentarily stunning him long enough for me to unbuckle Stella. But before I can drag her from the car, he's jamming a pistol into my jaw.

"Get out!" he roars. "Now."

"Dad!" Stella screeches as I wrap my hand around the barrel and meet his gaze dead on. It's obvious he isn't thinking about his daughter as he attempts to wrestle the weapon from my grip, and I'm running out of fucking options. Stella's trapped between us, and he's likely to discharge the firearm any second.

"Get out, Stella." I wedge my body into the open door, shoving against it as I struggle to maintain my hold on the gun. "Run, baby."

Her horrified eyes meet mine for a split second, and in that second, I wish I could convey all the things I should have said to her. But there isn't time now, and I need her to understand that more than I've ever needed anything else in my life.

"Go!" I demand. "I'll be right behind you."

She doesn't believe me, and if I'm being honest, I don't either. But if it comes down to my life or Stella's, it will always be hers. A sob rips from her throat as she slides her body out of the narrow gap I've created for her, and when her father tries to pull her back, I leverage the weight of the gun to jam his fingers back with a satisfying crunch.

"Motherfuck!" he hisses as his hand falls limp in my grasp.

I can't pry the weapon from his broken fingers, but regardless, he won't be firing it anytime soon. With that disaster narrowly avoided, I turn my attention back to Stella and untangle myself from the car. To my horror, she's surrounded by agents who still have their weapons drawn as they shout orders at her.

"Lay down on the ground!"

"She's pregnant!" I yell. "She can't lay on the goddamned ground!"

But they can't hear me over the noise, and when I move to shield her body with mine, someone tackles me from behind. The air deflates from my lungs as I hit the pavement, and Stella screams at the same time a piercing shot rings out. Terror claws at me as I attempt to fight off whoever's on top of me. *I need to get to Stella.* I need to make sure it isn't Stella. But the weight on my back triples as I frantically seek her out. Time seems to slow down, and I can't tell the difference between minutes or hours as I repeat the same mantra.

"Please," I beg. "She's pregnant!"

"Sebastian!" Stella cries out. "I'm okay. It isn't me. I'm okay."

I don't trust her assurances. Not until the agents drag me to my feet and I see her. Somewhere during the chaos, my pitiful pleas must have registered because Stella is sitting in the back of an ambulance with her cardigan off while the EMTs examine her. And against all odds, she's still breathing. My body sags into itself as I focus on that one simple fact. *Stella is alive.*

In a separate ambulance, her father is strapped to a stretcher with a bullet wound in his arm. And apart from appearing stunned and disoriented, it looks like he'll be enjoying a long stay in prison after a brief hospital visit.

After the adrenaline crash, the uniformed officer releases me from his hold as an agent appears and begins to question me. But nothing else registers. My only focus is on Stella as they strap her in and prepare to take her away from me.

"I can't do this right now," I argue. "If you want to question me, you'll have to do it at the hospital. I'm not leaving her." The agent glances at his superior, and she nods in agreement. Two minutes later, I'm sitting in the ambulance with Stella and a federal agent as our escort. The ride to the hospital is a blur. When I reach for Stella's hand and feel her warmth against me, nothing else exists outside of this moment. I know that nothing is okay, but I need to hear her lies right now.

"Tell me you're okay." My voice fractures as I study every square inch of her body.

I almost lost her. I almost fucking lost her.

"I'm okay," she insists, but I still can't believe it. Not until the hospital staff examines her, and I hear it directly from the doctor.

As soon as we arrive, the agent tries again to separate us, but I refuse to leave Stella's side.

"We need to question you both separately, sir," he tells me.

"That's not fucking happening."

"Sebastian," Stella rasps. "Please just do what they say so this can be over with."

The exhaustion in her voice nearly breaks me. In her eyes, I can see she's barely fucking holding on to herself, and I know she's right. The sooner we can get this over with, the better. But it doesn't make it any easier to accept.

"We can talk in the hall," the agent says. "My colleague will stay with Stella, and she'll be safe here."

"I'll be right outside," I promise her. "If you need anything, tell the nurse to get me."

She nods, and I lean down to kiss her forehead, whispering the only truth I know. "You can't leave me, Stella."

Chapter Forty-One
Stella

After a lengthy conversation about how I ended up in a car chase with my father, the doctor comes to examine me and give me a few stitches for the cut on my head. She tells me my baby is fine, but they want to keep me overnight for observation anyway. I agree to stay until they tell me otherwise because right now it's all I can do to keep from breaking down. *My baby is safe. Sebastian is safe.* That's what I try to focus on, but eventually, I have to ask the question I've been dreading.

"Is my father okay?"

"He'll be fine," Agent Allison assures me. "He sustained a gunshot wound to his arm, so he'll be spending a couple days in the hospital before he's processed into jail. From there, he will be charged and tried for the crimes he's committed."

"I've never seen him like that." I squeeze my eyes shut as I recall him jamming the pistol into Sebastian's face all over again.

"Running from something like this changes people," Agent Allison says. "The isolation and paranoia leave them in a bad way sometimes. There's nothing you could have done to change that."

"Am I in trouble?" I ask her.

"No." She shakes her head. "We won't be pursuing any charges against you, Miss LeClaire. But might I suggest you take this as a life lesson and learn from it."

"Trust me, I have." I blink away the tears. "I already cut my mother out of my life. And honestly, after today, I'm not sure I'll ever want to see my father again either."

"Well, you'll likely have a very long time to think about it," she says. "He's looking at a lengthy sentence, and he won't be going anywhere."

"We have a room available for you," the nurse interrupts. "I can take you up now, if you're finished."

"We are." Agent Allison stands up and heads for the door. "What about Sebastian?"

"He's just down the hall," she informs me. "I'll let him know where he can find you."

As soon as my head hits the pillow, my eyes start to feel heavy, but I don't want to fall asleep until I talk to Sebastian. Fighting that battle is difficult because the events of the day are catching up with me. Too much has happened, and I haven't even begun to process the entirety of it.

I close my eyes just for a moment, and I can't tell if it's been a second or an hour when the door creaks open. I smell Sebastian's cologne before I feel his lips ghosting over my forehead as he breathes me in. When I open my eyes and meet his, he draws in a ragged breath and pulls me upright into his arms.

"God, Stella." His entire body trembles against me. "I almost fucking lost you."

Despite everything that's happened between us, I can't reject this source of comfort right now. There are still so many uncertainties ahead of me, but Sebastian is right. I could have lost my life today because of my father's recklessness. And worse yet, I could have lost the baby and him. As much as my heart hurts, I can't even think about my anger and pain at this moment. I can only think about this second. This minute. The next hour. We are here. We're alive.

I wrap my arms around him and breathe him in too. "We're all okay. The baby is okay."

"Christ." He glances down at my belly and curves his palm over the bump there. It's such a simple gesture, but it's too much. The first sob rips from my lungs before I can stop it, and within seconds, I'm bawling uncontrollably. Sebastian squeezes me in his grasp, stroking my back while he whispers assurances I never thought would come.

"I'm here, baby. Everything will be okay now. I'm going to take care of you."

I can't even begin to respond to that statement, and he doesn't ask me to. He lets me remain in my feelings for as long as I need while he holds me and whispers promises I so desperately want to believe in my fragile state of mind. At least until a familiar voice startles us apart.

"Thanks for letting me know you're okay!" Sybil shrieks. "My God, Cherrybomb. I have been FREAKING the hell out."

"Oh my God." I wipe my eyes and look up at her. "I'm so sorry, Sybil. Everything just happened so fast, and then—"

"It's okay." She walks around the bed and sits in the chair next to me. "I'm just glad you're all right. That's the only thing that matters. You are all right, aren't you?"

"Yes." I trace over the bandage on my head as she examines it. "It's just a cut. But otherwise, I'm fine. They are keeping me overnight just to be safe."

She looks at Sebastian and raises her brows. "You were like Superman out there. I've never seen anything like that."

I peek at Sebastian, and a flush creeps up his throat as his gaze meets mine. It never occurred to me what he must have gone through trying to get to me. I don't even know how he did. One minute, he just materialized, and the next, he was shielding me with his body, risking his life... to protect me.

"I wasn't about to let anything happen to you," he murmurs. He squeezes my hand in his, and Sybil clears her throat to remind us we still have a visitor.

"I'm sorry, this whole day has just been insane," I tell her.

"So what happens now?" she asks carefully.

"Well, my father is going to prison," I choke out. "And I have no idea what will happen at Loyola. Do you?"

Sebastian looks down at me, and I know this is a conversation he'd rather have privately, but he should know Sybil isn't going anywhere.

"Headmistress Gilbert agreed to let you finish your studies through correspondence," he says. "I know it might be an adjustment, but this way, you can still graduate with a diploma from Loyola."

"Oh." A knot forms in my throat as I consider that I had based my entire plan for after graduation, and right now, I don't have anywhere permanent to go.

"I knew it." Sybil shakes her head. "That bitch is kicking you out. It's so unfair."

"It probably doesn't do well for their image to have a preggo on campus," I mutter.

"It's for the best," Sebastian tells me. "At least this way, you'll be safe, and you won't have to deal with Louisa or anyone else making your life hell."

"Do you think you'll be able to find an apartment that quickly?" Sybil worries her lip between her teeth. "We haven't even started looking yet."

"She'll be in Westport with me," Sebastian interjects as if there isn't even a question about it.

"That's over forty minutes away." Sybil pouts.

"Nothing is set in stone," I tell her, and Sebastian's grip on my hand tightens when I meet his eyes. "We still have a lot to discuss. I'm not entirely sure what my plan is yet, but I'll figure it out."

CHAPTER FORTY-TWO
STELLA

The ride to Westport is quiet and filled with tension. Sebastian's in the driver's seat, deftly navigating the freeway with a blank expression on his face while I stare out the passenger window, attempting to organize my thoughts. When the hospital released me, I agreed to visit his home, but I haven't promised to stay. What I said to Sybil has been weighing heavily on him, and though he hasn't left my side, he's been far too much in his head ever since.

"What are you thinking about?" I ask.

He gives me a sidelong glance, the muscle in his neck straining with unease. "I was wondering if you're punishing me."

"What?" I study him. "Why would you think that?"

"Because it's what I deserve."

"I'm not punishing you." I sigh. "But you ghosted me for months. Then you just popped back into my life yesterday, and everything is so insane right now I can't even process it. We have a lot to talk about before you start trying to make decisions for me."

"I fucked up," he answers in a gravelly voice. "I can't say it any other way. I wasn't right in the head when my father died. I've been so goddamned cruel to you, but I thought the only way to make things right was to leave you alone. I've pushed you away for so long because you just fucking terrify me, Stella. You brought me back to life. You made me feel again, and I didn't like it. I thought I had something to prove by breaking you, but it was the biggest mistake I've ever made in my life."

I swallow because that wound is still too raw to touch. I know Sebastian has been through a lot, and in the beginning, all I wanted to do was save him. But I have a baby to think about now, and I need to know he won't ever do that again. Not if he wants to be a part of our lives.

"I know how much I hurt you." His knuckles tighten around the steering wheel. "It's going to take time to repair that, and I'm trying not to push you. But I'm here and I'm not going anywhere. In time, I hope you will see that."

"I want to believe that," I admit. "But I just… I don't know yet."

"You're still wearing my necklace." His eyes drift to the gold bar hanging around my neck. "Does that mean there's hope?"

"I couldn't bring myself to take it off." My voice wavers. "I didn't want to. But that doesn't mean I never will."

"You're breaking my heart." His voice cracks.

"You broke mine too." Tears sting my eyes as I turn my gaze to the passing scenery.

"Don't go somewhere else," he pleads. "Talk to me. Tell me how we can work through this."

My hands squeeze together in my lap as I work up the courage to ask the scariest question. "Okay, well for starters, I need to know how you feel about this baby."

"I want the baby." He glances over at me. "Obviously, it was always a consideration."

"It wasn't a consideration." I glare at him. "It was a high likelihood, and you know it."

"Do you want me to say it?" His jaw clenches. "Do you want me to tell you that on some level, I wanted this? Because I guess I did. I knew what I was doing when I fucked you and came in you. It didn't stop me. I'm a twisted son of a bitch, but when it comes to you, I can't fucking help myself."

I take a moment to process his words, and I don't know if I should be mad, but his honesty is refreshing for once. Because if I'm being honest too, I knew exactly what we were doing.

"Do you want the baby?" he asks so softly I barely hear the question.

"Of course, I do." I lay a protective hand over my belly.

"So I haven't fucked up your life forever?" His voice is so raw, it physically hurts me to see him like this.

"No, Sebastian. You haven't."

He takes a moment to gather himself before continuing. "Because if you feel that way, on any level, I need you to know this isn't your fault. You can walk away. You can go to college, figure out your future, do whatever you want. I will raise this child and take responsibility for it, no matter what."

"You aren't raising my baby without me," I answer, horrified by the thought. "My child won't ever think for one second that she wasn't wanted by me. Never."

"I don't want to raise this baby without you." He reaches over and strokes my arm. "I just want you to know that I would if that's what it came down to. It would be the hardest thing I'd ever have to do to let you go, but I need to know that you'll be happy. It's the only way I can be at peace."

I don't know how to react to this version of Sebastian. I've never seen him so emotionally ravaged, and I want to give him my reassurances, but I'm not ready for that yet. Without a doubt, I am going to raise this baby. And when I imagine the future, I can't see any other reality where Sebastian isn't by my side. But the only way we'll ever get there is by taking it one day at a time. And right now, I'm too lost for words when he pulls into the drive of one of the most beautiful estates I've ever seen.

"Oh my God." I poke my head toward the windshield and stare at the sprawling brick manor on display before us. "This is your house?"

"Yes." His voice is terse, and he seems nervous as he studies me, but I don't understand why.

As soon as he turns off the ignition, I'm halfway out of the car before he can come around to assist me. Sebastian leads me up the stairs and opens the front door, revealing a huge reception area with vaulted ceilings and marble inlay floors. He wastes no time taking my hand in his and giving me the quickest tour in history, rattling off details as we wander from room to room.

The place is thirteen thousand square feet with six bedrooms, a cherrywood library, two living rooms, and a pool with a view of Long Island Sound. It truly is the most magnificent home I've ever seen, but Sebastian seems unaware of my wonder as he mentions oak floors and custom glasswork. On the second level, he points out a gym, a wine cellar, and a home theater. And after seeing this house, I can't even imagine him spending the last four years in a small cottage at Loyola.

"This place is insane," I murmur.

"I inherited it from my mother's estate," he tells me. "It's on a private peninsula, and the real estate is prime. I can tell you from experience it's a nice place to have a family, but if you don't love it, I'll buy you a house anywhere you want."

He says all of this as he stares out the window, and I realize that beneath his indifference, fear lurks. Sebastian wants my assurance that I'll live here with him. I just don't know yet if it's a promise I'm willing to make.

"I would never ask you to sell this place." I attempt to soften the blow of my uncertainty.

"Then tell me what I have to do to make things right." His eyes fall on me, and the anguish hidden in those green depths nearly destroys me. I want to vanquish it for eternity, and if I had the power, I would.

"I know about your sister," I say softly. "Were you ever going to tell me?"

The vein in his neck pulses, and he leads me over to the nearest sofa, making sure I'm comfortable before he retreats to the window. He doesn't like to be vulnerable, and I get that, but if we still have secrets between us, there's no chance this relationship will ever work. The last time I confronted him about his father's death, he left me, and I honestly don't know what to expect from him right now.

"It's not a topic I particularly like to revisit," he says. "That's why I didn't tell you."

"I just need to know that you can talk to me," I assure him. "That's it."

He bows his head and his shoulders tremble under the weight of his silent emotion. "I've spent the past five years being so goddamned miserable. She would hate me for doing that. Katie, I mean. She was an amazing person. She would have loved you."

"I wish I could have known her," I answer delicately.

"She was my biggest supporter," he explains. "She came out that night to help me celebrate my decision to go pro. It meant everything to her to see me playing soccer rather than following my father's chosen path. But he wasn't the type of man you could say no to. When he found out I was going to be drafted, he hired the men who mugged me. They were just supposed to shatter my knee, and Katie happened to be there. When they attacked me, she lost it. Everything happened so fast, there wasn't even time to react. One minute, I was on the pavement, and the next, her life was over with three bullets."

"My God, Sebastian." I curl into myself as I try to hold it together for his sake. "I had no idea your own father was responsible for that. I'm so sorry."

"He was a prick," Sebastian answers flatly. "But on some level, I think I still loved him regardless. Even after everything, when he died, it fucked me up."

"We can't help who our parents are," I tell him. "Or loving them, flaws and all."

"I was always afraid I'd turn out just like him," he admits.
"And I saw it happening with you. I did things I hated myself
for under the guise of helping you in some twisted way."
"It wasn't just you," I concede. "I was an active participant in
those twisted games too."
"I always knew you deserved better." He wheels around and
looks at me. "I still do. But I can't let you go. I don't want to."
I want so badly to tell him he doesn't have to, but there are
still so many things we need to work through.
"How can I know you won't go back to that dark place
again?" I ask.
"When I almost lost you, it woke me the fuck up. The notion
of a world without you was unbearable. Not even an hour
before, I saw you in that office, pregnant with my child, and it
felt like everything was falling together. In a single second, my
old life was gone, and my future was sitting right there in
front of me. I can't even explain it, but at that moment,
everything became so clear. And I promise you, if you let me,
I will spend the rest of my life proving myself worthy of your
love."
He approaches me slowly, and when he collapses onto his
knees in front of me, I struggle to keep my emotions in check.
"I will beg for your forgiveness if that's what it takes."
"I don't want you to beg." I reach out to touch his face. "That
isn't the man I know you to be."
"Then what?" He looks up at me as his hands come to rest on
mine.
"Tell me about Megan."
"Megan?" He looks confused, as if he doesn't understand the
question. "What about her?"
"The papers said you were with her in New York. After the
funeral, you went to dinner with her."
"Christ, Stella." His face morphs from confusion to relief. "Is
that what you've been worrying about this entire time?"
My lack of response is enough for him to take that as a yes.

"Nothing happened with Megan," he assures me. "I haven't been with anyone but you."

"But you were with her," I argue.

"I was with her because she's in real estate, and she volunteered her help selling my father's penthouse along with his belongings."

"That's it?" I release a shaky breath.

"That's it," he swears. "You have my word. I might be a lot of things, but a liar and a cheat aren't one of them."

"Well, you could see how I might have misread the situation." I jump up and begin to pace the floor. "You never made it clear we were in a relationship, and that was the second time I saw you with her. How do you think it makes me feel that you opened up to her instead of me?"

"Like shit, I imagine." His shoulders fall. "I wasn't thinking when I met with her, and it wasn't about me opening up to her. She was aware of my family situation, and I asked her for a favor. That was it."

"I need to know stuff like that won't happen again," I tell him, and a smile curves his lips. "Why are you smiling?"

"I'm sorry." He tries and fails to hide it. "But you're so goddamned beautiful when you're jealous."

My cheeks burn as he hauls me into his arms, gripping my chin between his fingers while his lips caress mine.

"I belong to you, baby. From the day you walked into my life, that was it for me."

"Are you sure?" I challenge. "Because there are no refunds. You're stuck with me now."

"I'm so fucking sure I think there's only one way to prove it to you."

"What's that?" I arch a brow at him.

His eyes darken, and the dominance returns to his voice as he makes his demand in my ear. "Take off all your clothes."

Chapter Forty-Three
Stella

"You have no idea what this does to me," Sebastian murmurs as his hands come to rest on my belly in what can only be considered a form of worship.

He's kneeling before me in nothing more than his trousers, and I'm completely naked on his bed. His palms snake around my back and drag my ass over the edge of the mattress, the position forcing my legs apart. My fingers curl into his hair in anticipation as he peppers my inner thighs with tender kisses. The muscles in his back are rigid, and I can tell he's trying to maintain his self-control, but he's failing.

"I haven't had you in months." He drags his nose against my sex and inhales me. "I fucking need you, baby. But I don't know how to love you gently. I only know how to love you on fire."

"So, love me on fire." My nails scrape over his scalp as I arch into him. "Let us smolder until we both turn to dust."

He releases a growl and finally caves into his animal ways, diving into the most intimate part of my body like a man who's gone without for years. And I realize that he has. Sebastian has been emotionally starved, and his soul is fractured in so many places. But I vow here and now that I will love that broken soul and fill up every void with goodness and light.

He lashes at me with his tongue, and I close my eyes and surrender to the sensations. Everything feels so intense. Is it the hormones, or the walls we've finally managed to break down? I don't know, but when I orgasm around him, he groans and starts fumbling with his trousers so fast it's obvious he feels it too.

"I just need to be inside you," he murmurs.

He barely manages to free his cock from his trousers before he's on me, and then in me. Burying himself deep within my warmth, he kisses me so fiercely the scorching heat will be branded onto my lips for eternity. Sebastian grunts in pain as his hips thrust in and out of me while I dig my fingers into his flesh, anywhere I can reach, never getting close enough.

"I fucking love you, Stella," he confesses as he pulls back briefly to look at me. "I love you."

"I love you too." I drag his face back to mine, and he thrusts into me, his entire body trembling out his release.

"You're mine," he declares. "And I'm never letting you go."

"So what happens now?" I trace the hard lines of Sebastian's chest as I lie next to him in bed.

Neither of us has moved in hours, content to just hold each other as the daylight fades and darkness consumes us. But I'm getting hungry, and I'm still trying to wrap my head around the idea of living here. I don't have any of my things yet from school, and I need to figure out how this correspondence will work. There are a million things to do, but right now, admittedly, I don't have the energy for anything else.

"I'll send someone to get your things," he volunteers. "Or if you'd prefer, we can arrange for Sybil to bring them this weekend."

"I'd much rather have Sybil bring them," I admit.

He nods, as if he expected as much. "Headmistress Gilbert is aware of the incident that occurred, so you'll be starting correspondence next week. That should give you some time to rest and settle in."

"Okay."

"I need to go grab something," he says. "Wait here a minute."

I sink into the fluffy bed without protest because I have no intentions of going anywhere. Initially, I thought it would take me some time to feel comfortable here, but I realize that I already do. Honestly, though, it wouldn't matter if we were living in the tiny cottage together in Nantucket. The only thing that matters is that I'm with Sebastian.

It's crazy how much I miss him, even when he's only gone for a minute in the other room. I briefly wonder if this is normal, and then quickly realize I don't care. Nothing about our relationship is normal or typical, and I need to throw those expectations out the window.

"I have something I want to give you." He returns and sits down on the bed in nothing but his briefs, and I have difficulty concentrating with so much of his beautiful body on display. He seems to notice when a smile curves his lips. "Focus, Stella."

"Sorry." My eyes move to his. "You are just so… distracting."

"I'll take that as a compliment." His smile morphs into a different expression, and if I didn't know any better, I might think he was nervous.

"What do you want to give me?"

"I know we haven't done anything the traditional way," he says. "Everything has moved at lightning speed between us, and there's still a lot to figure out. So, with that being said, I'm not looking for an answer right now. In fact, I don't want one right now. I want you to finish school, and have our baby, and after you've given it adequate thought, you can tell me what you want."

My heart hammers against my rib cage as Sebastian opens his palm to reveal a ring. A stunning art deco piece with what appears to be a canary diamond right in the center.

"It was my mother's." He reaches for my hand and slides it onto my right ring finger, as if to prove that this doesn't mean we're engaged. But it doesn't change the way I'm staring at it, or the way my heart feels right now.

"Sebastian, I don't know what to say."

"Don't say anything," he insists. "Someday, when you're ready, I want you to be my wife. But until then, please just wear this and know without a doubt, I am devoted to you in every way. The past is behind us now, and every time you look at this ring, I want you to consider what your future looks like. With or without me."

I reach out to touch his face, and then drag his lips to mine. It would be so easy to give him an answer right now. In my heart, I know nothing will change. But we have all the time in the world to prove it.

Epilogue
Stella

"Holy mother effing shit," Sybil hisses as she nudges me in the side with her elbow. "Did you see this?"

"What?" I ask absently as I scan the room and offer a polite smile to the guests as they make their rounds.

"Look." She shoves her phone into my hand, and my eyes shoot up in surprise when I see the image in the article entitled *A Socialite's Fall from Grace*. The mugshot of Louisa isn't doing her complexion any favors, and it's obvious that prison orange is definitely not in her color wheel.

"What did she do?" I whisper.

"Apparently, she got caught skimming from her father's company after he cut her off. Fraud, embezzlement, there's a whole laundry list of charges."

"That's insane," I murmur.

"Not really." Sybil snickers. "She thought the whole world was her playground, and now she's getting her just desserts if you ask me."

"True." I shrug, but even as I say it, I can't help feeling a little disappointed that she never amounted to anything. In my mind, I always imagined there would be a day when Louisa had an awakening and grew out of her pettiness. But clearly that didn't happen.

"Want to hear the craziest part?" Sybil asks.

"There's more?" I cringe.

"Uh-huh." She nods. "She's going to the same prison as Lila."

"Why doesn't that surprise me?" I roll my eyes. "Now they can scheme together."

"Or against each other," she says. "At least for the next ten years."

I shake my head, and as I consider it, I realize that it doesn't bother me in the least. When Lila was arrested for fraud and extortion a year ago, I wasn't even shocked. I haven't seen her since the day I told her to get out of my life, and when Sebastian admitted that she'd blackmailed him, I had no interest in ever seeing her again. As for my father, he still has at least another fifteen years on his sentence. I've forgiven him for my own sanity, but I still haven't decided if I want to forget him entirely. If a day ever comes that I want to see him, it will be on my terms. For now, he's not going anywhere regardless.

"Holy crap." I hand the phone back to Sybil as I spot Miranda Kinkade whirling into my path like the hurricane she is. "Okay shoo, I have to work now."

Sybil flits off and leaves me to rub elbows with one of my idols.

"Stella, you really have outdone yourself this evening." Miranda gestures wildly around the gallery. "This is marvelous. Truly, you are one of the most gifted visual artists I have ever had the pleasure of knowing."

"High compliments coming from you." I offer her a shaky smile. Miranda has worked in the fashion industry and at some of the top women's magazines in the nation. I'm honored that she would even show up to my little slice of paradise.

"Truly, you better batten down the hatches," she says. "You will have *Vanity Fair* and *Vogue* at your door in no time."

"Well, I'd be honored," I confess. "But I think I'll stick to what I do best."

"Honey, that's your prerogative." She throws me a wink and breezes out of my life just as fast as she came.

I take a deep breath and look around the gallery to make sure everyone is comfortable and having a good time. And then it settles over me. These pictures on the wall are mine. These people came here to see them, and more importantly, they like them. It still feels surreal.

"You should be proud of yourself," a deep, warm voice purrs into my ear from behind me.

I turn to find Sebastian with an expression of utter awe on his face, and it's almost too good to believe.

"Did you call all of your contacts?" I accuse.

His lips tilt into a beautiful grin and his shoulders shake with laughter. "No, baby girl. This is all you. This is talent and hard work."

"And one fine ass subject if I do say so myself," Sybil announces as she rejoins us with Sariah in tow.

Sariah might be our daughter, but she is every bit the graceful worshipper of her 'aunty' Sybil.

"Mommy, Daddy!" Sariah does a little curtsy in her ballerina skirt. "Look what Sybil taught me today."

She spins around with stars in her eyes before Sebastian scoops her up into his arms and kisses her cheek. She giggles and squeezes her arms around his neck, and they look at each other with so much love and mutual admiration that my heart practically melts all over the floor.

"She is such a daddy's girl." Sybil rolls her eyes.

"Hey, she loves me too, right?" I poke her belly, and Sariah sticks her tongue out.

"Of course, I do, Mommy. You make way better cookies than Daddy does."

"Ha!" I smirk. "You hear that, Mr. Carter?"

"I won't argue that, Mrs. Carter." He leans over and kisses me while Sariah wiggles in his grasp. "You do make some damn good cookies. And beautiful photos. And even more beautiful babies."

"I had some help with that," I tease.

"You two are ridiculous," Sybil groans and steals Sariah away. "I'm going to go show the mini-me all the amazing photos of me dancing."

"Don't think I don't know what you're doing," I call after her as she walks away.

Sybil winks and shrugs her shoulders. "You said she could be anything she wanted. I'm just feeding her dancing addiction."

"We are going to have our hands full with that child." I sigh as Sebastian pulls me against his chest and wraps his arms around my waist.

"I don't doubt that for a second," he agrees. "So does that mean you aren't ready for another one just yet?"

I smile up at my husband, squeezing his fingers in mine. We've had five long years together, and it still feels like we are just getting started in some ways. Sebastian works with local soccer teams and runs mentorship programs, and I'm finally getting my gallery up and running. It's taken a lot of hard work and uncertainty to get to where we are, but I wouldn't trade a second of it.

There are some people who believe life is a series of milestones, meant to be achieved in one unfaltering order. But I disagree. Happiness is an ever-changing thing, and what I've learned along the way is that it's not about the goal, it's the journey that makes all the difference.

Truthfully, I'd much rather follow my heart than follow a dream that didn't make sense. I had to get to where I am to figure out who I am, and it's still something that changes daily. But there are a few things in my life I can be sure of. I love my husband and daughter more than anything else in this world, and if I had nothing else but them, I would be okay with that.

The beauty of my life is that I don't have to choose. I can have it all, and I want to have it all with Sebastian. Including a son, and maybe even a couple more. I drag his hand over my belly and look up at the most beautiful man I've ever known. My partner in life, and my rock.

"I can practically already feel him there," I whisper. "But you better take me home tonight, just to make sure you've done your job properly."

Sebastian kisses me and squeezes me in his arms like he'll never let me go, and I know without a doubt that he won't. "Always happy to oblige, Mrs. Carter."

The End.

Made in the USA
Coppell, TX
03 December 2019